国家出版基金项目
NATIONAL PUBLICATION FOUNDATION

朱小和 演唱

史军超 卢朝贵 杨叔孔 汉译整理

蔡蔚 张立玉 英译

[美] H. W. Lan 审校

哈尼阿培聪坡坡

"十三五"国家重点图书

中国南方民间文学典籍英译丛书

丛书主编 张立玉 丛书副主编 起国庆

MIGRATING EPIC OF THE HANIS

出品单位:

中南民族大学南方少数民族文库翻译研究基地

云南省少数民族古籍整理出版规划办公室

· 汉英对照 ·

WUHAN UNIVERSITY PRESS
武汉大学出版社

图书在版编目(CIP)数据

哈尼阿培聪坡坡:汉英对照/蔡蔚,张立玉英译.—武汉:武汉大学出版社,2021.4(2022.1重印)

中国南方民间文学典籍英译丛书/张立玉主编

2020年度国家出版基金资助项目 "十三五"国家重点图书

ISBN 978-7-307-21990-8

Ⅰ.哈… Ⅱ.①蔡… ②张… Ⅲ.哈尼族—史诗—中国—汉、英 Ⅳ.I222.7

中国版本图书馆 CIP 数据核字(2020)第 240754 号

责任编辑:邓 喆 责任校对:李孟潇 版式设计:韩闻锦

出版发行:**武汉大学出版社** (430072 武昌 珞珈山)

(电子邮箱:cbs22@whu.edu.cn 网址:www.wdp.whu.edu.cn)

印刷:湖北恒泰印务有限公司

开本:720×1000 1/16 印张:28.5 字数:344 千字

版次:2021 年 4 月第 1 版 2022 年 1 月第 2 次印刷

ISBN 978-7-307-21990-8 定价:80.00 元

丛书编委会

学术顾问

王宏印　李正栓

主编

张立玉

副主编

起国庆

编委会成员（按姓氏笔画排列）

邓之宇	王向松	艾　芳	石定乐	龙江莉	刘　纯
陈兰芳	汤　茜	李克忠	杨　柳	杨筱奕	张立玉
张扬扬	张　瑛	和六花	依旺的	保俊萍	起国庆
陶开祥	鲁　钒	蔡　蔚	臧军娜		

内容提要

《哈尼阿培聪坡坡》是一部完整地记载哈尼族历史沿革的长篇迁徙史诗，具有较高的历史价值。作为哈尼族人民的"史记"，全诗由歌头和以下七章组成：《远古的虎尼虎那高山》《从什虽湖到嘎鲁嘎则》《惹罗普楚》《好地诺马阿美》《色厄作娘》《谷哈密查》《森林密密的红河两岸》。该史诗以现实主义手法记叙了哈尼族祖先在各个历史时期的迁徙情况，并对其迁徙各地的原因、路线、途程，各个迁居地的社会生活、生产、风习、宗教，以及与毗邻民族的关系等，均作了详细而生动的辑录，因而该作品不仅具有文学价值，而且具有重大的历史学、社会学及宗教学价值。

序

近年来，民族典籍英译捷报频传，硕果累累。韩家全教授等人的壮族系列经典翻译陆续出版，王宏印教授等人的系列民族典籍英译研究著作已经问世，李正栓教授等人的藏族格言诗英译著作不断在国内外出版，王维波教授等人的东北民族典籍英译著作纷纷付梓，李昌银教授等人的"云南少数民族经典作品英译文库"于 2018 年年底出版，其他民族典籍英译作品也在接踵而至。

近日，中南民族大学张立玉教授传来佳音：他们要出版"十三五"国家重点图书——"中国南方民间文学典籍英译丛书"。虽叫民间文学，其实基本上都是民族典籍。这一系列包括十本书，它们是：《黑暗传》《哭嫁歌》《哈尼阿培聪坡坡》《彝族民间故事》《南方民间创世神话选集》《查姆》《召树屯》《娥并与桑洛》《金笛》《梅葛》。其中，好几本是云南少数民族的。只有一本是汉族典籍，即《黑暗传》。很有意思的是，这些典籍展示了不同民族的创世史诗或诸如此类的东西。

《黑暗传》以民间歌谣唱本形象地描述了盘古开天辟地结束混沌黑暗，人类起源及社会发展的历程，融合了混沌、盘古、女娲、伏羲、炎帝神农氏、黄帝轩辕氏等众多英雄人物在洪荒时代艰难创世的一系列神话传说。它被称为汉族首部创世史诗。《哈尼阿培聪坡坡》是一部完整地记载哈尼族历史沿革的长篇史诗，堪称哈尼族的"史记"，长 5000 余行，以现实主义手法记叙了哈尼族祖先在各个历史时期的迁徙情况，并对其迁徙各地的原因、路线、途程，各个迁居地的社会生活、生产、风习、宗教，以及与毗邻民族的关系等，均作了详细而生动的辑录，因而该作品不仅具有文学价值，而且具有重大的历史学、社会学及宗教学价值。《南方民间创世神话选集》包括一些创世神话，主要是关于世界起源和人类起源的神话。本书所列包括生活在广泛地域的民族，如门巴族、珞巴族、怒族、基诺族、普米族、拉祜族、傈僳族、毛南族、德昂族、景颇族、阿昌族、布朗族、佤族、独龙族、水族、仡佬族、布依族、仫佬族、高山族和侗族等。这些神话不仅讲述了世界的起源，也讲述了人类的始祖，以及人类对世界的改造。《梅葛》是彝族的一部长篇史诗，流传在云南省楚雄州的姚安、大姚等彝族地区。"梅葛"本为一种彝族歌调的名称，由于人们采用这种调子来唱彝族的创世史，因而创世史诗被称为"梅葛"。《查姆》是一部彝族史诗，是彝族人民唱天地、日月、人类、种子、风雨、树木等起源的长篇史诗，被彝族人民当作本民族的历史来看待。

其余几本书展示了一些少数民族的风俗习惯、恋爱故事、斗争故事等。《哭嫁歌》是土家族文化典籍。"哭嫁"是土家族姑娘在出嫁时进行的一种用歌声来诉说自己在封建买办婚姻制度下不幸命运的活动，是指土家族姑娘的抒情歌谣，富有诗韵和乐感，融哀、怨、喜和乐为一体，以婉转的曲调向世人展示土家人独特的"哭"文化。《彝族民间故事》是一部以流传于云南楚雄彝族自治州彝族人民中间的民间故事为主体，同时覆盖全省包括小凉山等彝族地区的民间故事集。这些故事丰富多彩，从中能看到民族民间故事的各种形态和生动、奇妙而颇具彝族民族特色的文化特征。《召树屯》是傣族民间长篇叙事诗，叙述了傣族佛教世俗典籍《贝叶经·召树屯》中一个古老的传说故事。这部叙事诗一直为傣族人民所传唱，历久不衰。《娥并与桑洛》是一部优美生动的叙事诗，一个凄美的爱情悲剧。《金笛》是一部苗族长篇叙事诗，富于变幻性和传奇性，尽情铺叙扎董乎冉与蒙诗彩奏的悲欢离合，热情赞颂他们在与魔虎的激烈斗争中所表现出来的坚贞不屈、英勇顽强的精神，许多情节含有浓郁的民族特色。

这些故事都很引人入胜，都很符合国家文化发展需求，向世人讲述中国故事，传播中华文化，并且讲述的是民族故事，充分体现了党和国家对各民族的关怀。

民族典籍英译是传播中国文化、文学和文明的重要途径，是中华文化"走出去"的重要组成部分，是国家战略，是提高文化"软实力"的重要方式，在文化交流和文明建设中起着不可或缺的作用，对提升中国国际话语权和构建中国对外话语体系以及对建设世界文学都有积极意义。

中国民族典籍使世界文化更加丰富多彩、绚丽多姿。我国各民族典籍中折射出的文化多样性极大地丰富了世界多元、特色鲜明的文化。人们对多样性形成全新的认识角度和思维方式，有助于开阔视野，丰富思考问题的角度，挖掘这些经典中的教育价值和文化价值，对世界其他民族都有指导和借鉴意义，并且有助于建设我国的文化自信。

民族典籍翻译与研究事业关乎国家的稳定统一，关乎民族关系的和谐发展，关乎世界多元文化的实现。在中国，民族典籍资源极为丰富，有待进一步挖掘、翻译，仍有许多少数民族典籍亟待拯救，民族典籍翻译与研究工作任重而道远，民族典籍翻译事业大有可为。

李正栓[①]

2019 年 7 月 19 日

[①] 李正栓，中国英汉语比较研究会典籍英译专业委员会常务副会长兼秘书长；中国中医药研究促进会传统文化翻译与国际传播专业委员会常务主任委员。

前　　言

　　《哈尼阿培聪坡坡》是一部哈尼族的迁徙史诗。哈尼族是
云南重要的少数民族，有一百六十多万人口，源自游牧于青
藏高原的古代羌族。哈尼族向南迁徙后，目前主要聚居在滇
南的红河、澜沧江沿岸和无量山、哀牢山地带，分布在云南
省的红河哈尼族彝族自治州、普洱市、玉溪市以及西双版纳
傣族自治州。他们主要从事农业，善于开垦梯田，善于种
茶。从前哈尼族没有文字，但口头文学资源较为丰富，特别
是神话传说和史诗。一代代贝玛（演唱史诗的歌手）口耳相
传，将哈尼族传统文化中美好而珍贵的诗章传承下来。《哈
尼阿培聪坡坡》这部广泛流传于红河流域的迁徙史诗，就是
哈尼族口头文学中的一颗耀眼明珠，由于其系统完整记载了
哈尼族历史沿革，还被称为"哈尼族人民的'史记'"。

　　《哈尼阿培聪坡坡》中，"阿培"意为祖先，"聪坡坡"意
为从一处搬到另一处，也有逃难之意，因此诗名意为"哈尼
族先祖的迁徙"。这部史诗长达五千余行，内容丰富，情节
曲折，细节动人，人物丰满，语言优美流畅，以哈尼哈八
（哈尼族酒歌）的形式吟唱了哈尼族历尽艰辛，从远古的虎尼
虎那高山，来到红河南岸定居的悲壮、曲折而又漫长的迁徙
历程。全书以哈尼人主要迁徙路线为线索，按主要定居点分
为七个章节，分别是神奇荒凉的虎尼虎那高山、水草丰满的
什虽湖和龙竹成林的嘎鲁嘎则、雨量充沛的温湿河谷惹罗普

1

楚、诺马河边的好地诺马阿美、得威海边的平坝色厄作娘、平坦宽广的平原谷哈密查，以及森林密密的红河两岸。《哈尼阿培聪坡坡》勾勒了哈尼族先民在不同历史时期的迁徙史路，并对其迁徙的原因、路线、途程，在各迁居地的社会生活、生产、风习、宗教以及与毗邻民族的关系等作了详细而生动的辑录，是研究哈尼族历史与文化极其珍贵的史料。

本次英译本的汉语原文本采用 1985 年云南省少数民族古籍整理出版规划办公室整理出版的版本，根据元阳县洞铺寨歌手朱小和的演唱进行整理翻译。据搜集者称，朱小和家三代贝玛，家学渊博，功底深厚。他的演唱充满感染力，生动形象，气势磅礴。由此整理的诗章语言节奏明快，琅琅上口，生动感人，具有明显的口传文学特点和较高的艺术价值。《哈尼阿培聪坡坡》中较为广泛地使用了排比、比兴、比喻、拟人、通感和夸张等修辞手法，语言表达上具有鲜明的哈尼族民族特色。在译文中我们尽量保存其原汁原味的表达，力图再现这些修辞手法体现的文学效果、文化信息和民族特色。史诗中丰富细致的描写能够使读者和听者浮现出栩栩如生的画面，还有声音、气味等多种感受，试举两例：如描写北边大河厄地西耶，"它的脾气又野又犟；粗大的身躯扭动翻滚，搅起无数漩涡浊浪，大河像一只下山的饿虎，怒吼声震动四面八方"，气势惊人；再如描述刚到迁居地时哈尼人的日常生活，"七个扎密去背水，七股笑声丢在后边，七个阿妈去背水，七个扎谷把衣角牵"，画面感极强，仿佛能看到小孩跌跌撞撞牵着妈妈衣角走路的样子，能听到姑娘们银铃般的笑声。在翻译的过程中，译者主要采用直译方式，为保留原诗中的独特形象和生动比喻，尽量还原其语言特色和文化韵味。另外，这部史诗在汉译时保留了哈尼族对人对物的独特称呼，如上文中将姑娘称为扎密，小孩称为扎谷；哈尼族还喜欢用人的关系来定义大自然事物，将田地称为"田小伙"，秧苗称为"秧姑娘"，火和水称作"火娘"和"水娘"。英译时我们均用音译或直译的方式将这些称呼予以体现。特别值得提到的是，这一版本是史军超先生领军搜集整理并汉译的，其哈尼族背景和学者身份给这一版本增加了文化特色和学术气息。汉译本中有较多注释，如介绍哈尼族的独特文化，解释哈尼族不同史诗中对相同事件的不同表述等，在英译中我们都予以保留。为了更好地进行文化阐释，我们也加了少量译者注释，希望将史先生严谨的学术态度和本书的学术和文化兼有的独特风格一并传达。

翻译过程中译者多次与担任审校工作的美国威斯康星大学拉克罗斯分校英语系的 H. W. Lan 教授深入交流讨论，并得到她的悉心指导。为了尽量理解和再现原文本中所包含的生态语境，译者还进行了大量的文献研究和实地调研，希望尽量减少误读与误译，力求英译忠实原文，并传递哈尼族的语言和文化。但由于水平有限，翻译过程中难免有未竟疏漏之处，恳请广大读者朋友批评指正，以便修订时更正。

蔡蔚　张立玉

2020 年 10 月

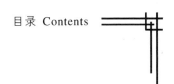

目　录

歌头 ……………………………………………………… 2

一、远古的虎尼虎那高山 ……………………………… 6

二、从什虽湖到嘎鲁嘎则 ……………………………… 34

三、惹罗普楚 …………………………………………… 52

四、好地诺马阿美 ……………………………………… 84

五、色厄作娘 …………………………………………… 194

六、谷哈密查 …………………………………………… 236

七、森林密密的红河两岸 ……………………………… 368

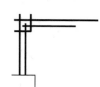

Contents

Prologue ·· 3

Chapter 1   The Ancient High Mountain Hunihuna ··········· 7

Chapter 2   From the Shisui Lake to Galugaze ··········· 35

Chapter 3   Reluo Puchu ·································· 53

Chapter 4   A Nice Place Nuoma Amei ················· 85

Chapter 5   Se'ezuoniang ·························· 195

Chapter 6   Guha Micha ·························· 237

Chapter 7   Dense Forest along the Red River ··········· 369

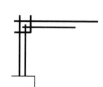

歌　头

歌手：

萨——依——！

讲了，

亲亲的兄弟姐妹们！

唱了，

围坐在火塘边的哈尼人！

让我饮一口辣酒润润嗓门，

来把先祖的古今唱给你们！

先祖的古今呵，

比艾乐坡①独根的药还要好，

先祖的古今呵，

像哀牢山的竹子有枝有节有根。

瞧呵，

今晚的月光这样明亮，

---

① 艾乐坡：哀牢山南段主峰，是哈尼族艾乐支系主要聚居区。

Prologue

Singer:

Sa—ee—!

Let us tell stories,

My dear brothers and sisters!

Let us sing songs,

The Hanis who are sitting around the fireplace!

Let me moisten my throat with a gulp of spicy liquor,

And share with you the stories of our ancestors!

The stories of the ancestors,

Were better than the single-rooted herbs on the Mount Ailepo①.

The stories of the ancestors,

Were like the bamboo in the Ailao Mountains

With its branches, joints, and roots.

Look,

The moonlight is so bright tonight,

---

① Mount Ailepo: The main peak in the southern part of the Ailao Mountains. It is the main settlement area of the Aile branch of the Hani.

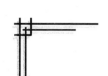

蘑菇房①里的人们像过六月年②一样欢腾。

我们正合唱一唱，

先祖怎样出世，

我们正合讲一讲，

先祖走过什么路程。

每支歌都是先祖传下来的，

是先祖借我的舌头把它传给后代子孙！

众人：

萨——依——萨！

---

　　① 蘑菇房：哀牢山区哈尼族居住的蘑菇状房屋。

　　② 六月年：哈尼族的重大节日之一，也称苦扎扎，一般在六月
二十四日前后，节期三至六天，届时以村寨为单位杀牛祭祖，亦称祭
秋房，青年们聚集一起荡秋千、摔跤、狩猎、唱山歌。

And the people in the mushroom houses① are so festive as if celebrating the June Festival②.

Let us sing their songs,

About how the ancestors were born.

Let us share,

What the ancestors underwent.

Each song has been passed down from the ancestors,

Through my tongue, to their descendants!

Audience:

Sa—ee—sa!

---

① Mushroom house: The mushroom-shaped house of the Hani people in the Ailao Mountains.

② June Festival: One of the most important Hani festivals, also called the Ku Za Za Festival in their own language. It is celebrated around June 24th of the Chinese lunar calendar and lasts for three to six days. During the festival, villagers kill an ox for sacrificing to their ancestors, which is also called the Qiufang Sacrifice. Young people enjoy the festival by participating in turn-swinging, wrestling, hunting and singing.

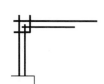

一、远古的虎尼虎那高山

（一）

歌手：

萨——依——！

先祖的古今是这样开头的呵，

一娘生的亲人们！

在那远古的年代，

天边有个叫虎尼虎那①的地方，

红红的石头像天火在燃烧，

黑黑的石头像黑夜笼罩，

奇怪的巨石成千上万，

垒成了神奇的巍峨高山。

世间原没有高山大河，

天上也不见星月闪光，

---

① 虎尼虎那：即红色石头和黑色石头，此处指红色和黑色大石
垒成的高山，具体所指不详。

Chapter 1　The Ancient High Mountain Hunihuna

1.1

Singer:

Sa—ee—!

The life of the ancestors begun like this,

Kinsfolk born from one mother!

In that ancient time,

At the end of the sky, in a place named Hunihuna①,

Red rocks were like the burning fires

And black rocks were like the dark nights.

Thousands of strange rocks,

Piled up into a mysterious towering mountain.

There were originally not great mountains and rivers in the world,

And no shining stars and bright moon in the sky.

_____

① Hunihuna: Red and black rocks. It refers to the high mountain of red and black rocks. The specific reference is unclear.

天神地神杀翻查牛造下万物，①
粗大的牛骨造成这座大山。

虎尼虎那岩石一层高过一层，
凸凸凹凹像天狗的牙齿一样；
凸起的石头顶着天的脚掌，
凹下的石头压在地的头上。

虎尼虎那神奇又荒凉，
五彩云霞在岩石上飘荡；
最高的山峰天神也不敢歇脚，
那道山梁像巨人高高的鼻梁。

陪伴山梁的是两条大水，
滔滔波浪拍打着山岗，
好像大山也有伤心的眼泪，
两条河日夜向着东方流淌。

北边的大河叫厄地西耶②，
它的脾气又野又犟；

---

① 哈尼族创世史诗《烟本霍本》中记叙：远古时，天神已造好
日月星辰，但日月无光，于是天地之神杀倒查牛，用牛眼做月亮、太
阳，使之有光。查牛，从土中拉出的神牛。
② 厄地西耶：流黄水的大河。

The gods of heaven and earth killed the sacred cow to create everything,①

And used its thick bones to build this mountain.

The rocks on the Hunihuna were layer upon layer,
Uneven like dogs' teeth.
The rocks at the peaks supported the sky,
While those in the valleys held down the earth.

The Hunihuna was miraculous and desolate.
Colorful clouds floated above the rocks.
Its highest peak even the gods would not dare to rest at,
And its ridge was like the nose bridge of a giant.

Accompanying the mountain were two great rivers,
Whose surging waves beat against its hills.
As if the mountain had tears of sorrow,
Both rivers flowed to the east day and night.

The one to the north was called Edi Xiye②,
And it was rather wild;

---

① According to the Hani genesis epic *Yanben Huoben*, in ancient times, the gods of heaven and earth had already made the sun, the moon and the stars, but the sun and the moon had no light, so the gods of heaven and earth killed the sacred cow Chaniu and made the eyes of the cow the moon and the sun that give out light. Chaniu, a sacred cow that was pulled out from the earth.

② Edi Xiye: A big river of yellow water.

粗大的身躯扭动翻滚，
搅起无数漩涡浊浪，
大河像一只下山的饿虎，
怒吼声震动四面八方。

南边的大河叫艾地戈耶，
像青色的宝剑劈开山岩，
滔滔流水像闪电一样，
常常惊落蹦跳的岩羊；
宽大的水帘如飞流直下，
雪样的泡沫像白云飞扬。

远古的虎尼虎那，
先祖的古今是这样讲：
双角的马鹿结队奔驰，
大嘴的老虎到处窥探，
麂子在剑麻丛里啃草，
刺猪在芭蕉林里游荡，
老熊把大树扳倒，
猴子把石块推进波浪。
泉边的小树上，
画眉争着唱歌；
山边的木姜子林里，
龙子雀上下奔忙；
猫头鹰不停地鸣叫，
老鼠吓得慌慌张张。

Its bulky body twisted and rolled,

And stirred up vortexes of turbid waves.

The river was like a hungry tiger coming down from the

mountain,

And its roar shook all sides.

The river to the south was called Aidi Geye,

And it was like a rock-splitting turquoise sword;

The rushing water was like a lightning,

Often startling the rock-climbing goats;

The broad curtains of water flew straight down,

And the snow-like foams were like the floating clouds.

The ancient Hunihuna,

The ancestors described like this:

The two-horn red deer running together,

The big-mouth tigers spying around,

The muntjacs grazing in the sisal,

The porcupines wandering in the banana forest,

The bears pulling down the trees,

The monkeys pushing the stones into the waves.

On the trees and by the spring,

Thrushes were singing;

In the litsea bushes by the hills,

The dragon-finches were jumping up and down;

The owls kept hooting,

Terrifying the mice.

虎尼虎那的飞禽走兽数不尽，
虎尼虎那的游鱼跳虾数不完，
绿色大地到处都充满生气，
哈尼先祖就出生在这个地方。①

众人：
萨——依——萨！

（二）

歌手：
萨——依——！
虎尼虎那山花，
花开花落历经七十七万次，
山坡上生出了七十七种飞禽走兽；
虎尼虎那大水涨了又落，
水涨水落也历经七十七万回，
大水里有七十七种动物生长；
先祖的诞生也经过了七十七万年，
到我这一辈八十代已经算满。②
亲亲的弟兄们，
要说哈尼先祖是什么样，

---

① 哈尼族史诗《汗交交本本》（人类从哪里来）中又说，哈尼祖先诞生在色厄（大理）以北的欧什山上。
② 歌手朱小和的家谱有八十代。

There were countless birds and animals in the Hunihuna,

As well as innumerable fishes and shrimps.

The green land was filled with vigour,

The place where our ancestors were born.①

Audience:

Sa—ee—sa!

1. 2

Singer:

Sa—ee—!

Flowers in the Hunihuna bloomed and withered,

For seven hundred and seventy thousand times,

And seventy-seven kinds of animals were born to the slope.

The rivers in the Hunihuna rose and fell

For seven hundred and seventy thousand times,

And seventy-seven kinds of animals were born to the water.

Till my generation, the eightieth generation②,

It has been seven hundred and seventy thousand years since the births of the ancestors.

Dear brothers,

What our Hani ancestors were like,

①　Another Hani epic *Hanjiaojiaobenben* (where humans came from) has a different account of the Hanis' origin. It states that the Hani ancestors were born on the Oushi Mountain, north of Se'e (the Dali County).

②　Zhu Xiaohe, the singer of this epic, can trace his family tree back to eighty generations.

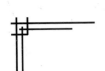

等我细细唱来慢慢讲。

先祖的人种种在大水里，
天晴的日子，
骑着水波到处飘荡；
先祖的人种发芽在老林，
阴冷的季节，
歪歪倒倒走在地上。
最早的人种是父子俩，
布觉是腊勒的阿爸；
布觉像水田里的螺蛳，
背上背着硬壳，
腊勒像干地上的蜗牛，
嘴里吐出稠稠的浆。

第二对人种是俄比和腊千，
她们是亲亲的母女俩，
娘两个分不开走不散，
走路像分窝的蜂群挤挤攘攘。

跟着出来了第三对人种，
那是阿虎和腊尼兄弟俩，
他们和前辈截然不同，
走路像蚂蚁排成行。

三对人种发芽了，
人芽和草芽不一样，

Listen to me and I will tell you in detail.

The human seeds of the ancestors were planted in the water.

In sunny days,

They floated around with the waves;

The human seeds of the ancestors sprouted in the forest,

And in cold and damp days,

They stumbled around on the earth.

The earliest human seeds included a father and a son,

Bujue was the father of Lale.

Bujue was like a spiral shell in the paddy field,

With a hard shell on his back;

Lale was like a snail on the dry land,

Spitting out thick mucus.

A second pair was Ebi and Laqian,

Mother and daughter.

They were inseparable,

Walking like two bees from the same swarm, bustling around

each other.

Following them was the third pair,

The brothers Ahu and Lani.

They differed very much from their predecessors,

Walking in a row like ants.

These three pairs of the human sprouted like seeds,

But they differed from the grass that sprouts.

一代人用手走路，

他们里面有嫁给豹子的姑娘；

一代人蹲在地上攒动，

屁股常常磕碰在地面上；

一代人和我们现在一样，

腰杆就像挺直的棕树站在山坡上①。

换过二十三次爹娘，

人种像大树成长，

二十四代塔婆②出世了，

她的英名人人敬仰。

塔婆是能干的女人，

她把世人生养。

在她的头发里，

生出住在白云山顶上的人；

---

① 《汗交交本本》中关于人类、各族祖先的诞生是这样说的：在矮山的坝子里，觉多和多娜开始繁衍人类，他们生下七个儿子，一个儿子一样肤色，世上的土地是七块，一人居住一地。七个儿子分别是汉族、哈尼族、彝族、傣族等的祖先，汉族祖先"召来"住在欧什山以北，哈尼族祖先——生着乌黑翅膀的血娜（一种鸟）住在欧什森林里，彝族祖先尤先和龙鼠玛（均为动物）住在欧什山腰，傣族祖先同推、篾西玛（两种红尾雀）住在江边坝子里。

② 塔婆：传说塔婆是人类始祖母，她以前的"人"是动物，她以后才开始出现真正的人类。

A generation walked on their hands,

Some of the young women were married to leopards.

Another generation moved around squatting on the ground,

Their butts often bumped against the ground.

Yet another generation was like us now,

Their back was like the straight palm tree standing on the hillside.①

After twenty-three generations,

Men grew like big trees.

To the twenty-fourth generation Granny Tapo② was born,

And her great name was respected by everyone.

Granny Tapo was a capable woman.

She gave birth to people in the world.

In her hair

Were born the people living on the top of the White-Cloud Mountain.

---

① *Hanjiaojiaobenben* explains the origin of human beings and ancestors of different ethnic groups as follows: in the flat land of the low mountains, Jueduo and Duona gave birth to seven sons, each one with a different skin color, and living in a different place. They were the ancestors of seven Ethnic groups: the Han, the Hani, the Yi, the Dai, etc. The Han ancestor Zhaolai lived in the north of the Oushi mountain; the Hani ancestor — Xuena, a bird with black wings, lived in the Oushi forest; the Yi people's ancestors Youxian and Longshuma (both animals) lived in the Oushi mountainside; and the Dai ancestors Tongtui and Miexima (two kinds of red-tail sparrow) lived in the flat land by the river.

② Granny Tapo: It is said that Granny Tapo was the grandmother of all human beings. It was only after her that the human race really began to appear.

在她的鼻根上，
生出在高山上骑马的人；
在她白生生的牙巴骨上，
生出的人住在山崖边；
在她软软的胳肢窝里，
生出的人爱穿花衣裳。
粗壮的腰杆上人最多，
雾露和他们来做伴；
脚底板上人也不少，
河水对他们把歌唱。
塔婆生出的孩子里，
她最心疼的是哈尼；
哈尼生在肚脐眼里，
祖祖辈辈不受风霜。①

（三）

歌手：

萨——依——！
虎尼虎那时代的先祖，
从不把父母挂在心上，
阿哥不认得阿弟，

———————————

① 传说塔婆生出了瑶、蒙古、苗、彝、哈尼、汉、傣、壮等二十一种族姓人，因为她最爱哈尼人，便把他们生在肚脐眼里，这是对哈尼寨子多在山坳里的神化解释。

At the tip of her nose

Were born the people riding horses in the high mountains;

On her white jawbone

Were born the people residing by the edges of the mountains.

In her soft armpit

Were born those who loved to wear colorful clothes.

Numerous were those on her stout waist,

With the dew and mist keeping them company;

And many lived on the soles of her feet,

With rivers singing to them.

Among her children,

She loved the Hanis the most.

As the Hanis were born in her navel,

Their descendants were kept away from sufferings of wind and frost.①

1.3

Singer:

Sa—ee—!

The ancestors in the Hunihuna era,

Never worried about their parents.

Brothers did not know each other,

---

① It is said that Granny Tapo gave birth to twenty-one ethnic groups such as the Yao, the Mongolian, the Miao, the Yi, the Hani, the Han, the Dai, the Zhuang, etc. It was because the Hanis were her favorite that they were born in her navel. It is a mythological explanation for why most Hani villages are set in the col.

阿妹不知阿姐的长相，
阿舅是谁他们不管，
阿婶是谁他们不想。
撵跑豹子，
他们就搬进岩洞；
吓走大蟒，
他们就住进洞房；
找着吃食，
他们吃撑肠肚；
找不着东西，
他们饿倒地上；
看见猴子摘果，
他们学着摘来吃；
看见竹鼠刨笋，
他们跟着刨来尝；
看见穿山甲鳞甲满身，
他们也穿起树叶衣裳；
听见鹦哥鸣叫，
他们也学着把话讲。

天上响起百面打鼓的声音，
炸雷把大树劈倒在地上；
老林里烧起了七天不熄的大火，
火光把先祖的眼睛照亮。
先祖把火种捧回山洞，
把它小小心心保藏。
有了火再不怕抓人的豹子，
有了火再不怕吞人的大蟒。

And sisters knew not each other's looks.

They did not know their uncles

And did not think about their aunts.

Once they drove away the leopards,

They moved into their caves;

Once they scared away the boas,

They found their sleep chambers.

When there was food,

They ate to their fullest;

When there wasn't any,

They fell to the ground from hunger.

Seeing the monkeys picking the fruits,

They learned to pick and eat them, too.

Seeing the bamboo rats digging the bamboo shoots,

They dug and tasted them.

Seeing the pangolins covered with scales,

They also put on the clothes of leaves.

And hearing the parrots talking,

They also learned to speak.

From the sky came the drumming sound from all sides,

And thunders split the big trees that then fell;

For seven days a great fire burned in the forest,

The fire that lit up the ancestors' eyes.

The ancestors brought the seeds of the fire back to the cave,

And preserved it with great care.

With fire, they were no longer afraid of leopards;

With fire, they were no longer afraid of boas.

热乎乎的身子力大无穷，
先祖就像老象到处敢闯。
火是先祖的胆子，
火是先祖的力量，
火是哈尼的命根，
火是哈尼的亲娘。

（四）

歌手：

萨——依——！
哈尼先祖生养下了大群儿孙，
石洞不能再当容身的地方。
看见喜鹊喳喳地笑着做窝，
先祖也搭起圆圆的鸟窝房。
鸟窝房上搭树杈，
冷天暖和热天荫凉，
圆圆的房子开着圆圆的门，
堵起大门不怕虎狼。

有了"火娘"① 和房屋，
先祖找着落脚的地方，
老人嗨嗨地笑了，
娃娃爬满草房。

---

① 火娘：即火。哈尼族对与自己生活关系密切的事物都有亲切
的称呼，如将火称作"火娘"，将谷子称作"金谷娘"，等等。

The strength of the heated body was infinite,

And the ancestors dared to venture far and wide like the ele-

phants.

Fire gave the ancestors courage,

Fire gave the ancestors strength,

Fire was the lifeblood of the Hanis,

Fire was the birth-mother of the Hanis.

1. 4

Singer:

Sa—ee—!

The ancestors gave birth to numerous descendants,

And the caves could no longer serve as their shelter.

Seeing magpies chirping and making nests,

The ancestors also built the round birdhouses.

With branches on top,

The houses were warm in the winter and cool in the summer.

With the round door that could open up the round house,

And the closed door protected them from the beasts.

With "Mrs. Fire" ① and the house,

The ancestors found the place to settle down,

The elderly laughed,

And the toddlers crawled all over the hut.

---

　① Mrs. Fire: Fire. The Hani people have affectionate names for the
things closely related to their lives, e. g. fire is called Mrs. Fire, and grain
is called Mrs. Golden Grain, etc.

你见我也喜欢，
我见你也高兴，
一个见着一个会招呼，
一个遇着一个会礼让。
摘回野果，
先祖们又唱又跳，
高高低低的声音，
高山峡谷里回荡。
喜欢的时候，
男人就比试力气，
力气大的人，
得到众人的赞扬。

力气最大的是先祖惹斗，
他打主意像刮风一样快当。
当千百只蚂蚁走来，
抬着死鼠运回土房，
他急忙跑向人群，
拍着手把话讲：
"小小的蚂蚁抬得起老鼠，
比蚂蚁大的人抬得起大象！
老老少少都跟我上山去，
齐心合力把野物敲翻！"

九个最老的先祖点头了，
九个最小的先祖也喜欢，
惹斗领着大家去打猎，
从这山爬到那山。

They liked seeing each other.

They loved meeting each other.

They greeted each other

And respected each other.

Returning with the wild fruits,

The ancestors sang and danced,

Their high and low voice

Reverberating in the mountains and valleys.

When happy and leisurely,

Men tried to test their strength.

Those of great strength,

Were praised by the crowd.

The strongest was the ancestor Redou,

Who could make up his mind as quickly as the blowing wind.

When thousands of ants came,

Carrying the dead rat to the nest,

He ran to his people,

Clapped his hands and said:

"Little ants can carry a mouse,

And we, bigger than ants, can also carry the elephant!

Follow me up the mountains, old and young,

To work together and knock over the wild animals!"

Nine oldest ancestors nodded their heads,

And nine youngest ancestors also agreed,

So Redou led everyone to go hunting

From this mountain to that mountain.

遇着大象，

先祖把它摔下深涧；

遇着麂子，

就敲断它的脊梁；

见着豹子，

就扛起木棒吆喝；

见着野猪，

就拿起石头壮胆。

惹斗的主意比蜂儿还多，

他的眼睛像星星闪亮，

黄茅草①戳穿了脚背，

他比着做成竹箭，

先祖们都学他做，

弓箭成了男人的靠望。

摔山的时候，

利箭像流星飞去，

中箭的老虎像麻蛇扭成团，

最恶的豺狗也不敢下山岗。

众人：

萨——哝——萨！

———————

①　黄茅草：一种尖端如箭镞、质地异常坚硬的尖头茅草。

With elephants,

The ancestors chased them into the ravine;

With muntjacs,

They broke their backs;

With leopards,

They shouldered the sticks and shouted;

With wild boars,

They picked up the stones to embolden themselves.

Redou had more ideas than there were bees.

His eyes shone like the stars.

When the yellow thatch① pierced his instep,

He got the idea of making a bamboo arrow.

The ancestors all did what he did,

And the bows and arrows became men's resort.

When they hunted in the mountains,

Arrows flew like meteors.

The tigers shot by arrows twisted like snakes,

And even the cruellest dholes were afraid of coming down the
hills.

Audience:

Sa—nong—sa!

_____

①　Yellow thatch: A kind of unusually hard and pointed thatch with an
arrowhead at the tip.

（五）

歌手：

萨——依——！

麂子马鹿下儿，

一年只得一窝，

猎野物的先祖，

一天一天增多。

从前人见野物就跑，

现在野物逃到远方，

先祖们找不着肉了，

两座"山峰"戳伤肩膀。

先祖到处找食，

他们来到艾地戈耶河边，

抬眼望见飞虎捕鱼，

翅膀张开好像蛛网一样，

他们扑通扑通跳进河水，

丢上岸的鱼儿闪着银光。

火堆边围着大群先祖，

啃骨头撕鱼肉吃得真香，

有个阿波①牙齿不快，

---

① 阿波：即阿爷，也含有对英雄、智者的尊敬之意，如称呼起义女领袖多沙为"多沙阿波"。

1. 5

Singer：

Sa—ee—!

When muntjacs and red deer gave birth,

They have only a litter a year.

The hunting ancestors

Gradually increased in number.

In the past people ran away from the beasts,

But now it was the beasts that escaped afar.

The ancestors had nothing to hunt any more, and

Like barren mountains, their shoulders were skins and bones.

When the ancestors looked for food everywhere,

They came to the Aidi Geye River

And saw the flying squirrels fishing

With their wings spreading like cobwebs,

So they themselves plopped into the river,

And the fish they threw ashore glistening like silver.

Around the fire were a large group of the ancestors,

Nibbling on the bones and tear-flaying the fish.

An apo① had slow teeth,

---

①　Apo：Grandpa. It connotes respect for the courageous and the wise. For example, Duosha, a female leader of the Rebellion, was actually referred to as Apo Duosha.

手里的青鱼跳进火塘，
转眼间鱼被烧熟，
样子像枯叶又焦又黄，
香甜的气味四处飘散，
先祖的鼻子像细草搔痒。
阿波舍不得丢掉食物，
抢出火堆尝一尝；
味道从来没有这么鲜美，
他的嘴巴嗒得直响。
先祖们把鱼肉丢进大火，
从此晓得熟肉比生肉香。

听我讲呵，哈尼的子孙！
听我唱呵，先祖的后人！
仓里的红米撮一碗少一碗，
撮到底半碗也不够装。
两条大河里的鱼越捞越少，
虎尼虎那不再是哈尼的家乡。

顺着野兽的足迹走呵，
先祖离开住惯的山岗；
随着大水淌呵，
先祖走过无数河滩。
艾地戈耶把先祖领到新的住处，
这里有宽宽的水塘；
水塘像眼窝深凹下去，

Letting the herring jump into the fire,

And in a moment the fish was cooked.

The cooked fish looked like withered leaves,

Burnt and golden, with a sweet smell

That tickled the ancestor's nose like it was teased by the fine

grass.

The apo would not waste any food,

Snatching the fish from the fire for a taste.

It was so delicious,

He chewed with a happy noise.

The ancestors threw the fish and meat into the fire

And learned that meats cooked tasted better than raw.

Listen to me, the Hani offspring;

Listen to me, the descendants of the ancestors!

The rice in the granary became less and less

Until it hit the bottom.

The fish in the two big rivers became fewer and fewer

Until the Hunihuna was no longer the hometown to the Hanis.

Following the footsteps of the wild beasts,

The ancestors left the mountains they had learned to live;

Walking along the flowing waters,

The ancestors went through countless rivers and beaches.

The Aidi Geye River led the ancestors to their new living

place,

Where there was a wide pond

That was like a sunken eye socket,

先祖就在什虽湖①边盖起住房。

众人：

萨——哝——萨！

---

① 什虽湖：湖名。

The ancestors built their houses on the shores of the Shisui Lake①.

Audience:

Sa—nong—sa!

---

① Shisui Lake: The name of a lake.

二、从什虽湖到嘎鲁嘎则

（一）

歌手：

萨——依——！

亲亲的兄弟姐妹们，

先祖爱上新的家乡。

七十七双眼睛四方看，

七十七只手指指点点，

大湖边山岭连着山岭，

密林里野兽见人不慌。

七十七双耳朵一齐听，

七十七双脚走遍山岗，

大湖静得像睡着的小娃，

山林把大风拦在远方。

哈尼女人走到湖边背水，

哈尼小娃在草坡上吵嚷。

老林的绿荫下，

到处望得见哈尼支下的扣子，

Chapter 2　From the Shisui Lake to Galugaze

2. 1

Singer:

Sa—ee—!

Dear brothers and sisters,

Our ancestors fell in love with their new hometown.

Seventy-seven pairs of eyes looked around.

Seventy-seven pairs of hands pointed at here and there.

Around the great lake were mountains after mountains.

Beasts in the forest were not afraid of men.

Seventy-seven pairs of ears were listening,

And seventy-seven pairs of feet stepped upon all the hills.

The great lake was as still as a little sleeping child,

And the mountains kept the wind at a distance.

The Hani women walked to the lake to fetch the water,

And the Hani children clamoured on the grassy slope.

Under the shade of the old green forest,

Traps were set everywhere.

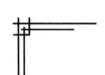

尖尖的山脊上，
哈尼围猎声如雷响，
成群的豺狼野狗，
跌进了深深的陷阱。
成群的野猪麂鹿，
被利箭射穿了胸膛。

什虽山上成群的野物，
像湖边铺满的沙子，
先祖敲死了老野猪，
把它的小儿逮回住房。

先祖奥遮的姑娘遮姒，
又把新的主意想：
"才发的草芽汁不甜，
才下的小猪肉不香，
不如把它豢养，
再破它的肚肠。"
遮姒把小猪抱去，
从此把野物饲养。

先祖逮回十七种野物，
十七种野物闹闹嚷嚷。
遮姒做成木栏，
树桩围在四方。

木栏里野猪野马一处吃草，
木栏里野牛野羊一处游逛。

On the cusp of the mountain ridge,

The sound of hunting was like thunders.

Herds of jackals and dholes

Fell into the deep traps.

Herds of wild boars and muntjacs

Were shot by the sharp arrows.

The wild beasts around the Shisui Mountain

Were like the sand by the lake.

The ancestors killed a wild boar,

And brought its cubs back to the house.

Zhesi, the daughter of the ancestor Aozhe,

Got an idea:

"Like the newly-sprouted grass is not sweet,

The newly-born cubs are not delicious.

Better raise them

And then slaughter them."

Zhesi brought the piglets home

And started to domesticate the wild animals.

The ancestors brought back seventy-seven kinds of them,

Which made all kinds of noises.

Zhesi made the wooden fences,

With stakes set in all directions.

In the stockade, wild boars and wild horses grazed together,

And bisons and wild goats wandered side by side.

野鸡野鸭也关进来，
野狗野猫成了同乡。
一年两年过去了，
动物分出野生家养。
野生的有一百二十种：
龙，蛇，虎，豹，麂，鹿，狼……
家养的有十二种：
鸡，猪，鸭，鹅，马，牛，羊……

什虽湖边热闹了，
人欢马叫闹嚷嚷，
生着七十七层红冠的公鸡，
拖长声音啼鸣，
一夜不睡的看家狗，
见人就把尾巴摇晃。

六畜家禽越来越多了，
串串干巴挂满屋梁，
遮姒姑娘人人敬重，
件件大事和她商量。

哈尼还有一位能人，
遮努的名声飞遍八方。
她摘来了饱满的草籽，
种进最黑最松的土壤，
姑娘又去背来了湖水，
像雨神把水泼在籽上。
草籽发出了粗壮的芽，

Pheasants and ducks were also brought in,

And wild dogs and cats became fellow-villagers.

After a couple of years,

The animals were separated as wild and domesticated.

There were 120 species of the wild animals:

Dragon, snake, tiger, leopard, muntjac, deer, wolf...

There were twelve species of the domesticated animals:

Chicken, pig, duck, goose, horse, cow, sheep...

The shores of the Shisui Lake were getting lively,

With people bustling and horses neighing.

The rooster with seventy-seven layers of red cockscomb

Crowed long and loud;

Watchdogs who stayed up all night

Wagged their tails on seeing people.

Domestic animals were all thriving,

And jerkies were hanging from the beams of the houses.

Ms. Zhesi was respected by all,

And people consulted her for every important matter.

There was another one of great ability among the Hanis,

Her name Zhenu spreading far and wide.

She picked the healthy grass seeds

And planted them into the darkest and softest soil.

She then carried the water from the lake

And watered the seeds like a goddess of rain.

The grass seeds grew stout sprouts

草籽长出了高高的杆。
当树叶落地的时候，
黄生生的草籽结满草秆，
先祖们吃着喷香的草籽，
起名叫玉麦、谷子和高粱。

遮努的收成有好有差，
细想想是节令没有合上，
她请教养牛放羊的遮姒，
遮努姑娘有了主张。
她指着十二种动物，
定下了年月属相，
一年分做十二个月，
一月有三十个白天夜晚；
哈尼算日子从鼠起头，
算到胖猪一轮就满。
有了属相按时栽种，
遮努种出吃不尽的米粮。
她又用五谷酿出美酒，
美酒成了哈尼离不开的伙伴。

众人：
萨——哝——萨！

And then into tall stalks.

When the leaves fell down in the autumn,

The yellow grass seeds grew all over the stalks.

The ancestors ate fragrant seeds

And named them corn, millet and sorghum.

Zhenu did not always have good harvests,

And she figured the growing had to match the solar cycles.

After consulting Zhesi who cared for cows and sheep,

Zhenu had an idea.

Pointing to twelve animals,

She assigned the year, months with animal signs.

A year had twelve months,

And a month had thirty days and nights.

The Hanis started counting with the rat

And ended the cycle with the pig.

With the animal signs as a guide for farming,

Zhenu grew an inexhaustible supply of food.

She then made wine out of the grains,

And the wine became the indispensable companion of the
Hanis.

Audience:

Sa—nong—sa!

（二）

歌手：

萨——依——！

粗树围得过来，

长藤也能丈量，

什虽湖好是好了，

好日子也不长久。

先祖去撵野物，

烈火烧遍大山，

燎着的山火难熄，

浓烟罩黑四方，

烧过七天七夜，

天地变了模样。

老林是什虽的阿妈，

大湖睡在老林下方，

这下大风吼着来了，

黄沙遮没了太阳，

大湖露出了湖底，

哈尼惹下了祸殃。

栽下的姜秆变黑，

蒜苗像枯枝一样，

谷秆比龙子雀的脚杆还细，

出头的嫩芽又缩进土壤，

天神地神发怒了，

2. 2

Singer:

Sa—ee—!

The thickest trees can be embraced by many people holding hands,

And long vines can be measured with rulers.

Good as the Shisui Lake was,

The good times had to end.

To keep away the wild animals,

The ancestors set the fire to the mountains,

But they couldn't put the fire out,

Black smoke covering everywhere.

After seven days and nights of burning,

Heaven and earth changed the appearance.

The forest was the mother of the Lake Shisui,

Which lay beneath the forest.

Once the wind was howling,

The sand blocked the sun,

The great lake showed its bottom,

And the Hani people were in trouble.

The planted ginger stalks turned black;

The garlic shoots were like withered twigs.

The stalks of the crops were thinner than the feet of the dragon-finch,

And the budding shoots shriveled back into the dirt.

The gods of heaven and earth were infuriated,

灾难降到了先祖头上。
身背不会走路的婴儿，
手牵才会蹦跳的小娃，
哈尼先祖动身上路了，
要去寻找休养生息的地方。

走走停停，停停走走，
几百个人做一队，
一个也不漏掉；
停停走走，走走停停，
几千个人做一群，
一个也不走散。
先祖走过的高山，
七十七双手也数不清。
先祖涉过的河滩，
七十七张嘴也说不完。

熬过多少干季和冷季，
耐过多少雨天和热天，
哈尼来到南方的群山，
来到嘎鲁嘎则地方。

这里巨石满地，
这里龙竹成行，
清亮的溪水绕着竹篷，
竹鸡的鸣叫响在耳旁。

And disaster befell the ancestors.

Carrying babies who couldn't walk yet,

Holding the hands of toddlers who had just started to jump and skip,

The ancestors set off

To look for another place to live.

Going and stopping, stopping and going,

Hundreds of people formed a team,

Leaving no one behind;

Stopping and going, going and stopping,

Thousands of people were in a group,

Letting no one go astray.

The mountains that our ancestors climbed

Cannot be counted even with seventy-seven hands.

The rivers that our ancestors crossed

Cannot be numbered even with seventy-seven mouths.

After having undergone many dry and cold seasons,

And endured many days of rain and heat,

The Hanis came to a mountainous area in the south,

An area called Galugaze.

There were huge stones everywhere

And dragon bamboos in rows.

Clear spring flowed around the bamboos,

And the crowing of the bamboo partridges was in the air.

竹林里住着阿撮①，
说话像清清的波浪；
阿撮见人嘻嘻地笑，
拉着哈尼问短问长。
先祖放下背箩，
娃娃爬到地上，
女人在溪边梳好头发，
男人把脸洗得放光，
哈尼跟阿撮走进竹林，
竹间绿荫像溪水清凉。

好客的阿撮拿出竹鸡竹笋，
远方的哈尼拿出玉麦酒浆，
两处人都像火塘一样热情，
不断的话像溪水流淌。

阿撮教哈尼破竹编篾，
哈尼换上滑亮的竹筐；
阿撮教哈尼织帽子，
笋壳帽轻巧又凉爽。
哈尼把鸡鸭分给阿撮，
雄鸡帮阿撮叫起太阳；

---

① 阿撮：据传为傣族，不详。

In the bamboo forest lived the ethnic group Acuo①,

Who spoke with a voice like clear waves;

They smiled when meeting people

And visited with the Hanis friendly.

The ancestors put down the back baskets,

And the children crawled onto the ground.

The women combed their hair by the brooks,

And the men cleaned their faces shining.

The Hani people followed their new friends into the bamboo forest,

And it provided the green shade as cool as the spring water.

The hospitable Acuo people shared the bamboo partridges and bamboo shoots.

And the Hani guests from afar took out the corn wine.

Both of them were as friendly to each other as the warming fireplace,

And their constant talks flowed like the spring.

The Acuos taught the Hanis how to cut split bamboos to weave bamboo baskets,

And the Hanis now had shiny baskets;

The Acuos also taught the Hanis how to weave hats

That, made of bamboo-shoot shells, were light and cool.

The Hanis shared the chickens and ducks with the Acuos,

So that the cocks woke up the Acuos at sunrise;

---

① Acuo: It is said to be the Dai people, but it is not known for sure.

哈尼教阿撮种五谷，
阿撮的篾箩装满玉麦高粱。
酿酒的方法阿撮也学会了，
阿撮男人们天天喝红脸膛。

先祖在嘎鲁嘎则住了两辈，
竹林刚遮掩着哈尼的住房；
只可惜龙竹刚刚成林，
苦难又落到哈尼头上。

阿撮的头人岩扎，
脾气比老熊还鲁莽，
他的女人突然死掉，
岩扎一天哭了七场。
他的咒骂像七月的暴雨，
咒骂哈尼带来不祥，
发誓要把哈尼撵走，
像把麂子撵下山岗。
哈尼送的干巴他当柴烧，
哈尼给的美酒他泼地上；
哈尼老人遭他骂了，
小娃也尝到他的棍棒。

七十七个老人站出来说话，
七十七个老人走来商量：
"我们还是走吧，
嘎鲁嘎则不是我们的家乡；
我们还是搬吧，

48

The Hanis taught the Acuos to grow crops,

And the Acuos' wicker baskets were filled with corn and sorghum.

The Acuos also learned how to make wine,

And the Acuo men drank their faces red everyday.

The ancestors lived in Galugaze for two generations,

With the bamboo forest growing just to cover their huts;

Unfortunately, when the dragon bamboos just became forest,

The scourge fell upon the Hanis again.

Yanza, the head of the Acuos,

Had a temper as bad as an old bear.

His wife died a sudden death,

And he cried seven times a day.

His curse was like the rainstorm in the seventh month,

Claiming that the Hanis brought the ill omen.

He vowed to drive the Hanis away,

Like driving the muntjacs down the hill.

He burned the Hanis' gift of the beef jerky as firewood;

He sprayed their gift of the wine on the ground.

He cursed the old Hani men

And beat the Hani children with clubs.

Seventy-seven old Hani men came together.

Seventy-seven old men talked over and said:

"Let's leave.

Galugaze is not our homeland.

Let's move away

离开阿撮居住的地方；
和和气气地来和和气气地走，
不要把眯细的眼睛变成睁大的眼睛！
喜喜欢欢地来喜喜欢欢地走，
不要用抬酒碗的手去抬弓箭棍棒！"

哈尼要搬了，
要到遥远的山岗；
哈尼要走了，
要到遥远的溪旁。
挖一蓬龙竹带上呵，
哈尼没有把阿撮的好意遗忘；
挖一蓬龙竹背上呵，
让哈尼不管走多远，
都有嘎鲁嘎则的竹林遮太阳。①

众人：

萨——哦——萨！

---

① 哈尼族贝玛在念诵葬词时要敲响竹筒，表示对嘎鲁嘎则的怀念。自此之后，哈尼族每到一地都要在寨脚栽竹子，竹子成为哈尼的一种标志。栽竹时要选三颗洁白的石子和三棵草放进塘底，而且只能由三十岁以上的男子栽，否则竹子发不出来，栽竹的人也会有一生的苦难。

From the place where the Acuos live.

Let's come in peace and leave in peace.

Do not wait till the small smiling eyes turn into big angry ones!

Let's come happily and leave happily.

Do not wait till the hands that raise the wine cups turn into the ones that wield weapons!"

The Hanis were going to move

To the faraway mountains.

They were going to leave

For the distant rivers.

Digging up a clump of the dragon bamboos and bringing it along,

The Hanis did not forget the kindness of the Acuos.

They carried the clump of the dragon bamboo

So that no matter how faraway they traveled,

The Galugaze bamboo forest would provide a shelter from the sun.①

Audience:

Sa—nong—sa!

---

①　The Hani priest "beima" knocked a bamboo tube when chanting at the funeral ceremony to memorialize Galugaze. From then on, the Hanis began to plant bamboos at the foot of their village wherever they went, so the bamboo had become a symbol of the Hanis. When planting the bamboo, they chose three white stones and three plants and put them in the bottom of the pond. This planting job could only be done by men over thirty years of age. Otherwise, the bamboo could not grow, and the planter would suffer a lifetime of hardship.

三、惹罗普楚

（一）

歌手：

萨——依——！
讲了，哈尼的后代儿孙！
唱了，亲亲的兄弟姐妹！
今晚火塘里添进新柴，
茶水在壶里快活地歌唱，
酒碗喝干了又倒满，
先祖的古今又开始一章。
老牛忘不记它的脚迹，
白鹇忘不记找食的草场，
麂子忘不了出生的岩洞，
哈尼忘不了惹罗①——
那头一回安寨定居的地方！

不知是哈尼找到了宝地，
还是哈尼感动了上苍，

---

① 惹罗：地名。

Chapter 3　Reluo Puchu

3. 1

Singer：

Sa—ee—!

Let's tell stories, the Hani descendants!

Let's sing songs, dear brothers and sisters!

Let's add firewood to the fireplace,

And let the water sing happily in the pot.

Fill up your emptied wine bowls,

Now that the lives of the ancestors were to enter a new chapter.

The old cow won't forget where it came from;

The silver pheasant won't forget its pasture;

The muntjac won't forget the cave where it was born;

And as the Hanis wouldn't forget Reluo①—

The first place they settled in!

Perhaps because the Hanis had found the treasured land

Or they had moved heaven,

———————————

①　Reluo: The name of a place.

53

先祖踏进了一块低低的凹地，

茫茫大雨跟着飞过山梁。

太阳带着阳光的热和，

簌簌地洗掉先祖脸上的黄尘；

大雨带着泉水的清凉，

哗哗地冲掉先祖身上的泥浆。

先祖欢喜地呼叫："惹罗！惹罗！"①

从此用惹罗来称这个地方。②

惹罗的土地合不合哈尼的心意？

惹罗的山水合不合哈尼的愿望？

先祖抬眼张望：

高山罩在雾里，

露气润着草场，

山梁像马尾披下，

下面是一片凹塘③。

先祖西斗见多识广，

指着大山把话讲：

---

① 惹罗：哈尼语，意为大雨倾盆。

② 另一歌手演唱中又说人类发源在惹罗，并由此迁往虎尼虎那，
但多数歌手与朱小和演唱则不同此说。惹罗又称惹罗普楚，即寨子很
多的惹罗地方；"普楚"，即大寨。下文中讲到寨子尚有"蒲玛"之
说，即大寨之意，如"厄戚蒲玛"。

③ 凹塘：山凹。

The ancestors stepped onto a basinal area,

As the heavy rain followed them, flying over the mountain ridge.

The sun with its warmth,

Washed away the dust on the ancestors' faces;

The rain with the coolness of the spring,

Washed away the mud on the ancestors' bodies;

They shouted happily: "Reluo! Reluo!"①

Hence it became the name of the place.②

Would Reluo meet the Hanis' expectations?

Would Reluo make their wishes come true?

The ancestors looked up:

The mountains were veiled in the mist,

And the meadows were moistened by the dew.

The ridge was like a horse's tail,

And below the ridge was the aotang③.

The ancestor Xidou, who was very wise,

Pointed to the mountain and said:

———————————

① Reluo: Heavy rain in the Hani language.

② According to another singer, the mankind originated in Reluo and then moved to the Hunihuna, but most singers and ZHU Xiaohe disagreed with that view. Reluo is also known as Reluo Puchu, which means Reluo with many large villages; Puchu means large village. "Puma" is another word for large village, e. g. Eqi Puma.

③ Aotang: (Notes from translater) It refers to a concave terrian. It is what the Hanis call an area in the mountain like a navel, round and dented, which they think is the best place to set up their village.

"哈尼人，快看吧，
天神赐给我们好地方：
横横的山像骏马飞跑，
身子是凹塘的屏障，
躲进凹塘的哈尼，
从此不怕风霜！"

智慧的老人点着白头，
赞成用惹罗做哈尼的家乡，
他们坐下说了长长的话，
把安寨大事细细商量。
从此哈尼不像雾露漂浮，
安寨有了惹罗的式样！

上头山包像斜插的手，
寨头靠着交叉的山岗；
下面的山包像牛架，
寨脚就建在这个地方。
寨心安在哪里？
就在凹塘中央。

这里白鹇爱找食，
这里箐鸡爱游荡，
火神也好来歇，①
水神也好来唱。②

---

① 此句意思是凹塘里背风暖和。
② 此句意思是哈尼族居住的地方清泉四季长流。

"Hani People, look,
The god of heaven has given us a good place:
The mountains are stretched like a running horse,
Its body shielding the aotang.
Now settled here,
The Hanis won't be afraid of the wind and frost any longer!"

Other wise old men nodded their heads
In agreement with building their homes in Reluo.
They sat down and had a long talk
And discussed the settlement in detail.
From then on, the Hanis no longer drifted like fog and dew,
And Reluo became the model of their setting up villages.

The higher mountains were like two slanted hands,
And the head of the village leaned against where the hills
connected.
The lower mountains were like a cattle rack,
Where the foot of the village was built.
Where was the center of the village?
It was right in the middle of the aotang.

It was where silver pheasants foraged
And bamboo pheasants wandered.
It was where the god of fire rested①
And the god of water sang.②

---

① It means the aotang had the wind blocked out and was thus warm.
② It means there were always spring waters flowing in all seasons
where the Hanis lived.

选寨基是大事情，
不是高能不能当。
先祖推举了西斗做头人，
希望他贡献出智慧和力量。
西斗拿出三颗贝壳，
用来占卜凶险吉祥：
一颗是子孙繁衍的预兆，
一颗代表禾苗茁壮，
一颗象征着六畜兴旺，
贝壳寄托着哈尼的愿望。
贝壳立下一天，
大风没有把它们刮倒，
贝壳立下两天，
大雨没有把它们冲歪，
三天早上公鸡还没叫，
西斗头人来到贝壳旁：
"昨夜老虎咬翻百只马鹿，
哈尼的贝壳安然无恙。
尊敬的阿波阿匹①，
亲亲的兄弟姐妹，
寨基选在这里，
哈尼的子孙会好，
哈尼的六畜会多，
哈尼的庄稼会旺！"
西斗又把肥狗杀倒，
拖着绕过一圈。

———————————

① 阿匹：阿奶。

Choosing the village foundation was an important matter,

And only the most capable would do.

The ancestors elected Xidou as the chief,

Hoping that he would use all his wisdom and power.

Xidou took out three shells,

And used them for divination:

One shell represented the propagation of the Hanis,

One the potential for the harvests,

And one the outlook for the domestic animals,

All representing the hope of the Hanis.

The first day the shells were set up,

The wind did not blow them over.

Another day had passed,

The rain did not push them tilted.

On the third day and before the cock had crowed,

Xidou came by the shells and said:

"Last night the tiger bit over a hundred of red deer,

But the shells remained safe.

Respectable apos and apis①,

Dear brothers and sisters,

If we made the foundation here,

The descendants will prosper,

The domestic animals will multiply,

And the crops will be abundant!"

Xidou then killed a fat dog

And then dragged it around in a circle.

①　Api: Granny.

鲜红的狗血是天神的寨墙，
它把人鬼分开两旁；
黑亮的血迹是地神的宝刀，
它把豺狼虎豹阻挡。

先祖的直系后裔，
真正的哈尼子孙，
牢牢记住吧，
惹罗是哈尼第一个大寨，
惹罗像太阳永远闪光，
不管哈尼搬迁千次万次，
惹罗是世上哈尼的亲娘！

众人：
萨——哝——萨！

（二）

歌手：
萨——依——！
惹罗的哈尼是建寨的哈尼，
一切要改过老样。
难瞧难住的鸟窝房不能要了，
先祖们盖起座座新房。
惹罗高山红红绿绿，
大地蘑菇遍地生长。
小小蘑菇不怕风雨，

The fresh red dog blood stood for the village wall by the god
of heaven,

Separating people and ghosts.

The shiny black blood stain stood for the swords by the god
of earth,

Keeping the beasts away.

Direct descendants of the ancestors

And true Hani offsprings,

Bear in mind:

Reluo was the Hanis' first large settlement village,

Like the sun that always shines;

No matter how many times the Hanis move,

Reluo is their beloved mother!

Audience:

Sa—nong—sa!

3. 2

Singer:

Sa—ee—!

The Hanis in Reluo were the generation of builders,

Building their new village.

They abandoned the ugly-looking nest-shaped houses

And built many new ones.

The Reluo mountains were red and green

With mushrooms growing everywhere.

Small mushrooms could stand wind and rain,

美丽的样子叫人难忘；
比着样子盖起蘑菇房，
直到今天它还遍布哈尼家乡。①

阿烟家三父子，
是哈尼最早的木匠。
他们砍来的梁柱，
像龙神飞天一样标直。
他们筑起的泥墙，
像早晨的太阳一样金亮。

哈尼姑娘和媳妇，
盖房时候最忙。
姑娘上山来割茅草，
媳妇下箐砍来竹竿，
她们的草排，
扎得像大雁展翅，
千百只雁翅落在蘑菇盖②上。

---

① 哀牢山区的哈尼族以蘑菇房为骄傲，有"谁不盖起蘑菇房，
谁就不是真正的哈尼"之说。

② 蘑菇盖：指蘑菇状房顶。

And their beauty was unforgettable.

The mushroom-shaped houses were built,

And till today they are everywhere in the Hani hometowns.①

The father and sons in the Ayan household

Were the first Hani carpenters.

They chopped down trees and used them as beams and pil-

lars

That were as straight as the Deity Dragon flying up into the

sky.

They built the mud-walls

That were as shiny as the golden morning sun.

The Hani women, unmarried and married,

Were the busiest when houses were built.

Unmarried young women went up to the mountain to cut the

thatch,

While married women went down to the valley to cut bam-

boos.

Their grass rows

Were weaved like the wings of the wild geese,

Hundreds and thousands of them falling over the mushroom

caps②.

---

① The Hani people in the Ailao Mountains are proud of their mushroom houses. There is a saying, "He who does not build a mushroom house
is not a real Hani."

② Mushroom cap: It refers to the mushroom-shaped roof.

最后要立大门，
黄心树扛到寨旁，
做成的门板像蛋黄般好瞧，
开门声像鸡叫一样响。①

众人：
萨——哝——萨！

（三）

歌手：
萨——依——！
大田是哈尼的独儿子，
大田是哈尼的独姑娘；
西斗领着先祖去挖田，
笑声和沟水一起流淌。

在落叶季节去砍树，
树灰是土地的米粮，
先种两年玉麦荞子，
试试土地对哈尼的心肠；
土好再来打埂犁耙，
地要松得像蒸糕一样。
田小伙②打扮好：

---

① 哈尼族喜欢会响的门，认为它会报告客人来到。
② 哈尼族把田地称为小伙子，与前面的"火娘"相同。

Finally, the gate,

The yellow-heart trees were carried to the side of the village

And was made into the doors, whose color was as nice-loo-

king as the egg yolk.

The sound of the door opening was like cocks crowing.①

Audience:

Sa—nong—sa!

3.3

Singer:

Sa—ee—!

The field was the Hanis' only son

And their only daughter.

Xidou led the ancestors to cultivate the lands,

Their laughter and the water running together.

They cut down the trees in the season of falling leaves,

And the tree ashes were the food for the land.

They first planted corn and buckwheat

To see if the field was kind to the Hanis;

They then plowed the kind field,

Making it as soft as the steamed buns.

When the field was ready like the groom②,

---

①　The Hani people like creaky door as it will announce the arrival of guests.

②　The Hanis call the field the groom, similar to Mrs. Fire as seen above.

又来养秧姑娘①，
秧姑娘出嫁的日子，
哈尼就在田里奔忙。
秧苗长高结谷穗，
像顶顶金帽发光；
新谷回家的时节，
脚碓像啄木鸟把树敲响；
清香的新米煮好了，
头一碗给阿波阿匹先尝。

从前惹罗只有老林，
现在惹罗金谷满山②，
最老的阿波坐在火塘边，
张开瘪嘴把话讲：
"哈尼人啊，我的儿孙！
我们再不用到处漂游，
再不用摘野果充饥肠！
快牵起我的手，
去看马尾一样奄下的谷穗，
去看酸汤杆③一样壮的荞麦。
哈尼的儿孙们，
能吃苦才得甜，

---

① 哈尼族把秧苗称为姑娘。
② 哈尼族惯以开垦梯田著称。
③ 酸汤杆：一种可食植物。

The seedlings arrived like the bride①.

On the day the bride leaves her home,

The Hanis were busy working in the fields.

The seedlings grew tall and yielded ears of grains,

Like the shining golden crowns.

By the time the new harvest was brought home,

The husk pounders sounded like the woodpeckers' pecking.

The first bowl of rice was cooked

And was given to apos and apis to taste.

Reluo had only forests before,

But now it was covered with golden harvest②.

The oldest apo, sitting by the fireplace,

Opened his toothless mouth and said:

"Hanis, my children!

We no longer need to wander and drift,

No longer need to pick the wild fruits as food.

Quickly, hold my hand

And let's go see the ears of grains hanging like the horses'

tails

And the buckwheat strong like the giant knotweeds③.

Remember, Hani children,

Only those who can endure the hardship can taste the sweet

harvest.

---

① The Hanis call the seedlings the bride.

② The Hani people are famous for cultivating terraced fields.

③ Giant knotweed: An edible plant.

做活要像土狗打洞，
不怕黄泥沾在身上，
栽秧收谷时尽管去苦去累，
死了晚娘也不消忙。"

众人：
萨——哝——萨！

（四）

歌手：
萨——依——！
惹罗的哈尼，
像蚂蚁上树结队成形，
扳着指头算算，
六千已经算满；
二月祭树①的时候，

---

① 祭树：即祭祖节，过去译为"祭龙节"，不确切，时间在十月后（哈尼以十月为岁首，故有"二月祭树"之说），主祭人类保护神"艾玛"（寨神）。每个家族有自己的神树，全寨又有共同的神树，由眯谷（祭司）主持祭祀，届时杀牲献祭，饮酒歌舞，狂欢二三日。妇女不能参加祭树，但在元阳下主鲁等地，主祭人又须男扮女装，这也许与祭树产生于遥远的母权制时代或与下文所叙的哈尼民族英雄戚姒有关。

Work as hard as the dogs digging the hole,

Fearing not the dirt covering your bodies.

Work so hard during the planting and harvesting seasons

That stop not even for the death of your stepmother."

Audience:

Sa—nong—sa!

3. 4

Singer:

Sa—ee—!

The Hanis in Reluo

Lined up like ants climbing the tree.

According to their counting,

The population was more than six thousand.

When making sacrifices before the sacred tree① in the
second lunar month,

---

① Making sacrifices to the sacred tree: Ancestor Worshipping Festival, also translated as "Dragon Worshipping Festival". It has not a fixed date
but is usually celebrated after the October Festival (October is the beginning
of a year in the Hani calendar and that's why there is the saying "making
sacrifices to the sacred tree in the second lunar month"). The chief goddess
in the rituals is "Aima" (Village God), the protector of human beings. Each
family has its own sacred tree, while the village has a common one. Migu
(the priest) presides the rituals in which animals are killed to offer sacrifices. People drink wine, sing and dance, and have a carnival for two or
three days. Women are not allowed to participate in the tree sacrifice, but in
places such as Zhulu Village in Yuanyang County, the chief worshiper has to
dress up as a woman, a practice that may be traced back to the origin of the
rituals in the distant era of matriarchy or to the Hani national heroine Qisi,
who will be described in the later chapters. (Notes from translator: It is also
called the Aimatu Festival. For three to five days people stop all their activities and celebrate.)

肥猪杀翻在山上，

腿快的人，只分得手指厚的一片，

脚慢的人，树叶薄的一片也不想要。

一家住不下分两家，

一寨住不下分两寨，

老人时时为分家操心，

头人天天为分寨奔忙。

寨里出了头人、贝玛①、工匠，

能人们把大事小事分掌。

头人坐在寨堡里，

蜜蜂没有他忙碌；

贝玛天天诵读竹排经书②，

哈尼的事书里栽③得周详；

工匠在溪边拉起风箱，④

---

① 贝玛：哈尼族传统歌手，民族古老文化的主要保存者，也参加一些祭祀活动。贝玛分大小，能者称牛腿贝玛，祭祀时可分得一只牛腿；小贝玛称鸡腿贝玛，可分得一只鸡腿。但其生活来源绝大部分依靠自己的农业劳动。

② 竹排书：哈尼族无文字，传说从前有过，书写于穿孔竹片之上，称竹排书，类似汉族竹简。

③ 栽：也许是书写工具的原因，哈尼语中没有"写字"，只有"栽字"。

④ 哈尼族工匠的工场多设在小溪边，意为财源不断。

Pigs were killed up in the mountains.

Those who were fast got a slice as thin as a finger.

Those who were slow barely got a slice as thin as a leaf.

A family could no longer live under one roof and was divided into two,

And the villages need to be divided too.

The elderlies were busy with dividing the families

And the headmen were bustling about with dividing the village.

There were now headmen, beimas① and craftsmen,

The capable men taking on different responsibilities.

The headmen working in the fort of the villages

Were busier than the bees.

The beimas read aloud everyday the classics on the bamboo slips②,

On which were planted③ the Hanis' stories in detail.

The blacksmiths operated the bellows by the river,④

---

① Beima: The traditional Hani singer, the main conservator of the ancient Hani culture; he also participates in some sacrificial activities. A senior beima is called the ox-leg beima as he can receive an ox leg during the sacrificial ceremony. A junior beima is called the drumstick beima as he can receive only a drumstick. Most of them make a living by farming.

② Bamboo slips: The Hani people have no writing now. But according to a Hani legend, they used to have writing on bamboo slips with holes for strings, similar to the Han's bamboo slips.

③ Plant: Perhaps due to the writing tool, in the Hani language they do not "write" but "plant" words.

④ The Hani blacksmiths' workshops were often set by the river. They hoped that the sources of fortune would run nonstop like the river.

那里是他发财的地方。
惹罗大寨美名远扬，
各山各坝的那扎①来来往往，
矮山的汉族来了三伙，
河坝的傣族来三帮。②

汉族夸矮山田里水多，
枯水的三月也满满当当；
傣族夸坝子里鱼胖，
支起篾笆鱼吃不完。
他们要换惹罗的大田，
先祖摇头不让。
汉族又夸瓦房明亮，
上楼就会咚咚作响；
傣族又夸竹楼凉快，
上去就会嘎嘎地唱。
他们要换哈尼的蘑菇房，
先祖摆手不让。
亲亲的兄弟姐妹们，

---

① 那扎：其他民族的统称。"扎"念 zā。下文皆同。

② 诗中多有同类描写，意思是说：哪怕汉族住在矮山上，傣族
住在平坝里，也没有哈尼住的地方好。

Where they made their fortune.

The Reluo village was famous.

The Naza① from other places came and went, including

Three groups of the Hans from the lower mountainous areas and

Three groups of the Dais from the riverside area.②

The Han people praised how much the water was in the hilly fields,

Brimming even during the dry seasons.

The Dai people admired how fat the fish were in the rivers,

And using the bamboo fences, they caught more than they could eat.

They wanted to trade for the lands in Reluo,

But the ancestors shook their heads and refused.

The Han people complimented how shiny the roof tiles were,

Making "dong dong" sound when they walked up the stairs.

The Dai people applauded how cool their bamboo houses were,

Singing "ga ga" as they went up the stairs.

They asked to trade with the Hanis for the mushroom houses,

The ancestors waved their hands and refused.

Dear brothers and sisters,

---

① Naza: Other ethnic groups are collectively called Naza.

② There are many similar descriptions in the epic. It means that even though the Han people lived in the lower mountains and the Dai people lived in the flat land, those places did not compare with the Hani's settlements; in other words, Hani villages were good.

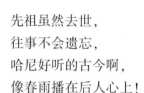
先祖虽然去世，
往事不会遗忘，
哈尼好听的古今啊，
像春雨播在后人心上！

众人：
萨——哝——萨！

（五）

歌手：
萨——依——！
哈尼有句古话，
老人常常爱讲：
"喜欢的时候不要太喜欢，
悲伤的时候也不要太悲伤。"

管病的天神心肠比黑蜂还毒，
他把病种撒遍惹罗的土壤。
力气最大的牛吐出白沫，
跑得最快的马虚汗流淌，
猪耳里流出黑血，
狗拖着尾巴发狂，
人吃不下饭喝不进水，
大人小娃两眼无光。

老实伤心啰，
亲亲的姐妹，
惹罗一天出了七十个寡妇！

Even though our ancestors have passed away,
Their stories should never be forgotten.
The Hanis' good stories of the past and today
Are like the spring rain moistening the hearts of all the Hanis.

Audience:

Sa—nong—sa!

3.5

Singer:

Sa—ee—!
There is an old Hani saying
That the elderlies like to use:
"When liking something, don't like it too much,
Nor be too sorrowful when feeling sad."

The god of plagues, more venomous than the black bees,
Spread the virus in Reluo.
The strongest oxen foamed at the mouth;
The fastest horse sweated the cold sweat;
Pigs bled through their ears;
Dogs became rabic dragging their tails;
People had no appetite for food or water;
And everyone, old and young, had no shine in their eyes.

It was so sad,
Our dearest sisters,
In Reluo seventy women were widowed in one day!

老实悲惨啰，
亲亲的兄弟，
惹罗一夜有七十个独儿子死亡！
生谷子的大田闲了，
牙齿草有一拃长；
蒸饭的甑子闲了，
绿霉比头发还长；
背水的竹筒闲了，
白木耳生在筒上！
……

寨堡里聚齐了老人，
头人请阿波们来商量。
人人头低得像熟透的谷穗，
个个脸色比蜂蜡还黄。
七座大山压住人们的舌头，
能说会道的人也无力开腔。
缺了十七颗牙齿的老阿波，
把大家不愿讲的话来讲：

"水浇过的火塘吹不着，
刀砍过的树长不长。
快快离开惹罗土地，
去那瘟神够不着的地方！
快趁哈尼还没绝种，
去到别处繁衍兴旺！"
阿波的眼睛哭出鲜血，
身子像枯树倒在地上！

It was so miserable,

Our dearest brothers,

In Reluo seventy only-sons died overnight!

The fields that produced crops were unattended,

With the pondweed growing tall.

The rice steamers were unused for so long

That the green mildew grew longer than the hair.

The bamboo water tubes were so idle

That the tremella grew.

...

The elderlies gathered in the village castle,

And the chief invited all apos for a discussion.

Everyone hung their heads as low as the ears of mature grains,

And their faces were sallow like the beeswax.

As if seven mountains were weighing on their tongues,

Even the most articulate had no strength to utter a word.

The apo who had lost seventeen teeth

Said what others were unwilling to say:

"The fireplace that was drenched won't light,

And the tree that has been cut won't grow tall.

Quickly leave the land of Reluo

And go to a place where the god of plagues cannot reach!

Do so before the Hani become extinct

So as to thrive in some other place!"

The apo cried till his eyes bled

And then fell down like a dried-up tree!

不离不行了，
亲亲的惹罗大寨！
不走不行了，
生养哈尼的亲娘！
走过田坝，
舍不得田坝，
田坝是养活六千哈尼的田坝；
走过山岗，
舍不得山岗，
山岗是养活六千哈尼的山岗；
走过老林，
舍不得老林，
老林为我们把狂风暴雨阻挡；
走过凹塘，
舍不得凹塘，
凹塘是阿妈生下我们的地方！

哈尼头人走上神山，
要把寨石搬到别处安放；
他的手像大风吹抖的草叶，
他的脚跪倒在寨石上。
哈尼阿波来到畜圈，
要牵走圈里的牛羊；
牛羊也恋着老圈，
眼泪像滴水崖的水往下流淌。

最不愿走的是哈尼女人，
最不愿离的是哈尼姑娘。

The Hanis had to leave now,
Leaving the beloved Reluo village!
The Hanis had to go now,
Going from the beloved mother of the Hanis!
Passing by the paddy fields,
They could not bear to part with the fields,
The fields that nourished 6,000 Hanis.
Crossing the hills,
They couldn't bear to part with the hills,
The hills that provided for 6,000 Hanis.
Walking through the old forests,
They couldn't bear to part with the forests,
The forests that protected them from the fierce storms.
Passing by the aotang,
They couldn't bear to part with the aotang,
The aotang where the Hani mothers gave birth to so many of us.

The Hani chief walked up the sacred mountain
To move the village sacred stone to the new place.
His hands were shaking like the leaves in the gale,
And he knelt on the village sacred stone.
All the Hani apos came to the pens
To fetch the cattle and sheep,
Which also did not want to leave their old pens,
Tears running like the water from the cliff.

The most reluctant were the Hani women
And especially the young women.

她们的伤心大山也支不住，
听来句句断人肝肠：
"哈尼尊敬的头人阿波，
你们的话女人从来不敢顶撞。
你们叫哈尼离开惹罗的田地，
是惹罗出了不懂规矩的媳妇，
还是出了不肯出力的姑娘？
你们叫哈尼离开惹罗的山林，
是嫌媳妇摘回家的猪菜太少，
还是嫌姑娘背回家的泉水不凉？"

"孝顺的姑娘媳妇哟，
世上再找不着你们这样的好心肠！
你们的心贴在惹罗的火塘上，
你们的心拴在惹罗的田坝上。
开大田数你们最出力，
盖蘑菇房数你们最忙。
想离开惹罗的人心最狠呵，
是灾难叫我们把狠心人来当！"

啊哟，不离不得啰，
先祖又要把家搬！
啊哟，不走不得啰，
哈尼又要走向陌生的山岗！
身背着不会走路的婴儿，
手牵着才会蹦跳的小娃，

Their sadness could crush even the mountains,

Every word heartbreaking:

"Respected Hani chief and apos,

Your words we never dare to contradict.

But now that you ask us to leave the fields in Reluo,

Is it because the daughters-in-law broke the rules

Or because the daughters did not work hard?

Now that you ask us to leave the Reluo forests,

Is it because the daughters-in-law brought too little vegetables

home

Or because the springwater the daughters carried home is not

cool enough?"

"Dutiful daughters and daughters-in-law,

The world has no kinder heart than yours!

Your hearts are as warm as Reluo's fireplaces;

Your hearts are tied to Reluo's paddy field.

You worked the hardest in cultivating the fields.

You are the most helpful in building the mushroom houses.

It is indeed cruel-hearted to leave Reluo,

But it's the disaster that has forced us to be so cruel!"

Alas, being forced to leave,

The ancestors had to move again!

Alas, having no choice but to leave,

The Hani people had to brave the unknown hills again!

Carrying the babies who couldn't walk,

Holding the hands of the toddlers who just learnt to skip,

六千哈尼告别了家乡。
手拉着不愿上路的老牛，
哄乖了汪汪叫着的小狗，
先祖走向南方的万道山梁。

众人：
萨——哦——萨！

Six thousands of Hanis bid farewell to their home.

Pulling the old cattle that were unwilling to move along,

And coaxing the puppies that were barking,

The ancestors moved south towards thousands of mountains and ridges.

Audience:

Sa—nong—sa!

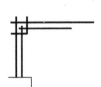
四、好地诺马阿美①

歌手：

萨——依——！

讲了，

亲亲的兄弟姐妹们！

讲了，

围坐在火塘边的寨人！

先祖传下的古今，

像鲜花开满山间；

先祖留下的古歌，

像画眉在树上婉转。

我已唱过了三个夜晚，

你们得了三夜喜欢；

我已唱赢七个贝玛，

七朵金花插在耳边。②

今天啊，我提提精神，

又要唱出新新的一篇。

---

① 诺马阿美：有两种解释，一为诺马河边的平原，一为水源诺马。

② 在盛典中演唱贝玛带有竞赛性质，主持人将金花银花插于席间，优胜者可夺而戴之。

Chapter 4　A Nice Place Nuoma Amei①

Singer：

Sa—ee—!

Let us tell stories,

My dear brothers and sisters!

Let us tell stories,

Villagers who are sitting around the fireplace!

The stories handed down from the ancestors

Are like flowers blossoming in the mountains.

The ancient songs passed down from the ancestors

Are as lovely as the singing by the thrushes in the trees.

I have sung over three nights,

And you have been entertained for three nights.

I have outdone seven other beimas

With seven golden flowers worn by my ears.②

Today, I am prepared

To sing another new chapter.

---

① Nuoma Amei: There are two explanations. One is the plains by the Nuoma River, and the other is the water source Nuoma.

② Beima's performance gave the ceremony a competitive characteristic. The host put the golden flowers and silver flowers on the table, and the winner could take them away and wear them.

（一）

歌手：

萨——依——！
麂子离不开在惯的岩洞，
水牛离不开歇惯的老圈。
哈尼离不开生养自己的惹罗普楚，
走一步要望两眼。
走哟，望哟，
哈尼的铁脚翻过数不尽的高山；
望哟，走哟，
先祖的血汗把数不完的大河洒满。

为了找着惹罗一样的好地，
头人派出了七队人马：
"去吧，亲亲的兄弟，
你们长着马鹿的快脚，
你们生着老鹰的尖眼，
不要怕脚趾头踢掉，
不要怕膝盖骨走弯，
快快找到合心的土地，
不要白做哈尼的男人！"

出去的人像离弦的箭，
回来的人像老牛耙田，

4. 1

Singer：

Sa—ee—!

The muntjac couldn't leave the accustomed caves,

As the water buffalo couldn't leave the accustomed pens.

The Hanis couldn't live without Reluo Puchu that raised

them,

Looking back twice at every step.

Walking and looking,

The Hanis with their iron feet climbed countless mountains.

Looking and walking,

The blood and sweat of the ancestors were scattered in count-

less rivers.

To find a place as good as Reluo,

The chief sent out seven teams：

"Go, dear brothers.

You have the feet as fast as the red deer's

And the eyes as sharp as the eagles'.

Don't be afraid of losing your toes.

Don't be afraid of damaging your knees.

Quickly find a good land,

So as not to be the Hani men in vain!"

They left as fast as the arrows that just left the bows,

But returned like the old oxen drawing harrows.

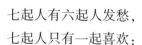
七起人有六起人发愁，
七起人只有一起喜欢：

"高能的头人，
亲亲的阿波阿匹，
赶紧背起竹箩准备上路，
赶紧捧起清水洗洗泪眼，
遇难的哈尼不消愁了，
万能的神降福到哈尼中间。

"我们走遍下方，
眼睛瞧涩瞧酸，
找不着一处合心，
瞧不着一处合肝，
不是见不到老林，
就是见不着清泉，
我们睡在山顶哭泣，
把尊敬的天神抱怨。

"天上响起呱呱的叫声，
头顶飞过一只大雁，
它的声音像雷鸣，
扇起翅膀像电闪。
我们尾着朝前走，
翻过一山又一山，
突然'嗖'的一声响，
大雁扎向地面，

Six of the seven were worried,

But one was delighted:

"Capable chief,

Dear apos and apis,

Quickly pack up the bamboo baskets and get ready to hit the
road.

Quickly use the clear water to wash your tearful eyes.

The suffering Hanis don't need to worry any more.

The almighty has sent blessings in our midst.

"We walked all over the places

Till our eyes were sour from looking,

Unable to find a place that had our heart's desire,

Unable to find a place that made us happy.

Either there was no old forest,

Or there was no clear spring.

We slept on the top of the mountain crying,

Complaining about the respected god of heaven.

"Then there was a croak in the sky,

And a wild goose flew by overhead.

Its voice sounded like thunders,

And its wings fanned like lightning.

We followed the goose,

Climbing one hill after another.

Suddenly, with a loud swoosh,

The wild goose swooped towards the ground.

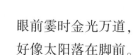

眼前霎时金光万道，
好像太阳落在脚前。

"睁大眼睛瞧瞧，
只见宽宽的平原，
一条大水汹涌澎湃，
湍急的水流分成两边。
大河像飞雁伸直的脖子，
平坝像天神睡在大水中间，
我们把这里叫作诺马阿美，
认定它是哈尼新的家园……"

男人的话还没有说够，
女人就像八哥嘴不闲：
"这块土地像不像手掌一样平，
这个坝子够不够女人绕个圈？"

男人"嗒嗒"地弹着舌头责怪：
"女人到底是女人！
那里平得像饭桌，
三天三夜也绕不完！"

娃娃们又叽叽喳喳：

Instantly, thousands of golden lights shone,

As if the sun had fallen in front of our feet.

"We opened our eyes

And saw a wide plain

And a great river with strong surging water.

Its torrential flow was parted in the middle.

The great river was like the stretched neck of the wild goose.

The flat field was like the god of heaven sleeping in the middle of the water.

We named it Nuoma Amei

And were certain it's the new home for the Hanis..."

The man had hardly finished

When the women started talking like starlings:

"Is this place as flat as the palm?

Is the bazi① big enough for women to saunter along?"

Clicking his tongue, the man complained:

"Women are women after all!

It's as flat as the surface of the dining table,

And sauntering three days and nights, you cannot see all of it!"

The children were asking, too:

---

① Bazi: (Notes from translator) Flat land, especially in the mountainous area.

"那里有没有花花雀，
有没有惹罗山上的树多，
有没有惹罗坝子好游玩？"

男人听罢高声回答，
呵呵笑出心里的喜欢：
"水牛一样宝贵的儿子呵，①
让我告诉你们：
那里的高山，
树林像头发一样密，
山下的坝子里，
鲜花一片挨一片，
那里的小河边，
乌黑乌黑的血娜雀不停唱歌，
那里的刺篷中，
恩西果维鸟②忙出忙进把蛋孵。
好儿子呵，
等阿爸们开出大田栽出秧，
你们就能绕着田埂尽情地玩。"

老头人又牵挂别样：

---

① 哈尼族视水牛为珍宝，故用以比喻儿子。
② 恩西果维鸟：一种小鸟。

"Are there colorful birds?

Are there as many trees as there were in Reluo?

Is it as interesting a place as Reluo?

On hearing the questions, the man answered in a loud voice,

Laughing with his heart's delight:

"Sons who are as precious as the water buffalo, ①

Let me tell you:

On the high mountain there,

The woods were as thick as the hair;

At the foot of the mountain,

The patches of blooming flowers were next to each other;

Along the small river,

The sooty xuena finch never stopped singing;

In the thorny bushes,

The enxiguowei finch② were busy hatching their eggs.

Good sons,

When your fathers have ploughed the field and planted seed-

lings,

You can enjoy yourselves around the tilled land as much as

you want."

The elderlies had different concerns:

---

① The Hanis see the water buffalo as a treasure, so they compare it to
their son.

② Enxiguowei: A kind of little bird.

杀牛的秋房①怎样盖，
拖狗的地方在哪里？
有没有地方安基石②，
有没有地方祭祖先？
样样问得详详细细，
头人阿波下令搬迁。

在那河水最大的七月，
先祖来到诺马河边，
奔腾的河水比豹子还凶，
撕破大地的吼声远远就听见。

头人想了三个夜晚，
把过河的事情安排周全：
牛马猪羊都会泅水，
老人小娃有人背牵，
只有先祖的字书难带，
叫人时时牵挂在心间。
他把字书扎好三道，
嘱咐的话也说过七遍，
这才带领队伍横渡大水，
好像一只领头的大雁。

贝玛阿波紧随着大队，

① 秋房：（译者注）祭祀用的房子。
② 基石：指神山上象征祖灵的石头。

How to build the sacrifice house qiufang① to kill the ox,

And where to drag the dog?

Would there be a place to lay the foundation stone②

And a place to worship the ancestors?

After the questions were addressed in detail,

The chief apo gave the order to relocate.

In the seventh month of the year, when the river crested,

The ancestors came by the side of the Nuoma River.

The rushing waters were fiercer than the leopards,

And their earth-tearing roar was heard from far away.

The chief planned for three nights,

Carefully making arrangements for crossing the river:

Cattle, horses, pigs, and sheep all could swim,

And the elderly and the young would be carried by some.

Only the ancestors' books were hard to bring along,

Which he worried about very much.

He wrapped and tied up them three times

And talked with the carrier seven times.

Only then did he lead the team to cross the water,

Like a leading goose.

The beima apo followed the group,

---

① Qiufang: (Notes from translater) The sacrifice house.

② Foundation stone: The stone on the sacred mountain. It symbolizes the ancestral spirit.

珍贵的字书搂在腰间。
越走大水越深越急，
好像大蟒在腿上乱钻。
贝玛阿波"呸呸"地吐着唾沫，①
连连把撵鬼的背词诵念。

大水慢慢淹到肚脐，
他把字书抱在胸前；
大水渐渐淹没胸口，
他把字书扛上了肩；
大水哗哗淹没肩膀，
他的脸变成绿叶一片。

贝玛大声喊：
"头人阿波，
七个水鬼来拖我，
阿波头人哦，
祖传的字书放哪里?"
头人大声告诉他：
"七十七个鬼来拖，
字书你也要保全；
要是两手拿不住，
你不会咬在嘴里边!"
贝玛刚刚咬好书，
大大的波浪打过来，

---

① 贝玛在念咒驱鬼时，第一句就是："呸！有我高能的贝玛在
这里，天鬼地鬼都滚开!"

Holding the precious book to his waist.

The farther they went, the deeper and the more rapid the water was,

As if the pythons were randomly running into their legs.

The beima apo kept spitting "Bah! Bah!"①

And chanting the incantation to banish the ghostly spirits.

The water slowly rose to his navel,

And he held the books close to his chest;

The water gradually reached his chest,

And he moved the books to his shoulders;

The water covered his shoulders,

And his face turned green like a leaf.

The beima shouted:

"Chief apo,

Seven water ghosts are dragging me down.

Apo chief,

Where should I put the books of the ancestors?"

The chief told him loudly:

"Even if seventy-seven ghosts came to drag you down,

You must protect the books.

If you can't hold them with your hands,

Hang on to them with your mouth!"

As soon as the beima held the books by his teeth,

A big wave came over him,

---

① When the beima chants, his first sentence is "Bah! The capable beima is here. Go away, the ghostly spirits!".

贝玛张嘴"呃"了一声，
转眼字书就望不见！

哈尼过了诺马大河，
头人把队伍细细查点，
猪羊牛马没有打失，
老老小小个个平安，
只是哟——
阿公阿祖的字书不见了。
问那管书的贝玛，
他用手指着老天，
说怕魔鬼来抢，
只好吞进肚子里面。
——可惜啰，亲亲的兄弟，
——可惜啰，哈尼子孙，
从此哈尼再没有文字，
世世代代受人欺压；
从此哈尼再没有老书，
先祖的古今靠什么来传？
——啊呀，胆小的先祖贝玛，
过河的时候不是哈八惹①的时候，

---

① 哈八惹：唱酒歌。哈八，酒歌，以一人主唱众人合唱的形式，在庄严的场合歌唱。本诗即是以此形式演唱的，一般主唱者先以"萨——依——萨——"的衬词起头，唱完一段或唱至情绪高涨处，众人举酒齐合"萨——依——萨！"以与歌手所唱内容相应和，其意为："合了！对了！是这样呢！"

And the beima opened his mouth and uttered "Ugh",

And the books disappeared in a trice.

Once the Hanis crossed the great Nuoma River,

The chief checked on his team.

No pigs, sheep, cattle, or horses were missing,

And the old and the young were safe.

But—

The ancestral books were nowhere to be found.

He asked the book-keeper beima,

Who pointed to the sky

Saying that he was afraid the devil was to rob him of the

books,

So he had swallowed them.

—What a pity, dear brothers.

—What a pity, Hani descendants.

Ever since then, the Hanis have had no written words

And have been oppressed for generations.

Ever since then, the Hanis have had no ancestral books,

How can the past and present of the ancestors be passed

down?

—Ah, timid ancestor beima,

Crossing the river is not the right time to "Haba Re"①.

---

　　① 　Haba Re: Sing drinking songs. Haba, drinking songs, sung on sol-
emn occasions with one singer singing and the audience chorusing to echo
him. The current epic is performed this way. The singer starts with "Sa—
ee—sa", and when he finishes a part, the audience raises a toast and chorus
"Sa—ee—sa!" which means "Yes! That's good! That's it!".

你为什么要把喝酒唱歌的嘴张开？
只怪你打失了先祖的文字，
哈尼成了只会说不会写的可怜人！①

众人：
萨——依——萨！

（二）

歌手：
萨——依——！
诺马阿美又平又宽，
抬眼四望见不着边，
一处的山也没有这里的青，
一处的水也没有这里的甜，
鲜嫩的茅草像小树一样高，
彩霞般的鲜花杂在中间。
一窝窝野猪野牛来来去去，
一群群竹鼠猴子吵闹游玩，
野鸡野鸭走来和家鸡家鸭亲热，

---

① 关于哈尼族遗失文字，诗中还有另一种唱法：哈尼族和彝族兄弟共同过河，彝族教哈尼族用嘴咬住字书，但哈尼族没有听清，以为是叫他吃进肚里，于是就把字书吃下去了，所以有这样的说法："哈尼的古书吃进肚里也不怕，先祖的古今深深埋藏在贝玛心中。"贝玛也用这种说法来解释自己的知识丰富。

So why did you open your singing and drinking mouth?

It is because you lost the writings of the ancestors,

The poor Hani people can only speak but not write[1]!

Audience:

Sa—ee—sa!

4. 2

Singer:

Sa—ee—!

Nuoma Amei was flat and wide,

So wide that its edges were out of sight.

There was no mountain greener than the mountains here

And no water sweeter than the waters here.

The fresh grass was as tall as the small trees,

With the fresh flowers like the rosy clouds in the midst of it.

Families of wild boars and bisons came and went.

Groups of bamboo rats and monkeys played noisily.

Pheasants and ducks, wild and domestic, came to play together.

---

[1]　There is another explanation for the Hani's lost written language. When two brothers Hani and Yi got across the river together, Yi taught Hani to bite the written books with the mouth, but Hani didn't hear that clearly and swallowed them. There is a saying: "It's okay that the Hani's ancient books had been eaten into the stomach, because the stories of the ancestors had already been buried deeply in the heart of the priest beima." Beimas themselves also use the same reason to explain why they are so knowledgeable.

麂子马鹿走来和黄牛骒马撒欢。
小娃爬上树顶，
逮得着一窝窝喜鹊，
大人去到水边，
常常把大鱼抱还。
好在的诺马阿美，
哈尼认作新的家园。
按照惹罗的规矩，
哈尼把寨子来兴建：
定居的基石是寨子的父母，
它从遥远的惹罗普楚搬来；
占卜的贝壳是神灵的嘴，
会告诉哈尼天神的意愿；
最直最粗的树选作神树，
它荫庇着哈尼子孙繁衍。

诺马阿美老实宽大，
哈尼建起了最大的大寨；
惹罗建寨要一个贝玛祭献，
诺马建寨要七个贝玛诵念；
惹罗祭寨要拖一条狗跑，
诺马祭寨要拖九条狗转。

Muntjacs and red deer were having fun with the yellow cattle
and mules.

The kids climbed to the top of the trees,

Catching nests of magpies.

The adults went to the water's edge

And often brought back big fish.

Nuoma Amei was beautiful,

And the Hanis took it as their new homeland.

According to the rules of Reluo,

When the Hanis built a village,

The foundation stone of the settlement became the parents of
the village.

The stone was carried there from the faraway land of Reluo
Puchu.

The shell for divination was the mouth of the god,

Which could tell the will of the god of heaven.

The straightest and thickest tree was chosen to be the sacred
one,

And it would protect the propagation of the Hanis.

Nuoma Amei was indeed big and wild.

The Hanis built the largest village.

Building a Reluo village required a beima to preside over the
sacrifice

And seven beimas to chant the scriptures in Nuoma Amei.

The Reluo sacrifice for the village required running with one
dog

And turning with nine of them in Nuoma Amei.

哈尼人口实在多，
一处在不下分在四面，
四个能干的头人，
轮流把诺马掌管，①
最大的头人叫乌木，
哈尼都听从他的指点。

乌木率领着哈尼涉过矣玛②大河，
把嘎鲁嘎则的竹子种下一蓬，
大家又来到吾玛③河边，
把大竹的种子埋进地面；
乌木指着两蓬竹子中间，
庄严地划下哈尼的界限。

诺马阿美的四面，
四个大寨依偎山边，
哈尼立起四个石墩，
一个石墩代表一寨，
每年祭寨的日子，
头人就带领寨人来祭奠。

---

① 哈尼妇女衣饰上爱缀以水车齿形的花纹，呈一线绕四结的形状，传说即是以此纪念诺马阿美的四个头人轮流执政。

②③ 矣玛、吾玛为诺马河的两条支流，两条支流之中就是诺马平原。

The Hani population was indeed large.

They couldn't stay in one place but in four places.

Four able headmen

Took turns to run Nuoma Amei.①

The most authoritative chieftain was called wumu,

And the Hanis all obeyed him.

The wumu led the Hanis to wade across the great river Ima②

And planted a clump of Galugaze bamboos.

They then came to the Wuma③ River bank

And planted the bamboo seeds.

He pointed to the space between the two clumps of bamboos

To mark solemnly the boundaries of the Hani land.

On the four sides of Nuoma Amei,

Four big villages nestled against the side of the mountain.

The Hanis set up four stone mounds,

Each symbolizing a village.

Annunally on the day to offer sacrifices for the village,

The headmen would lead the fellow villagers in worshiping activities.

---

① Hani women's dresses are decorated with a pattern of the water-wheel gear, with a line twinding around four knots. The pattern is said to commemorate the four headmen taking turns to rule over Nuoma Amei.

②③ Ima and Wuma are two tributaries of the Nuoma River. Between them is the Nuoma plains.

诺马阿美扎实好在，
哈尼爱上新的家园。
崖缝里冒出大股清泉，
像沸腾的水珠串串。
七个扎密①去背水，
七股笑声丢在后边，
七个阿妈去背水，
七个扎谷②把衣角牵，
七个伙子去打猎，
野物挂满了双肩，
七个阿爸去犁地，
地就像泡糕一样软。
早上起来瞧瞧，
十个女人笑了，
晚上睡下想想，
十个男人喜欢。

像野草一样扎根，
像石头一样站稳，
神赐的诺马好地，
哈尼又把蘑菇房兴建：
惹罗的蘑菇房盖到诺马，
先祖又把新的式样增添，
两层的房子又多建一层，

---

① 扎密：姑娘。
② 扎谷：小孩。

Nuoma Amei was a really nice place,

And the Hanis loved their new home.

Limpid spring water poured out from between the mountain rocks

Like strings of the boiling water beads.

Seven zamis① went to carry water,

Leaving behind them seven trails of laughters.

Seven mothers went to carry water,

And seven zagus② pulled on the edges of their clothes.

Seven men went hunting

And returned with wild games hanging from their shoulders.

Seven fathers went to plough the land,

And the land became as soft as a soaked cake.

Looking around in the morning,

Ten women smiled.

Thinking in bed at night,

Ten men were pleased

Taking root like weeds,

Standing firm like rocks,

On this divine land, Nuoma Amei,

The Hanis built the mushroom houses again:

When the mushroom houses of Reluo were built in Nuoma,

The ancestors added new stylistic touches.

Another floor was added to the two-story house,

---

① Zami: Girl.

② Zagu: Kid.

矮矮的耳房站在旁边；
房顶修成平平的晒台，
老人爱去烤太阳，
小娃爱去摔大跤，
女人爱去做针线。
高高的房子新落成，
谷雀就来祝贺寨人，
扇动着棕片般的翅膀，
来把勤劳的主人叫唤；
花花的喜鹊也来搭伴，
领着小儿搬来半边，
它也有自己的蘑菇房，
只是高高盖在树丫中间。

哈尼的牛马和猪羊，
也爱上这个新的家园；
看那寨脚的竹林边，
黄牛拖长声音在欢叫；
看那寨旁的平岗上，
马群一天到晚在游转；
看那寨头的黄泥坡，
早被猪群拱成蜂窝眼。

哈尼走到天涯海角，
不忘发家的宝贝是大田。
高能的乌木说话了，
像劲风把诺马坝子传遍：

With the low ear-chambers standing beside it.

The roof was made into a flat roof terrace,

Where the elderlies liked to bask in the sun,

The children liked to wrestle,

And the women liked to sew.

Now that the tall houses were newly completed,

A finch came to congratulate the villagers.

Flapping its brown wings,

It called upon the hard-working owners.

A colorful magpie also joined in,

Bringing along its hatchlings.

It had its own mushroom-shaped nest,

Only that it was built high in the tree branches.

The Hanis' cattle, horses, pigs and sheep

Also fell in love with this new homeland:

At the edge of the bamboo forest at the foot of the village

Were the cattle mooing with joy;

On the flat ground beside the village

Were the horses wandering all day long;

The yellow muddy slope in the front of the village

Had long turned into a honey comb by the pigs.

Even if going to the end of the earth, the Hanis

Would not forget that the treasure for building their fortune

was the land.

The capable wumu uttered powerful words

That, like a strong wind, spread over the Nuoma bazi:

"几千个人一个不要走散，
几千双手一双不要得闲，
快拿凿有八个孔的犁去开荒，
快拿开有十个孔的耙去平地，
开田不要怕挖绝土狗的种，
挖地不要怕把蚯蚓脖子斩断！①"

瞧啰，
在那高高的南罗山②下，
哈尼开出第一块肥田，
在那出名的南罗塞朋③，
秧姑娘露出甜甜的笑脸。

瞧啰，
头年过去，
一棵苞谷收三包；
二年过去，

---

① 一说哈尼族在诺马已开始号地，谁看中哪块地就去号住，方式有两种：一是以木刻、竹刻或结绳作记，一是在地旁大树上交叉砍两刀，别人就不再来耕种。
② 南罗山：诺马山名。
③ 南罗塞朋：南罗的秧田。相传哈尼族第一次在南罗学会育秧，与前所说在惹罗已会栽秧有出入。（来自原诗）

"None of the thousands of us should be spared,

And none of the thousands of our hands should be idle.

Quickly take up the plows with eight holes to cultivate the land.

Quickly take up the rake with ten holes to level it.

In cultivating the land, do not be afraid of destroying the mole hills,

Or cutting the earthworms in half!①

Look,

At the foot of the high Mt. Nanluo②,

The Hanis cultivated the first fertile field.

In the famous field in the Nanluo Saipeng③,

The seedling bride smiled sweetly.

Look!

The first year came and passed,

And one plant of maize became three packs of it;

The second year came and passed,

---

① One explanation is as follows: In Nuoma the Hani people had started to mark the land to cultivate. Those who preferred a piece of land could mark it in one of the two ways: to use carved wood, carved bamboo or knotted rope, or to mark with crosses on the trees beside the land. Other people would not farm this land if they saw the mark.

② Mt. Nanluo: The name of a peak of the Nuoma mountains.

③ Nanluo Saipeng: The seedling field in Nanluo. It is said that the Hanis learned to raise rice seedlings for the first time in Nanluo, which is inconsistent with what has previously been said that in Reluo the Hanis had already known how to plant rice seedlings. (Here we follow the original poem.)

一蓬芋头挖五背；
三年过去，
一穗红米收九碗。
开出大田，
公鸡伸长脖颈啼鸣了，
母猪也拖着大肚哼哼，
黄牛水牛也爱挑架，
哈尼夜里也不爱翻身。

攀枝花开了，
白鹇鸟唱了，
哈尼阿妈第一次把小娃在诺马生下，
哈尼阿爸第一次把衣胞埋在诺马山边，①
哈尼在诺马兴旺发达，
好像雨后的竹笋冒尖。
瞧啰，
哈尼小娃一对一对地出来，
好似一窝窝兔子乱蹦乱钻；
哈尼伙子一伙一伙地出来，
在寨脚的草坝上蹓马比赛；
哈尼姑娘一群一群地出来，
清脆的笑声像叮咚的山泉。

众人：
萨——哎——萨！

---

①　哈尼习俗，父亲要将儿子的衣胞埋在山上，并且面向东方，
以示吉祥。

And one clump of taros yielded five baskets of them;

The third year came and passed,

And one ear of red rice produced nine bowls of it.

Once the field was cultivated,

The roosters craned their necks and crowed;

The sows, too, dragged their bellies and oinked;

The cattle and buffalo liked to fight;

And the Hanis slept deep and sound at night.

The kapok blossomed,

And the silver peasant sang.

The Hani mother gave birth to the baby in Nuoma for the first time,

And the Hani father buried the afterbirth by the Nuoma mountains① for the first time.

The Hanis prospered in Nuoma,

Like bamboo shoots coming out of the ground after the rain.

Look!

The Hani babies came out in pairs,

Like litters of rabbits jumping and skipping;

The young Hani men came out in groups,

Horseracing on the meadow at the foot of the village.

The young Hani women came out in groups,

Their ringing laughter like the tinkling spring water.

Audience:

Sa—nong—sa!

---

① It is the Hani's custom that new fathers must bury in the mountains the baby's afterbirth, facing east, for good luck.

歌手：

萨——依——！

哈尼的头人像树根一样出来，①

威严地镇守自己的地盘，

头上的帽子像山巅高耸，

手握木杖象征权力无边；

哈尼的乌木说一句话，

四个头人把头点；

哈尼的头人说一句话，

没有人会来违反。

哈尼贝玛像树干一样出来，

他咒鬼的声音震动群山。

不要怪他打失那珍贵的字书吧，

先祖的古今一直在他肚子里面。

他是个神通广大的能人，

恶鬼恶魔遇着也要打颤。

他保护着哈尼躲灾免难，

使哈尼人像豹子般壮健。

哈尼的工匠像树尖一样出来，

他们是一个抵百个的能人，

---

① 哈尼族信奉大树崇拜，以树为尊，故有此喻。

Singer：

Sa—ee—!

The Hani headmen emerged like the tree roots①,

Protecting and guarding their land augustly.

The hats on their heads were like the towering mountain peaks,

And the wooden staffs in their hands symbolized their infinite power：

When the Hani wumu spoke,

The four headmen nodded their heads;

When the Hani headmen spoke,

No one would disobey.

A Hani beima came out like the tree trunk,

His incantation against the demons shook the mountains.

Do not blame him for losing the precious books,

For the ancestral past and present had always been in his belly.

He was a man of such great power

That even the evil ghosts trembled on meeting him.

He protected the Hanis from disasters,

Making them as strong and healthy as the leopards.

The Hani blacksmiths came out like the tips of the trees.

Each was as capable as a hundred men.

----

① The Hani people worship big trees so they have the metaphor like this.

115

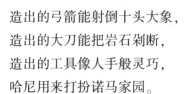

造出的弓箭能射倒十头大象，
造出的大刀能把岩石剁断，
造出的工具像人手般灵巧，
哈尼用来打扮诺马家园。

哈尼的寨子一个个增多，
像灿烂群星闪烁在天边，
最大最亮的水明星有一颗，
诺合大寨又平又宽。
诺合紧靠南罗山脚，
它的财富滚滚不断，
哈尼月月前来赶集，
头人日日把乌木进见。
赶街的哈尼挤挤搡搡，
好像鱼群在水里游玩，
背上背箩鼓圆肚子，
合心的东西装满装严。

头人们来到诺合议事，
忙出忙进像蜜蜂打转，
高高的寨堡站在大寨中央，
权威的乌木坐在里面。

亲亲的寨人，亲亲的弟兄，
要问诺马的哈尼有多少？
不到七年，

A bow and arrow they made could shoot down ten elephants,

And a broad sword they made could cut up the stones.

The tools they created were as dexterous as the human

hands,

And the Hanis used them to beautify their homeland in Nuo-

ma.

The Hani villages grew one by one,

Like the brilliant stars twinkling in the sky.

The largest and brightest was one bright mercury star,

Village Nuohe, flat and wide.

Nuohe was next to the foot of the Mt. Nanluo,

And its wealth billowing ceaselessly.

The Hanis came to the fair every month,

And the headmen visited the Wumu every day.

The Hani people came to the fair,

Crowded like a shoal of fish playing in the water.

Shouldering baskets on their backs with their bellies bulging,

They stuffed their baskets to their heart's content.

The headmen came to Nuohe to discuss official business,

Busy in and out like bees circling around.

The high castle was in the center of the village,

With the authoritative wumu sitting inside.

Dear villagers and dear brothers,

Do you wonder how many of the Hanis were in Nuoma?

In less than seven years,

就要以七千七百来计算；
要问哈尼在诺马有几代？
翻开家谱，
整整十三代人住在那边。

众人：
萨——哝——萨！

（三）

歌手：
萨——依——！
七月里最响的是打雷，
七月里最亮的是闪电，
诺马阿美像打雷扯闪，
好听的名字一节节传远。

诺马的美名传到东方，
传进了腊伯①高高的大城，
腊伯的乌木派大队马帮，
跋山涉水来到诺马河边，
他们用五彩丝线交换哈尼的红米，

---

① 腊伯：汉、彝、白等民族的总称，外族。

The Hani population must be counted by seventy-seven hundred;

Do you wonder how many generations of the Hanis were in Nuoma?

The family record showed

Exactly thirteen generations live there.

Audience:

Sa—nong—sa!

4.3

Singer:

Sa—ee—!

The thunders in the seventh month are the loudest,

And the lightnings in the seventh month are the brightest.

Nuoma Amei was like the thunders and the lightnings

With its beautiful names spreading far and wide.

When Nuoma's good name spread east,

It went to the great city of the Labo①.

The wumu in the Labo sent a caravan that

Traveled over land and water and arrived at the Nuoma River bank.

They traded colorful silk threads for the Hani rice,

---

①　The Labo: The collective name for other ethnic groups such as the Han, the Yi, the Bai, etc. Other ethnicities.

又用亮亮的金银来换哈尼的白棉。
诺马的美名传到南方，
那里坝子一片接一片，
出名的坝子名叫猛梭，
好心的摆夷住在那边。

摆夷头人也派来牛帮，
叮咚的牛铃整天不断。
生意人像河里的鱼虾来往穿梭，
多少人就有多少种心眼，
腊伯来时马背凸得像大虾，
走时就像母猪肚子拖在地下；
买卖又恶又奸滑，
好像乌鱼朝泥巴里钻，
哈尼摇着手说"麻卡①麻卡！"
腊伯说"卡呢②卡呢！"边把头来点。

哈尼头人去见乌木，
七嘴八舌说出心愿：
"尊敬的乌木，
亲亲的阿波！
哈尼的心像寨边的青竹一样直，

———————

① 麻卡：不行。
② 卡呢：行呢。

And the shiny gold and silver for the white Hani cotton.

Nuoma's good name spread to the south,

Where the settlements were one next to another.

In a famous one named Mengsuo

Lived the good Dai people.

The Dai's chief also sent a caravan to Nuoma,

The cattle bells ringing throughout the day.

Business people bustled like the shuttling fish and shrimp in

the river,

But everyone had their own interest on their mind.

The Labos came with hunched backs like shrimp,

But left with bellies dragged along like the sows' touching the

ground.

They were cruel and treacherous businessmen,

Like the mullets that liked to burrow into the mud.

The Hanis would shake their hands and say: "Maka, maka!"①

The Labos would nod their heads and say: "Kane, Kane!"②

The Hani headmen went to see their wumu,

Eagerly sharing their frustration:

"Respected wumu,

Dear Apo!

The Hani heart is straight like the green bamboo in the vil-

lage edge,

---

① Maka: It wont' do.

② Kane: That's okay.

腊伯的心像箐里的藤子一样弯。
因为不平，诺马河水才滚滚流淌，
因为贪心，腊伯才来到哈尼寨边。
请让我们拿起大刀弓弩！
把他们像麂子一样赶撵。"

乌木的心坝子样宽，
乌木的话棉花样软：
"亲亲的兄弟，
尊贵的头人，
哈尼心像金银样亮，
诺马的名声才像高飞的白鹇，
不要为了一棵稗子，
踩烂长满秧苗的大田。
诺马的哈尼比河沙多，
一人省一口，
要把腊伯的腰杆压断；
诺马的财富比河水旺，
一人出一把，
要把腊伯的背脊压弯。
客客气气地对他们吧，
不喝够酒不要让他上路；
亲亲热热地对他们吧，
不包好饷午不要让他回转！"

But the Labo heart is bent like the vine in the bamboo groves.

Just like the Nuoma River was rough due to the uneven river bed,

The Labo came to the Hani villages due to their greed.

Please allow us to take up the broadswords, bows and cross-bows

To drive them away like deer."

The heart of the Wumu was as wide as the bazi,

And his words were as soft as cotton:

"Dear brothers,

Respected headmen,

It is because the Hani heart is as shiny as gold and silver

That Nuoma has the reputation like the soaring silver pheasants.

Don't, for the sake of a weed,

Trample on the fields full of seedlings.

The Hani population in Nuoma is more than the sand in the river,

So if everyone spares a bite,

There is enough to break the backs of the Labos.

The wealth in Nuoma is greater than the water in the river,

So if everyone offers a handful,

There is enough to bend the backs of the Labos.

Be civil with them,

And don't let them leave until they have had enough to drink;

Be kind to them,

And don't let them return until they have had lunch!"

乌木的话就是天神的话，
头人们只好把腰弯。
哈尼的酒罐打开了，
倒酒的声音像雷神的笑声；
哈尼的火塘烧旺了，
煮肉的香气飞上云端。
哈尼的客气和财富啊，
被各路马帮越驮越远。

（四）

歌手：

萨——依——！
讲了，先祖的后世子孙，
我要把诺马的往事讲给你们！
听了，一寨的兄弟姐妹，
听我把伤心的古今来传！
我要讲啊，
腊伯怎样抢走哈尼的诺马，
先祖怎样被撵出诺马家园！
我要唱啊，
诺马河流过多少先祖的血泪，
有多少哈尼埋葬在诺马河边！

诺马阿美是园中的香椿，
不煮香味就四处飘散；

Since the words of the wumu were the words of the god of
heaven,

The headmen could not but obey.

The jars of the Hani wine were opened,

The sound of the wine pouring like Thor's laughter;

The fires in the Hani fireplaces were burning hard,

The aroma of the meat cooking rising into the clouds.

The Hani hospitality and wealth

Were carried farther and farther away by various caravans.

4. 4

Singer:

Sa—ee—!

Let's tell stories, the descendants of the ancestors.

I will tell you the stories of Nuoma's past!

Listen, brothers and sisters from the same village,

Listen to me to pass on the sad stories!

I want to tell

How the Labos robbed the Hanis' Nuoma,

How the ancestors were driven out of their home in Nuoma!

I want to sing about

How much the ancestors shed their blood and tears into the
Nuoma River,

How many of the Hanis were buried by the Nuoma River!

Nuoma Amei was the Chinese toon in the garden,

Without being cooked its fragrance already drifting everywhere;

到来的腊伯像蚂蚁，
肥美的诺马真逗人喜欢；
离开诺马就会后悔，
家里的妻儿也忘在一边；
七十个人逗拢驮子，
选出个伙子把他们管。

腊伯伙子和哈尼相好，
见人就喜笑颜开，
好像久别的亲人团圆，
拉着两手叙长问短。
雄鸡刚刚叫过头遍，
伙子来到乌木门前，
丰厚的礼物抬进大门，
动听的话说出一串：
"腊伯的京城高楼大厦数不清，
幢幢高楼用金银堆成。
见着哈尼的蘑菇房，
家乡的大房我不想。
尊敬的乌木阿波啊，
请你答应腊伯，
把房子盖在哈尼旁边。"

哈尼乌木似截竹筒，
直是直啦没有心眼，
答应了伙子的请求，
准他把房子盖在寨边。

The newly arrived Labos were like ants,

Who found the fertile and beautiful Nuoma really lovely;

They did not want the regret for leaving Nuoma,

Forgetting even their wives and children.

Seventy men gathered together

And elected a man to be in charge.

This Labo man tried to be friend of the Hani,

Smiling at everyone he saw,

As if they were long-lost relatives reunited,

Holding both of their hands and making a small talk.

The cock had just crowed for the first time

When the man came to the wumu's door,

With the bountiful gifts carried into the front gate

He said a string of sweet words:

"There are countless tall buildings in the capital of Labo,

Each is built with gold and silver.

But seeing the Hani mushroom houses,

I don't want to return to the big buildings in my hometown.

Respected wumu apo, please allow the Labos

To build our houses by the Hani houses."

The Hani Wumu was like a bamboo tube,

Really straight and guileless.

He granted the man his request

And allowed him to build the house beside the village.

刚刚喝过盖房的米酒，
腊伯又迈进乌木的家门：
"腊伯哈尼同饮一条河的水，
哈尼腊伯同住在一座山边，
亲兄弟也比不上这样亲密无间，
同甘共苦是哈尼腊伯的心愿。
亲亲的阿波，
尊贵的乌木！
听见你们的壮牛哞哞叫，
我们想起家乡的牛群；
望见你们的骏马在奔跑，
我们惦记着自己的马厩。
有钱的阿哥忘不记无钱的阿弟，
请把哈尼的牛马分我们一点！"

糯米粑粑又软又香，
缺牙的阿波百吃不厌。
哈尼乌木听见请求，
慷慨地答应分出财产。
领着腊伯走进马厩，
乌木请他自己挑选，
望见母马小马关一处，
腊伯伸手把小马牵。
乌木又走进牛圈，
把壮壮的牯牛指点，
腊伯伸手到母牛背后，
把细脚的小牛拉出了圈。

As soon as the rice wine for building the house was drunk,

The Labo man came again into the wumu's house:

"The Labo and Hani people drink from the same river

And live by the same mountains.

Blood brothers would not be any closer than this,

So sharing weal and woe is the wish of the Hani and Labo

people.

Dear apo,

Distinguished wumu,

Hearing your strong cattle moo,

We think of the cattle in our hometown.

Seeing your horses running,

We think of our horses' stables.

The rich elder brother remembers the poor little brother.

Please share some Hani cattle and horses with us!"

Glutinous rice pie was soft and tasty.

Apo, who had missing teeth, was never tired of eating it.

Hearing this request,

The Hani wumu generously agreed to share the property.

Leading the Labo man into the stables,

The Wumu let him choose.

Seeing that the mare and pony were in the same place,

The Labo man reached out to lead the pony.

Then the wumu went into the barn

And pointed to the strong bulls.

But the Labo man reached behind the cows

And pulled the calf out of its pen.

牵走小牛小马，
腊伯把自己夸奖七遍：
"贪心才牵母牛母马，
我的好心乌木望见？"
憨憨的乌木听了他的话，
心里一层一层喜欢。

——哦哦，
亲亲的兄弟姐妹，
先祖乌木比老牛还笨，
把无数灾难带到哈尼中间！
——啊哟，
权威的乌木大头人！
你的眼睛是被鬼抠掉，
怎么望不见灾难来到面前？
难道最小的道理你也不懂，
难道放鸭小娃还胜你十分？
水牛老虎同一山，
老虎张口了，
水牛还活得成？
薄荷香柳①共一园，
香柳高了，

---

① 香柳：一种高茎香料植物，常与薄荷栽在一处。诗中常用香柳薄荷的关系来比喻处事的安危，但有两种说法，贬义者说香柳长高，抢去阳光露水，薄荷难活；褒义者说香柳死了，薄荷失去扶持，也长不高。

Taking away the calf and pony,

The Labo man praised himself seven times:

"Only the greedy take the cow and mare,

So does the wumu see my kindness?"

The unsuspicious wumu listened to his words,

And his heart filled with layers of sheer delight.

—Oh oh,

Dear brothers and sisters,

The ancestor wumu was dumber than the old cow,

Bringing countless disasters to the Hanis!

—Alas,

The authoritative wumu, the leader of the headmen!

Your eyes must have been removed by the ghost,

Or else why couldn't you see the disasters coming?

Didn't you understand the smallest truth,

And was the kid who tended ducks ten times better than you?

If the buffalo and the tiger live in the same mountain,

When the tiger opens its mouth,

Can the buffalo stay alive?

If the mint and the fragrant willow① exist in the same garden,

When the fragrant willow grows tall,

---

①　Fragrant willow: A tall aromatic plant, often planted by the mint. In the poem, the relationship between the fragrant willow and the mint is often used to describe the safety of doing things, but there are two views. Derogatorily, if the fragrant willow grows tall, it will rob the sun and dew of the mint and the latter can hardly survive; commendatorily, if the fragrant willow dies, the mint will lose support and cannot grow tall.

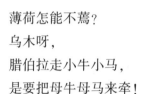

薄荷怎能不蔫？
乌木呀，
腊伯拉走小牛小马，
是要把母牛母马来牵！

阿波哟，
从此哈尼不能在诺马河边种田，
后世儿孙又要像麂子被人赶撵！
瞧啰，
腊伯拉走了小牛，
母牛哞哞叫着跟在后面，
腊伯牵走了小马，
母马嘶叫着跳出栏圈；
诺马的先祖呀，
没有牛也没有马了，
吃苦的哈尼哦，
望着空圈把乌木埋怨！

众人：
萨——哝——萨！

歌手：
萨——依——！
牵来的牛马还没有驯服，
腊伯又有新的盘算。

How can the mint not wither?

Wumu!

The Labo man took the calf and pony

In order to have the cow and the mare!

Apo!

From now on, the Hanis could no longer farm by the Nuoma

River,

And their children and grandchildren would be driven out

like the muntjac again!

Look!

Once the Labo man led away the calf,

The cow mooed and followed.

Once the Labo man led away the pony,

The mare neighed and jumped out of the stall.

The ancestors of Nuoma

Had neither cattle nor horses any more.

Poor Hani people,

Looked at the empty stalls and blamed the Wumu!

Audience:

Sa—nong—sa!

Singer:

Sa—ee—!

Before the cattle and horses had even been tamed,

The Labo man hatched another ploy.

听说乌木有一儿一女，
两个儿女比珠宝值钱；
儿子还是贪玩的扎谷，
放鹅放鸭常到溪边，
女儿已经长成扎密，
就像山上的腊哈腊芊①。
伙子穿上滑亮的外衣，
洗白手脚又站到乌木门前，
好听的话树叶样多，
细细的腰树枝样弯。
"阿波乌木啊，
你是我最喜欢的人！
我的马帮走过七座大山，
七座大山的姑娘，
没有你的扎密逗人惹眼；
我的马帮走过七个大海，
七个海边的伙子，
没有我聪明矫健。

"阿波哦，
麂子黄牛放一山，
箐鸡找伴找白鹇，
请你把金花戴在我头上，
让我把扎密讨进门！"

---

① 腊哈腊芊：杜鹃花，有些支系又叫妥底玛侬。

He had learned that the wumu had a son and a daughter,

Who were more precious than the jewelry.

The son was still a naughty zagu,

Often tending geese and ducks by the stream.

The daughter had grown into a zami,

Like the lahalaqian① in the mountains.

The Labo man put on his sleek coat,

Washed his hands and feet and appeared again in front of the

Wumu's door.

His nice words were as many as the leaves,

And his small waist bent like a twig.

"Apo wumu,

You are my favorite person!

My caravan went across seven mountains,

But none of the pretty young women there

Is as attractive as your daughter;

My caravan has traversed across seven great lakes,

But none of the men there

Is as wise and good-looking as I.

"Oh, apo,

Muntjac and cattle can exist in the same mountain.

Bamboo pheasants seek the companionship in silver pheasa-

nts.

Please put the golden flower on my head

By letting me marry your daughter to my home!"

---

① Lahalaqian: Azalea. Some Hani branches call it Tuodimayi.

漩涡卷昏了鱼头，
风沙迷瞎了马眼，
乌木答应了腊伯的婚事，
把扎密嫁到腊伯中间，
扎密不单带去鲜花的容貌，
还带去最平最肥的良田。

头人们听见消息，
一齐走到乌木面前：
"哈尼是粗粗的大树，
树根就是大田；
扎密拿走了诺马的珍宝，
那里栽一年够吃三年；
哈尼的姑娘为什么嫁外人？
先祖的土地为什么给他人来管？"

乌木的回答大家都不欢喜，
但是头人怎好违背乌木的心愿：
"我的独囡招了姑爷，
姑爷也是半个儿子，
一家人就要像一家人，
一碗饭一人吃一点。"

乌木的姑娘爱上了漂亮的男人，
腊伯的话像蜂蜜一样甜，
她走拢各位头人，

Like the whirl pool making the fish dizzy
And the sand wind blinding the horse's eye,
The wumu agreed to the marriage of the Labo man,
To marry his zami to the Labo's home.
Not only did the zami bring her beautiful looks
But also the most leveled and fertile land.

When the headmen heard the news,
They went to the wumu together:
"The Hanis are a thick tree,
And its roots make the land;
Your zami took with her Nuoma's treasure
That can be planted one year and yield enough to eat for
three years.
Why did the Hani girl marry an outsider?
Why let others manage the Hani ancestors' land?"

The wumu's answer was not satisfying to anyone,
But the headmen couldn't violate the wishes of the wumu:
"My only daughter attracted a son-in-law,
Who, too, is half of a son.
A family should act like one,
And when there is a bowl of rice, everyone should have
some."

The wumu's daughter fell in love with the handsome man,
So fed by the Labo's words sweet as honey,
She approached the headmen

为腊伯说话申辩:
"哈尼女人本不该多话,
但是水不舀干塘底不会露面。
哈尼从惹罗来到诺马,
几千人尾着高飞的大雁,
我也是扎密中的一个,
拉着阿妈的衣角来到新的家园。
安新寨的时候,
你们扛来粗粗的大树,
我和姊妹们背草到门前,
挖田的时候,
你们烧荒犁耙日日辛苦,
我送饷午天天去到田间;
今日我出门了,
只是从寨头嫁到寨尾,
没有离开阿爸阿妈,
没有去到地角天边;
阿波啊,
分田应当有我一分,
分房应当有我一间!"
头人们听了找不着答话,
只好随她分走大田。

扎密嫁到腊伯家,

In defense of him:

"As a Hani woman I should not talk much,

But unless the water is all emptied out the bottom of the

pond won't show.

The Hanis came from Reluo to Nuoma,

Thousands of us followed the goose flying high.

I, too, am one of the Hani zamis,

Holding onto a corner of my mother's clothes came to the new

home.

At the time of building the new village,

You carried the thick trees,

And my sisters and I carried straws to the door.

At the time of plowing,

You burned and harrowed the fields day by day,

And I took the lunch to the fields every day.

Now I am about to get married,

But moving just from the front of the village to the end of it.

I am not leaving my parents,

Nor did I go to a faraway place.

Apos,

I should have my share of the land

And my share of the house!"

The headmen did not know how to reply

And had to let her take the land.

Once married into the Labo family,

天天像过活夕扎①。
不香不糯的饭，
丈夫不添进碗；
不肥不厚的肉，
男人不帮她拣；
好好听听的话，
一日说三遍，
句句说出来，
冬蜜一样甜：
"亲亲的女人，
好瞧的白鹇，
为了让你日子过好，
我要把生意做起来，
为了当上权威的乌木，
我要多多地找钱。"

哈尼扎密格格地笑，
奇怪男人的歪心眼：
"哈尼乌木不是自己找，
没有高能众人不会选。
乌木力气要大过水牛，

---

① 活夕扎：尝新米节，时间在农历八月第一个属龙日（哈尼认
为龙的属相是增添上涨之意），届时全寨哈尼身着盛装品尝新米饭，
并祭献龙王欧罗和始祖母塔婆。

She ate good food every day and every day was like Huoxiza
Festival①.

Unless the rice was fragrant and glutinous,

The husband would not add to her rice bowl;

Unless the meat was fat and thick,

The man would not pick for her;

Words pleasing her ears

Were uttered three times a day.

Every word was

As sweet as the winter honey:

"Dearest woman,

My good-looking silver pheasant,

In order to let you live a good life,

I'm going to start a business.

In order to become an authoritative wumu,

I'm going to make more money."

The Hani zami giggled,

Wondering why the man had such a silly thought:

"The Hani wumu isn't sought

But only elected by the community because of high capabili-
ties.

The wumu needs to be stronger than the buffalo

---

① Huoxiza Festival: Taste-the-New-Rice Festival. It falls on the first
dragon Day in the eighth month of the lunar calendar (The Hanis take the
sign of dragon as increasing and rising), when all the Hanis in the village
are dressed up to taste new rice and offer sacrifices to Dragon King Ouluo and
Granny Tapo.

主意要像星星数不完，
只有这种人才能戴权帽，
宽宽的绶带才能挂胸前。①"

"阿爸从没说过这些话，
他们是粗心的老人！
亲亲的女人你细细说，
要紧的事情男人记心间。"

"哈尼来到诺马阿美，
攀枝花开过七十七遍，
哈尼像河边的竹林，
发得又密又快。
七十个能人也管不赢，
哈尼就分开坝子四面，
乌木是能人里的老虎，
祖传的珍宝就带在身边。
权帽不是拿来遮日头，
再滑的布也不比它轻软，
毛毛的虎皮又牢又花，
再硬的弓箭也射不穿。

"绶带也不是拿来扎腰，
十条豹筋也比不上它坚韧，

---

① 权帽和绶带是哈尼族古代头人权力的象征。传说绶带是用贝皮
（贝是一种传说中的动物，所有动物都怕它，大小如狗，皮极珍贵）做
成的，权帽则是用虎皮做成的，后垂貂尾，周围满插五彩羽毛。

And has ideas more than the stars.

Only this kind of people can wear a chief hat

And the wide sash on the chest." ①

"Father never said such things to me,

A careless old man just like the others!

My dearest woman, you tell it to me carefully,

And man remember the important things."

"When the Hanis came to Nuoma Amei,

Kapok had blossomed seventy-seven times.

The Hanis were like the bamboo forest by the river,

Growing fast and thick.

Seventy capable people could not manage them,

So the Hanis were divided among four areas in the bazi.

The wumu is the tiger among the capable people,

And the ancestral treasure is by his side.

The chief hat is not used to shade the sun,

And the smoothest cloth isn't lighter or softer than it.

The fuzzy tiger fur is so strong and colorful

That the hardest bow and arrow can't shoot through it.

"His sash is not used to tie the waist,

And ten tendons of leopard are not as tough as it.

---

① Chief's hat and sash: They were symbols of the power of the ancient Hani chieftain. According to legends, the sash was made of the skin of bei (a mythical creature that all animals were afraid of; it was in the size of dog, and its skin was extremely precious), while the hat was made of tiger skin, with a drooping sable tail and surrounded by multicolored feathers.

亮亮的带子像黑蛇的花皮，
再快的砍刀也难砍断。
权帽代表诺马的高山大岭，
绶带代表诺马的河流平原，
所有哈尼要对它低头，
它装着天神的意愿。"

诺马河里一层层大浪，
腊伯心里一阵阵喜欢：
"这样稀奇的宝贝，
怎不拿给我保管！
兄弟是三指长的嫩笋，
只知山上水边游玩，
阿爸是坡上的老树，
经不起雷打电闪，
丢失了先祖的珍宝，
哈尼的灾祸要到眼前！"

扎密生着大竹的直心，
听说赶紧把宝贝讨来，
托付给她的是阿妈，
女儿最讨阿妈喜欢。

乌木回到家中，
找不着帽子绶带，

The shiny belt is like the black snake's skin,

It is hard for even the sharpest broadsword to cut it in two.

The chief hat symbolizes the high mountains and the hills in Nuoma,

And the chief sash, the rivers and plains of Nuoma.

All Hanis bow to it

Because it contains the will of the gods."

Like the waves in the Nuoma river were strong,

The Labo man was delighted:

"Such rare and fancy treasures,

Why not let me keep them!

Your little brother is a tender bamboo shoot of three-finger high,

Knowing nothing but playing in the mountains and beside the rivers.

Your dad is an old tree on the slope

That can't afford being hit by the thunder and lightning.

If the ancestors' treasures are lost,

Disasters will befall the Hanis!"

The zami had a bamboo-straight heart,

And got the treasures as soon as she was asked.

The one who gave them to her was her mother,

Since she was her mother's favorite.

When the wumu returned home,

He could not find the chief hat and sash.

怒火比山火还旺，
声音像老虎叫喊：
"女人，
你的头生到脚的下面！
怎能把宝贝交给外人，
你难道要把哈尼送断？"

妻子像雨中的小雀发抖，
晓得事情干得太憨。
乌木撵到姑爷家中，
要把帽子绶带讨还。

腊伯不像花样好瞧，
话比花蜜还要香甜。
梁头的腊肉割下三块，
洗脚的热水抬到面前：
"我不是一个哈尼也是半个哈尼，
阿波阿匹的话我记在心间，
不吃不喝不是亲热，
山样的大事吃饱又款。"

乌木的怒火熄掉一半，
厚厚的肥肉送到嘴边。
尖牙的老虎掉进陷阱，
力大的牯牛穿上鼻眼。

He was more angry than a wild fire,

And yelled with a tiger's voice:

"Woman,

Your head grows under your feet!

How can you give the treasures to an outsider?

Or are you trying to ruin the Hanis?"

His wife was shaking like a bird in the rain

And realized she had done something foolish.

The wumu rushed to his son-in-law's house

To get back his hat and sash.

Though the Labo man wasn't as handsome as flower,

His words were sweeter than the flower honey.

He cut off three pieces of bacon hanging from the end of the

beam

And brought hot water before the wumu for washing the feet:

"Though I am not a total Hani man, I'm a half one,

Who will bear the words of apo and api in my heart.

Not eating and drinking together means not close with each

other,

So no matter how serious the matter is, let's eat first."

The wumu's anger extinguished by half

By the time the thick fat pieces of meat were sent to his lips.

Now the sharp-toothed tiger was trapped

And the strong bull's nose ring was installed.

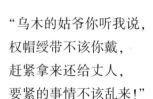

"乌木的姑爷你听我说，
权帽绶带不该你戴，
赶紧拿来还给丈人，
要紧的事情不该乱来！"

"阿妈耳聋听不清话，
腊伯怎能当哈尼头人？
两样东西扎实宝贵，
年幼的兄弟不会保管；
阿爸年老又爱出门，
打失宝贝对不起祖先；
扎密的心头发样细，
姑爷的心马鹿样善，
不给扎密收着真是粗心大意，
不给姑爷守着难道要给外人？"

"阿波哦，
我从远方来到诺马，
就像瓦雀歇在屋檐，
腊伯怎会要哈尼的宝贝，
只想等兄弟长大再归还。"

尖嘴的八哥叫得人高兴，
巧嘴的腊伯说得乌木心转，
他哪知腊伯是漏底的水塘，
多旺的水也装不满。

"Listen to me, wumu's son-in-law.
You shouldn't wear the chief hat and sash.
Give them back quickly to me, your father-in-law,
Not to mess with things as important as this."

"Mom is deaf and didn't hear me clearly.
How could a Labo man be a Hani chief?
The two things are truly precious,
And the young brother can't keep them safe;
Dad is old and loves to go out,
So if the treasures were lost you would feel guilty to the ancestors;
Your zami's mind is as detailed as the hair,
And your son-in-law's heart is as kind as a red deer's.
It's your oversight not to let your zami keep them
And, if not your son-in-law, should an outsider keep them?

"Apo,
I came to Nuoma from afar,
Like a sparrow resting under the eaves.
The Labos would never want to own the Hanis' treasures,
So I just want to return them to the young brother when he has grown up."

As the sound of the sharp-beaked black birds pleases people,
The sleak-tongued Labo man changed the wumu's heart.
Little did he know that the Labo man was a bottomless pond,
Which couldn't be filled up with no matter how much water.

（五）

歌手：

萨——依——！

诺马涨过几十次大水，

攀枝花红过几十次山岗，

夜鸟叫来不祥的时辰，

老乌木回到虎尼虎那故乡，

年轻的乌木接替了阿爸，

坐上高位管理四方。

得雨的秧稞一天天拔节，

诺马的腊伯一天天兴旺。

高脚的公鸡站满篱笆，

大耳的胖猪睡在路旁；

山上山下放着牛马，

坡前坡后盖着瓦房。

仗着人多马多，

腊伯的笑脸变成苦脸；

瞧着乌木细嫩，

腊伯由小羊变成老狼。

领着蜂子样的人群，

腊伯走进了寨堡，

4. 5

Singer:

Sa—ee—!

The Nuoma River had flooded a few dozen times,

And the kapok flower had colored the hills red many times.

When the night bird called at the ominous hours,

The old wumu returned to the Hunihuna, his home.

The young wumu took over the place of the father

And sat on the high position to manage the four directions of

Nuoma.

Day by day, the seedlings receiving the rain grew,

And day by day, the Labos in Nuoma became prosperous.

The long-legged cocks stood all over on the hedges,

And the big-eared fat pigs slept by the roadside.

Up and down the mountains the cattle and horses were graz-

ing,

And in front of and behind the slopes stood the tiled houses.

With more people and horses now,

The Labo man's smiling face turned into a bitter one.

Sicne the young wumu was still green like a seedling,

The Labo man changed from a lamb into an old wolf.

Leading a wasp-like crowd,

The Labo man walked into the village castle.

不像来吃酒玩耍,
声气像牯子叫嚷:
"我的兄弟你要听好,
诺马不是哈尼的地方,
阿哥的在处不够,
快领着你的族人到下方!"

年轻的乌木坐在高位,
说出话来硬硬邦邦:
"不到十月年①你就喝醉酒,
舌头倒着生话也不会讲。
一个老人不在,
规矩还是照样,
乌木的寨堡不准来吵闹,
这是说情讲理的地方!"

①　十月年:按哈尼历法,十月是岁首,所以十月年是大年,节期较长,将近半月,最为热闹。这时正是大春上场、圈中猪肥的时节,家家杀猪、春糯米粑粑、蒸年糕、染黄糯米饭献天地祭祖先;亲友们互相走访;请媒说亲;出嫁的姑娘也要带礼物回家过年;男女青年,欢歌跳舞。有的地方还有一种特殊风俗,即前一年出嫁的新娘们,要聚于村外山上互相诉说自己的新婚生活,而严禁男子偷听。

He did not sound like going there to drink or to play,

But like a bull, he yelled:

"My brother, listen carefully.

Nuoma is not a place for the Hanis.

Me, your elder brother, do not have enough space,

So quickly lead your people and move to the lower part!"

The young wumu sat in the high seat.

The words he spoke were hard and stiff:

"It's not yet the October Festival① and you're drunk,

Your tongue must have turned backward and you know not how to speak.

The old man is not here,

But the rules are the same.

The wumu's castle won't allow all this noise.

It's a place to process and review cases!"

---

①　October Festival: The grandest and longest (nearly half a month) festival as October is the first month of the year according to the Hani calendar. It is the season of harvest and every family kills pigs, makes glutinous rice cakes, steams niangaos (rice cakes) and dyes glutinous rice yellow to offer sacrifices to ancestors. Friends and relatives visit each other; parents ask matchmakers to make a match for their kids; married women bring gifts home for the Hani New Year; young men and women sing and dance merrily. There is also a special custom in some places, namely, the women who got married the year before will gather on the mountain outside the village to tell each other about their newly-married life, and the men are forbidden to eavesdrop.

"你不见一块块大田，
长满腊伯的稻谷高粱?"
"一块块大田，
都是我阿姐的嫁妆!"
"你不见腊伯的畜群，
像云彩盖满山岗?"
"你抢走哈尼的牛马，
来时哪见牛羊!"

"满坝走着腊伯，
你睁大眼睛望望，
不怕你是乌木，
我们要占诺马地方!"
"多多的腊伯是哈尼扎密生养，
先祖的土地半点也不能让，
你愿在就安分守己地在，
不愿在就赶紧搬回东方!"

"嗬哟哟!
都说你是高能的乌木，
怎么一点道理也不讲?
要说哈尼是诺马的主人，
就把权帽绶带拿在手上!"

"你是吃血的豺狗，
只会欺负鸡羊;
你是吃米的老鼠，
偷米还屙屎在米上!

"Don't you see that in the patches of the fields
Were filled with rice and sorghum that belong to the Labos?"
"Patches of the fields
Were the dowry for my older sister!"
"Don't you see herds of animals that are Labos',
Covering the hills like the clouds?"
"You robbed the Hanis of their herds,
Which you had none when you came!"

"Labos are all over the bazi:
Open your eyes wide and look around.
I don't care you are the wumu,
And we are to occupy Nuoma!"
"Many of the Labos were born and raised by the Hani women,
So none of the ancestors' land can be given up.
If you want to stay, know your place,
Or just hurry and return to the east!"

"My goodness!
Many say that you are a talented wumu,
But how can you be so unreasonable?
If the Hanis should be the maser of Nuoma,
Show your credential chief hat and sash!"

"You are a bloodthirsty dhole,
That can but bully chickens and sheep;
You are a rice-stealing mouse,
That steals some rice and defecates on the rest;

155

你的屁股老实大，
挤走别人的地位；
你们的手杆老实粗，
专把别人的饭碗抢。
你骗走权帽和绶带，
又打哈尼一巴掌。
我拿不出先祖的珍宝，
但指得出先祖开发的地方：
你到诺马河边去看看，
那里有先祖的石标；
你到南罗山上去望望，
那里有哈尼的石柱。
这神石从惹罗搬来，
和哈尼永远在一方！
你说出这样的丑话，
不怕天神降下祸殃？"

"天神管天上的事情，
忙不赢问人间的吉祥。
搬出神石也吓不倒人，
诺马定要做腊伯的家乡！"

"哈尼不是给人骑的快马，
也不是给人宰的肥羊，
你敢抬手我也敢抬脚，

You have a huge buttock,

Pushing others out of their seat;

You have the thick wrists,

Specializing in robbing others of their food;

You cheated the Hanis out of their chief hat and sash,

And then slapped them on their face.

I can't show you the ancestral treasures,

But I can point to the land explored by the ancestors:

Just take a look at the shore of the Nuoma River,

Where exists the stone marked by our ancestors;

Just go take a look at the top of the Mt. Nanluo,

Where stands the sacred stone pillar erected by the Hanis;

The sacred stone was moved from Reluo

And will stay with the Hanis forever!

How brazen of you to say what you did,

For don't you fear the punishment by the god of heaven?"

"The god of heaven is only in charge of the affairs in the
heaven,

Too busy to care about the fortunes of the world.

Using the god of heaven won't intimidate me.

Nuoma must be the Labos' homeland!"

"The Hanis will never just wait to be trampled upon by others at will,

Nor will we ever surrender to you like the lambs.

If you dare to raise your hand, we won't hesitate to lift our
feet.①

---

①　Notes from translator: Once you have done something offensive, we
also dare to counterattack. If you dare, then we dare.

你有弓箭我有刀枪!"

好话说完了,
丑话说完了,
乌木一句不听,
哈尼一步不让。

腊伯想出花招,
又对乌木讲:
"你当真舍不得诺马,
我也不再勉强,
该你在还是该我在,
请天神话说帮忙。
来吧,哈尼的乌木,
让我们到诺马河上放火,
看谁的火烟飘得最远,
诺马就是谁的家乡!"

年轻的乌木点头答应,
没有把腊伯的话思量。
他是才学撵山的小狗,
却遇到了豺狗的老娘。

乌木拿起刻纹的牛角①,

---

　① 牛角:指牛角号。传说这是天神召集各路神灵的号角,可吹出低沉悠长的单音,哈尼用来召集部族、指挥战斗,甚至谈情说爱。

You have arrows, and we take swords!"

Nice words were said.
And so were the bad.
The wumu compromised not a word.
The Hanis gave up not an inch.

The Labo man changed his tactic,
Saying to the wumu:
"If you really cannot let go Nuoma,
I won't force you.
Whoever should stay,
Let the god of heaven decide.
Come, Hani wumu.
Let's set fire to the Nuoma River.
Whoever's fire smoke floats farther,
They Whould claim Nuoma their homeland!"

The young wumu nodded his head in agreement,
Without thinking over the Labo man's proposal.
He was just a puppy who newly learned how to hunt in the
mountains,
But now playing against a mother dhole.

The wumu picked up the relief-covered buffalo horn①,

---

①　Buffalo horn: Buffalo horn trumpet. It is said that the gods used it
to call out various deities. With a deep, solome, and long sound, it was used
by the Hanis to gather the tribes, conduct battles, and even court a woman.

号声传遍河坝山梁，
"嗒嗒——呜——！嗒嗒——呜——！"
一声比一声响亮。

九山的哈尼赶来了，
九坝的哈尼跑来了，
九沟的哈尼奔来了，
各路哈尼聚在一方。

乌木说完放火的话，
七十个雄壮的男人走出来，
弯腰听从安排指点，
他们都是砍树的内行。

走遍诺马的大沟小箐，
走遍南罗的十道山梁，
找着最粗最大的干树，
扛到宽宽的诺马河旁。

架起山高的火堆，
干树烧得雷响，
火把节也比不上这样热闹，
全体哈尼来河边瞭望。

七百个贝玛齐声念咒，
请神灵保佑火烟飘扬，
杀倒壮牛献过公鸡，
哈尼把燃烧的大树推进波浪。

Its sound then covering the bazi, the river and the mountain
ridges.

"DADA—WU—! DADA—WU—!"

The sound became louder and louder.

The Hanis from nine mountains came.

The Hanis from nine bazies came.

The Hanis from nine ravines came.

The Hanis were gathered together.

As soon as the wumu finished talking about the match,

Seventy strong men came out,

Bending over and ready to follow his instructions,

All good at cutting trees.

Combing through furrows and valleys in Nuoma,

And all the ten mountains in Nanluo,

They found the biggest, thickest tree trunks

And carried them to the side of the wide Nuoma River.

The firewood was piled as high as a hill,

And the sound of the dry trunks burning was like thunders.

Livelier than the Torch Festival,

The riverside was filled with the Hanis who came to watch.

The 700 beimas incanted together,

Praying for the deities to bless their fire smoke.

The Hanis killed oxen and roosters to make the sacrifice

And then pushed the burning wood into the river.

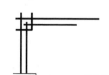

奸狡的腊伯不进山箐，
不砍大树不烧火塘，
拾来干干的牛屎，
点着的青烟细线一样。

哈尼的火堆呼呼燃烧，
火光把河水照得红亮，
随着波浪时起时落，
好像傍晚江心的太阳。

——哦嗬，可惜啰！
漂过短短一截，
干树浸成湿树，
火苗唑唑哭着，
慢慢不见亮光。

腊伯的牛屎浮在水面，
不怕漩涡不怕风浪，
火苗越烧越旺，
浓烟飘满大江，
江风呜呜作鸣，
浓烟飘扬远方。

啊哟，哈尼的后代子孙，
我们的火烟就这样熄灭！
苦啰，亲亲的兄弟姊妹，
哈尼把眼泪洒进波浪！

The cunning Labo man didn't make fire with treetrunks,
Nor did he go into the mountains.
He picked the dry cattle dung
To make a plume of blue smoke as thin as a thread.

The fire set by the Hanis was snapping,
And its flames lit up the river bright and red.
Floating up and down with the waves,
It was like the early evening sun in the river.

—Oho! What a pity!
Having moved for only a short distance,
The dry wood turned wet.
Flames were weeping
And eventually went off.

The Labo man's cattle dung was floating along.
Desspite of the whirlpool or the waves,
The flames are burning higher and higher;
The smoke floated over the river;
The wind wailed around the river;
And the intense smoke floated farther and farther away.

Alas, the Hani descendents,
Our flame died out just like that!
How bitter, my dear brothers and sisters,
The Hanis' tears fell into the waves.

听啊，腊伯说话了：
"哈尼！
快快牵起牛马，
赶紧背起小娃，
顺着火烟的去处，
搬出这块地方！"

哈尼的乌木说话了，
一边捶打自己的胸膛：
"不服气啊，
老实不服气！
黑心的腊伯啊，
为什么要叫哈尼搬家？
阿爸的身子才埋进新土，
坟草还没有眼睫毛长，
你这细手细脚的腊伯，
为哪样把乌木的恩情遗忘？
不搬，硬是不搬，
哈尼要守住自己的家园；
不走，硬是不走，
哈尼要护住先祖的坟场！"

乌木硬硬地抵着，
腊伯又把主意来想：
"是啰是啰，
再对你们让让，

Listen, the Labo man said then:

"The Hanis!

Hurry and lead your cattle and horse.

Hurry and carry your young children.

Follow the smoke

And move out of here."

The Hani wumu spoke,

Fist beating his chest:

"We cannot accept the result!

We are not willing to give up!

You the brutal Labo man,

Why do you force the Hanis to move away?

Our father has just been buried,

And the newly-growing grass on the tomb is not yet eyelashes
tall.

You the Labo man who doesn't work with your hands and
feet,

How can you be so ungrateful to him?

No way, we won't move;

The Hanis must guard our own homeland!

No way, we won't leave;

The Hanis must guard the cemeteries of our ancestors!"

The young wumu being tough,

The Labo man came up with another trick:

"Okay, okay,

I will make one more concession.

老乌木对我有情有义，
这回看在他的面上，
哪个合在诺马，
再请天神来讲。

"诺合是哈尼的头寨，
寨头岩石像堵大墙，
岩脚伸进诺马河水，
波浪日夜在那里喧嚷。
让我们去射那堵岩石，
谁射得上石头就把主人来当!"

乌木听说扎实高兴，
满口赞成腊伯的主张，
晓得腊伯不会撵山放箭，
哈尼的箭法人人高强。
乌木的宝弓从老辈传下，
射倒的野物堆成小山。
漆黑的弓身像木炭，
白润的弓把像月亮，
虎筋绷成筷子直的弦，
漂亮的箭羽拔自老鹰的翅膀。

乌木来到河边，
腊伯在那里张望，
拿把嫩竹捂成的小弓，

The old wumu was indeed kind to me,

So for his sake this time,

Whoever should settle in Nuoma,

Let the god of heaven decide again.

"Nuohe was the head Hani village,

The giant rock in front of the village standing like a wall.

Its foot plunging down into the Nuoma River,

With waves thundering day and night;

Let's go and shoot at the rock,

And let the winner be the master of Nuoma!"

The wumu was happy on hearing that,

Agreeing with the Labo man,

Knowing that the Labos were not good at shooting

While all the Hanis were ace shooters.

The wumu's bow was inherited from the ancestors,

With which the preys shot having piled up like small
mountains.

The body of the bow was black like the charcoal,

And the handle was white like the crescent moon.

The string of tiger's tendons was taut and straight like a
chopstick,

And its beautiful feather was from the eagle's wings.

When the wumu came to the riverside,

The Labo man was there looking,

Holding a small bow made from the tender bamboos,

好像扎谷玩的一样。
乌木呵呵地好笑，
拉弓像大树伸手掌，
"嗖"地一箭射去，
"啪"的一声响亮——
箭头断成两截，
像鹞鹰折断翅膀！

难道是力气不大？
还是瞄不稳当？
乌木又使出大力，
一枝枝射空了箭囊，
岩石射出一窝白点，
箭杆纷纷掉进波浪。

腊伯把箭头涂上蜂蜡，
"卟"的一声射向岩石，
竹箭像轻轻的雀毛，
在河上飘飘荡荡，
刚刚挨着岩石，
它就牢牢粘上。

腊伯说了：
"天神不爱哈尼，
岩石已把话讲；
不要再说不搬的话啦，
还是快到别的地方！"

乌木流出大股眼泪，
好像利箭戳穿胸膛：

Like a zagu's toy.
The wumu was amused,
Pulling the bow like a big tree reaching out its hand.
Whoosh, went the arrow,
But cracked—the arrowhead broke into two pieces,
Like a harrier eagle breaking its wings!

Wasn't he strong enough,
Or wasn't he accurate enough?
The wumu tried harder,
One by one, and finally his quiver was empty.
But the rock showed some white dents,
And the arrows, one by one, fell into the waves.

The Labo man applied the beeswax to the head of his arrows,
Pop, the arrow being shot to the rock.
The bamboo arrow was light like a feather,
Floating above the river.
The moment it touched the rock,
It was stuck tightly to it.

The Labo man then said:
"The god of heaven doesn't like the Hanis,
And the rock has spoken;
Stop refusing to move away,
And better find yourselves a new home!"

In tears, the wumu
Felt as if the sharp arrows were stabbing his chest:

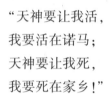

"天神要让我活，
我要活在诺马；
天神要让我死，
我要死在家乡！"

"咳！
出口话不算，
怎么做乌木？
哼！
不想迁的哈尼，
要被腊伯杀光！"
乌木抱起巨石，
丢进滚滚的河浪；
乌木朝天怒吼，
天上听见雷响：
"那扎！①
应该离开的不是哈尼，
倒是你们这些野羊！

瞧瞧诺马有多少哈尼，
有多少蘑菇房盖在山上！
数数杀牛的秋房有几座，
神山的神树多粗多长！
要说动手抬脚的话，
就把你的号角吹响！"

---

① 那扎：异族，前已有注。此处含从诺马河上游来的人、住在上边的人的意思，兼有不讲道理的人的意思。

"If the god of heaven wants me to live,
I want to live in Nuoma;
If the god of heaven wants me to die,
I want to die in my homeland!"

"Hey!
Breaking your own promises
How can you be a wumu?
Huh!
Any Hani that refuses to move
Will be killed by the Labos!"
The wumu picked up the huge rock
And pushed it into the rolling waves;
He shouted at the sky,
Like the thunder claps in the sky:
"Naza!①
It's not the Hanis that should leave,
But you the wild sheep!

See how many Hanis are in Nuoma,
How many mushroom houses are in the mountains!
Count the number of the sacrifice houses qiufang,
And the tall and thick sacred trees in the sacred mountain!
If you want to fight,
Just blow your horn!'"

----

① Naza: Someone who does not belong to the Hani, as noted previously. Here it refers to someone from the upper Nuoma River and has the connotation of a unreasonable person.

腊伯抬头四望，
见哈尼河沙一样多，
腊伯只是几棵细草，
风吹草动会被拔光。

腊伯的念头像只鱼雀，
拍拍翅膀飞得快当：
"乌木啊，
你还没脱下碗大的包都①，
我就背你上山游玩，
看在亲戚的情分，
我愿和你商量。

哈尼实在不想搬走，
就拿牛马来做抵偿，
今后腊伯也是主人，
大事小事要和我讲。"

听见腊伯话变，
乌木眼睛闭上：
"哈尼不是咬人的老虎，
也不是给老虎喂肉的肥羊，
你说话像拿尖刺戳人，
再不能把哈尼的亲戚来当！"

---

① 包都：哈尼族的儿子一生下地，就戴碎布缝成的小圆帽，称
为包都。

The Labo man looked up and then around.

He saw the Hanis as many as the sand in the river

But the Labos like a few thin grasses

That could be uprooted by the wind.

The Labo man changed his mind like a flying bird,

Flatting its wings and flying fast:

"Wumu,

Before you stopped wearing the baodu① as big as a bowl

I was the one who carried you up the mountains to play,

So since we are relatives,

I am willing to negotiate with you.

If the Hanis really don't want to move,

Pay me with your cattle and horses.

From now on the Labos will also be the master,

But everything, big or small, must let me know."

Hearing the Labo man changing his mind,

The wumu closed his eyes:

"The Hanis are not the man-eating tigers,

Nor are we the lambs to be fed to the tigers.

You speak with words harsh like thorns,

So you can no longer be a relative to the Hanis!"

---

① Baodu: As long as the sons of the Hani were born, they wore small
round caps made of rags, called Baodu.

两个恨恨地分手，
一个不让一个，
嚷闹打架的日子到了，
诺马阿美像河水动荡。

众人：
萨——哝——萨！

<h1 style="text-align:center">（六）</h1>

歌手：
萨——依——！
讲了，亲亲的兄弟姊妹，
伤心的古今唱出口，
像青青的老藤一样长，
七十七句唱不完，
等我慢慢地说细细地讲。

大水翻过无数波浪，
大山茅草青了又黄，
放火射箭的乌木去世了，
一个能人把乌木来当。

好听的名字就叫扎纳，
扎纳的古今人人会唱，
他生着漆黑发亮的脸膛，
像棵大树挺立山岗。

The two parted their ways in resentment,

Neither willing to compromise.

The days of quarrelling and fighting arrived,

Nuoma Amei to be as turbulent as the river.

Audience:

Sa—nong—sa!

4. 6

Singer:

Sa—ee—!

Let me tell stories, my dear brothers and sisters.

Tell the stories of the sad past,

As long as the green old rattans,

That seventy-seven sentences cannot tell them all.

Let me tell them slowly and in detail.

After the waves in the river had turned countless times,

After the grass on the mountains turned green and yellow,

yellow and green,

The wumu who set the fire and shot the rock died,

And an able man became the wumu.

His nice name was just Zhana,

His life experience familiar to all the Hanis.

His face was shiningly black,

His strong figure like a tall tree standing on the hill.

175

十颗虎胆没有他胆大，
十双鹰眼比不上他眼亮，
哈尼走过长长的路，
他是领群带路的头羊，
在他掌事的年月，
腊伯不敢来吵嚷。

寨头的棕叶一月一匹，
扎纳阿波也上了高龄，
手脚像枯藤样苍老，
又会气喘又会心慌。

腊伯头人换过三代，
换了头人换不过心肠，
望见扎纳年老体弱，
天天都来偷猪牵羊。

狗咬人人不会咬狗，
哈尼只愿平平安安。
扎纳叫来腊伯头人，
要他把腊伯管理顺当。

腊伯说出难听的话，
好像沤臭沤脏的水塘：
"偷是偷着啦，
抢嘛也得抢，
不偷不抢不会在，
头人不能把百姓绑。"

He was more courageous than ten tigers
And his eyes, brighter than ten eagles' eyes put together.
On the journey of the Hanis,
He led like a head-sheep of the flock.
During the years he was in charge,
The Labos dared not to mess with the Hanis.

The aging palm tree changed each month,
And Apo Zhana also aged,
With old wrinkled limbs,
And asthma and palpitations.

The Labos' chief changed three times,
But the heart stayed the same.
Seeing that Zhana was aging,
They came to steal pigs and sheep everyday.

Like people who, bitten by dogs, won't bite the dogs back,
The Hanis just wanted peace.
Zhana called the Labo chief,
Asking that he manage the Labos well.

The Labo chief replied with words
As dirty as the sewage:
"We did steal,
And we had to rob.
Without stealing and robbing we couldn't make a living.
The chief cannot arrest the folks.

"诺马的腊伯有一百，
大田只得一小块，
腊伯的牛马上一千，
只得一个小山岗；
要说不偷不抢，
哈尼和腊伯来分地方！"

乌木扎纳不开口，
烟筒咂得咕嘟响，
四个头人一齐把话说，
答应和腊伯划地分疆。

划地日子定在四月，
诺马山上青草正旺，
大风吹过刀口样的山顶，
青草像姑娘的头发披开两旁。

扎纳阿波爬上山顶，
舍不得把一山分做两岗；
舍不得也要舍得啰，
他猛地劈下手掌。
两边的地界划定了，
各人把住各人一方。

要提防黑心黑肠的腊伯，
扎纳阿波结下了第一个草结，
千百个哈尼一齐动手，
草结结成一道大墙。

"One hundred Labos live in Nuoma
But they have only a small piece of land.
They own more than a thousand cattle and horses
But have only a small hill.
If you don't want us to steal and rob,
The Hanis and Labos must divide the land!"

Wumu Zhana was silent,
Burbling away his bong.
The four headmen had a discussion
And agreed to divide the territory with the Labos.

The day to divide was set in April,
When the Nuoma Mountain was lush with grass.
A gale blew over the edge-like mountain peak,
And the grass split like young women's parted tresses.

Apo Zhana climbed to the top of the mountain,
Not wanting to divide the mountain into two parts,
But he knew he had to.
Swiftly, he swung his palm down,
And the divide between the two territorial parts was set,
And each party was expected to be in charge of its side.

To guard against the cruel Labos,
Apo Zhana tied the first grass knot,
And then hundreds and thousands of Hanis joined in
And built the grand wall of the grass knots.

179

哈尼阿培聪坡坡 Migrating Epic of the Hanis

高高大山分成两半，
腊伯不再来闹来嚷。
这座大山哈尼都记得，
"扎纳米波"① 世代名扬。

诺马的腊伯有七颗心，
七颗心都贪得无厌，
划界分地不打草结，
一块块石头抱上山岗。

到了天干风大的七月②，
一山绿草变成金黄，
腊伯放起烧天野火，
先祖的草结变灰堆。
一阵狂风灰堆尽，
地界随风飞天上。

趁着青草难长难发，
腊伯把石头趱到这边，
好山好水被他们把尽，
好田好地被他们占光。

扎纳阿波火冒三丈，

---

① 扎纳米波：哈尼语，扎纳划界的山。
② 此处仍按哈尼族以十月为岁首的说法，七月相当于夏历的十月。诗中记历均沿用哈尼历法。

The majestic mountain was divided into two territories,

And the Labos should no longer mess with the Hanis.

This mountain was remembered by all the Hanis,

And "Zhana Mibo" ①was known to all generations.

The Labos in Nuoma had seven hearts,

And all were greedy.

They did not tie the grass knots

But they carried stone blocks onto the hill.

In the dry and windy July②

When all the green grass turned golden,

The Labos set fire,

And the ancestors' grass knots turned into ashes.

A gale blew away the ashes

Together with the territorial boundary.

Before the green grass could resprout,

The Labos moved the rocks into the other side,

Taking more favorable mountains and rivers,

And good land and field.

Apo Zhana was furious

---

① Zhana Mibo: The Hani language, which refers to the mountain Zhana demarcated.

② According to the Hani calendar, October is the beginning of the year, so July is the equivalent of October in the Hani lunar calendar. The calendar referred to in the poem is the Hani calendar.

也把石头排满山岗。
腊伯头人走来说话,
要哈尼让出地方。

扎纳阿波说了:
"腊伯,
你烧得了草结的地界,
烧不了扎纳米波大山;
你搬得动山上的石头,
搬不动哈尼的山场!
我乌木对着诺马的大山说话,
你要听清你要细想:
划定了地界你们又撒赖,
诺马就没有你们的地方!"

腊伯的头人大声吼:
"年老的扎纳,
你也听我腊伯头人把话讲:
哈尼快快搬出诺马,
这里是我们的家乡!"

哦哦!
腊伯实在欺负人,
一点不把道理讲。
水牛忍不得气,
也会挑起尖角,
哈尼忍不得气,
个个摩拳擦掌。

And also piled up rocks all over the top of the hill.

The Labo chief came

Demanding that the Hanis give up their land.

Apo Zhana replied:

"Labo man,

You may burn the boundary made of grass knots,

But you can never burn out the Zhana Mibo Mountain;

You are able to move the rocks on the hill,

But you could never move the Hani land in the mountains!

Now me, the wumu, vow to the majestic mountains in Nuo-

ma,

And you'd better listen and consider carefully:

Violating the boundaries after they were set,

You have no place in Nuoma!"

The Labo chief roared back:

"Old Zhana,

You had better also listen to me the Labo chief carefully:

The Hanis should move out of Nuoma quickly,

For this is our homeland!"

Oh oh!

The Labo man pushed it too far,

Being completely unreasonable!

Even the water buffalo, having taken too much,

Would arch its horns.

The Hanis could not take it anymore

And all were ready to fight.

听啰,
扎纳的话传遍四方:
"诺马是哈尼的好地,
不能给野狗来屙屎;
诺马是哈尼的家园,
不能给乌鸦来歇翅膀。
九山九寨的哈尼,
不要再等再望,
快快吹响九道刻纹的牛角,
快快集合犁田种地的兄弟,
快快磨亮闪光的大刀,
快快削尖戳人的竹枪,
快快跟着我扎纳,
把心厚的腊伯攆光!"

打了,亲亲的弟兄,
哈尼和腊伯开了战。
河边遇着河边打,
田坝遇着田坝打,
喊打的声音传遍四方;
山上遇着山上杀,
箐里遇着箐里杀,
喊杀的声音叫人心慌!

哈尼的竹刀啊,
挑不破腊伯的肚皮;
哈尼的竹箭啊,
穿不透腊伯的胸膛。

Listen,

The words of Zhana were spreading everywhere:

"Nuoma is a good place for the Hanis

And can't be desecrated by wild dogs;

Nuoma is the homeland of the Hanis,

And can't be the resting palce for crows.

The Hanis of all nine mountains and nine villages,

Do not wait and hesitate any more.

Quickly blow your buffalo horns with nine carved lines,

And gather your plowing brothers in the fields,

Polish your shining broadswords,

And sharpen your bamboo swords.

Quickly follow me

To drive out all the greedy Labos!"

The battle had begun, my dear brothers,

The battle between the Hani and the Labo had started.

When they met by the river, they fought by the river;

When they met in the field, they fought in the field.

The shouting spread everywhere.

When they met in the mountains, they killed each other there,

And when they met in the valley, they killed each other there.

The sound of killing was chilling!

The Hanis' bamboo knives

Could not cut through the Labos' bellies;

The Hanis' bamboo arrows

Could not pierce through the Labos' chests.

腊伯的铁刀啊，
像剃头刀一样快，
把大树样的哈尼，
砍倒在山上！
腊伯的铁箭啊，
像尖刺一样硬，
把大象样的哈尼，
射翻在坝旁！
水急的诺马河，
漂起数不清的死人死马；
宽大的诺马坝，
哈尼人倒地睡平！
七千个女人变成寡妇，
七千个小娃望不见爹娘，
高高的秋房倒塌了，
三层的蘑菇房被烧光。

只怪忠厚的先祖乌木，
把田地牛马分给豺狼；
只怪老实的先祖乌木，
嫁出了不该出嫁的姑娘；
只怪昏头的先祖乌木，
不把权帽绶带珍藏！

扎纳召集全体哈尼，
把最大的事情商量，
权威的乌木决定离开诺马，

The Labos' iron swords

Were as sharp as the razor.

The Hanis, like the big trees,

Were cut down on the mountain.

The Labos' iron arrows,

Were as hard as stiff thorns.

The Hanis, like the elephants,

Were shot down by the field!

In the turbulent Nuoma River

Were floating countless dead people and dead horses;

On the wide Nuoma bazi,

Almost all the Hanis fell.

Seven thousand women became widows.

Seven thousand kids became orphans.

The tall sacrifice houses were pushed down,

And the three-story mushroom houses were burned to the ground.

This was all because of the straightforward ancestor wumu

Who gave the field and livestock to jackals and wolves.

This was all because of the guileless ancestor wumu,

Who married his daughter to a wrong person.

This was all because of the dippy ancestor wumu,

Who did not take good care of the chief hat and sash.

Zhana gathered all the Hanis

For the most important decisions.

The authoritative wumu decided to leave Nuoma,

走出这多灾多难的故乡。

扎纳叫妻子带领老小，
顺着大河走向下方，
自己带领勇敢的男人，
把凶恶的腊伯抵挡。

贤惠的扎纳玛①
哭瞎了双跟，
泪水浇湿烧倒的老房：
"麂子死了，
也要死在出生的岩洞；
白鹇死了，
也要死在出生的凹塘；
大树一样的哈尼，
不能离开生根的家乡！"

"哈尼人啊，
怎能丢下座座大山，
那里有先祖的尸骨埋藏；
怎能丢下棵棵神树，
哈尼在那里乞求过吉祥；
怎能丢下滚滚的诺马河啊，
那滴滴河水是哈尼的血浆！"

---

① 扎纳玛：扎纳的妻子，哈尼族的习称。

To leave this hometown riddled with misfortunes and mis-
haps.

Zhana asked his wife to lead the old and the young,

To go downstream along the river.

He himself led the brave Hani men,

To hold off the ferocious Labos.

The virtuous Zhana Ma①

Cried her eyes blind,

Her tears quenching the burn-down old house.

"When muntjacs die,

They die in the cave they were born.

When silver pheasants die,

They die in the aotang they were born.

The tree-like Hanis

Cannot leave the hometown, their roots.

"How can the Hanis

Leave these mountains

Where their ancestors were buried?

How can the Hanis leave these sacred trees

Where they prayed for good fortune?

How can they leave the rolling Nuoma River

Where every drop of water was the Hanis' blood!"

———————————

①　Zhana Ma: Zhana's wife, the way the Hanis refer to her customari-
ly.

听见扎纳玛的话，
七千个哈尼一齐停下，
七千哈尼纷纷跪倒啊，
求乌木带他们去拼杀疆场。

扎纳摇动满头白发，
声音又老又悲怆：
"亲亲的扎纳玛啊，
和我同老的女人，
鸭子不能和老鹰共一林，
人不能和魔鬼共一方。
起来走吧，
起来领着搬迁的人群，
快快走吧，
快快离开这熟悉的老房。"

"瞧你面前的棵棵柱子，
都是我从山上砍来；
瞧你脚边的块块石头，
都是我亲手砌上。
瞧着它们抵得瞧着亲儿子，
望见它们好像望着亲姑娘，
我也舍不得啊，
和你一样悲伤！

"哦哦，
不能了，
再不能舍不得了，
花鹿最宝贵的是角，

On hearing Zhana Ma's words,
All seven thousand Hanis stopped what they were doing
And, one after another, they dropped to their knees,
Begging the wumu to lead them to the battle field.

Zhana shaked his head full of white hair,
His voice old and sad:
"My dear Zhana Ma,
The woman who has grown old with me,
Ducks cannot stay in the same wood with eagles,
And humans cannot stay in the same place with devils.
Get up and go
And lead the migrating people!
Hurry up and go
And leave this familiar old house!

"Look at the pillars in front of you.
I chopped and carried them from the mountains.
Look at the stones by your side.
I laid them one by one.
Seeing them is like seeing my own son.
Looking at them is like looking at my own daughter.
It is just as sad for me to part with them
As it is for you!

"Oh oh,
We cannot do this any more.
We cannot not let go.
The most precious of the sika deer is their horns.

人最宝贵的是命，
哈尼还想有后代，
就要到远远的下方。"

"走吧，亲亲的女人，
草结烧掉，
来年还会转青；
房子倒掉，
石脚还会在地上。
大山不会变心，
平坝不会变肠，
只要哈尼没有死光，
总有一天会回到诺马河旁！"

听见扎纳的劝说，
扎纳玛离开了老墙，
走到诺马河边，
拾起一块石头，
她把这诺马的石头，
装进了披火披斗①，
让这珍贵的石头啊，
睡在靠心贴肉的地方。
她说一声："走啊！"
就带着大队离开了家乡。

众人：
萨——依——萨！

---

①　披火披斗：大襟衣，哈尼族常穿的衣服。

The most valuable of the humans is their lives.

If the Hanis want offsprings,

We have to move to very remote places.

"Go, my dearest woman.

The burnt grass knots

Can turn green the next year.

The fallen house

Still has the foundation stone on the ground.

The big mountains won't change their hearts,

Nor will the flat bazi.

As long as the Hanis don't die out,

One day we will return to the side of the Nuoma River!"

On hearing Zhana's words,

Zhana Ma left the old wall.

She came to the side of the Nuoma River,

And picked up a stone.

She put this stone from Nuoma

Into her Pihuo Pidou garment①,

Letting this precious stone

Sleep snugly in the place closest to the heart.

She called out: "Let's go!"

And led the people in leaving the hometown.

Audience:

Sa—ee—sa!

---

① Pihuo Pidou: Common garment of the Hani people, like a jacket with two pieces of clothes making up the front of it.

193

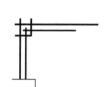
五、色厄作娘①

（一）

歌手：

萨——依——
九山的树叶又细又密，
诺马河翻滚着树叶样的波浪；
九山的藤子又扭又弯，
诺马河像弯藤爬向远方。
顺着河水走过七日马路，
哈尼大队停下来歇歇脚掌。
河水在这里转了个弯，
折头流向东升的太阳；
宽宽的水湾正合洗脸洗脚，
哈尼在这里安下营帐。

背上的鸡鸭还没有放好，
马上的驮子还没有卸光，
小娃刚刚攀住阿妈的奶头，

---

① 色厄作娘：海边的大坝子。

Chapter 5　Se'ezuoniang①

5. 1

Singer:

Sa—ee—!

Thick and dense, were the leaves in the nine mountains,

And just like the leaves, the waves were swirling in the Nuoma River;

Twisted and bent were the vines in the nine mountains,

And just like the vines, the Nuoma River was crawling far away.

Having walking along the river for seven days,

The Hani group stopped to have a rest.

The river took a turn here,

Flowing back towards the rising sun in the east.

The wide inlet was perfect for washing the face and feet

So the Hanis set up their camp here.

Before the fowls carried on the back had all been put away,

Before the horses had all been unloaded,

As the babies were just about to suck the mothers' breasts,

---

①　Se'ezuoniang: The wide embankment by the sea.

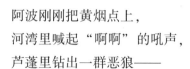

阿波刚刚把黄烟点上，
河湾里喊起"啊啊"的吼声，
芦蓬里钻出一群恶狼——

亲亲的兄弟们，
恶人早就等在这方，
一寨的姐妹们；
腊伯想把哈尼杀光！

扛着铁刀铁矛，
腊伯大声闹嚷：
"哈尼，
赶紧扎好你的驮子，
快快收好你的营帐，
远远地走高高地飞吧，
像领你们来的大雁那样；
不准再吃诺马的水，
不准再上诺马的山！"

九死一生的哈尼，
不像尖角的野牛强壮；
筋疲力尽的哈尼，
没有四蹄的马鹿快当。

但是哈尼人啊，
又抽出锋利的竹箭，
又拿起三拃的竹枪，
像拼命的老熊，

And the apos had just lit up the tobacco,

The hawling sounded in the bay,

And a group of fierce wolves came out of the reeds.

My dear brothers,

The bad people had been waiting here.

My dear sisters,

The Labos wanted to kill off the Hanis!

With iron swords and iron spears on the shoulders

The Labos shouted loudly:

"Hanis,

Hurry and load your horses

And pack up your tents!

Go far away and fly highly

Like the geese that led you here.

Don't drink from the Nuoma River any more,

Nor go up the Nuoma's mountain."

The Hanis, who narrowly escaped death,

Were not as strong as bison with sharp horns;

They, completely exhaused,

Were not as fast as red deer with four hoofs.

But, the Hanis

Once again pulled out the sharp bamboo arrows

And picked up the three-hand-long bamboo spear.

Like the desperate old bear,

197

像发怒的老象，
把短路的强人杀倒，
把恶辣的腊伯砍伤！

后代的儿孙们啊，
牢记这伤心的往事吧：
哈尼从此离开了亲亲的诺马河水，
爬上了野羊才走的陡峭山冈。

众人：
萨——依——萨！

歌手：
翻过一山睡一夜，
走过一箐歇歇肩，
涉过一水喘口气，
爬过一坡吃嘴干粮。

女人抱紧了小娃，
小娃是哈尼繁衍兴旺的人种；
男人牵牢了牛马，
牛马是哈尼开发新地的靠望。

搬家的哈尼受尽苦难，
像雨中的蜻蜓颤抖着翅膀；
受难的哈尼不说山陡水急，
只怨先祖乌木太憨太犟。

Like the furious old elephant,

They killed the robbers who were blocking the road,

And wounded the vicious and ferocious Labos.

Children and grandchildren,

Bear in mind this heartbreaking past:

From then on, the Hanis left the dear Nuoma River,

And climbed the steep hilly paths used only by the wild goats.

Audience:

Sa—ee—sa!

Singer:

After climbing over a mountain they slept for one night.

After walking across a valley they rested their shoulders.

After wading through a river they paused a breath.

After going over a slope they had a bite.

The women held tightly their babies,

Who were the seeds of the Hanis to flourish and thrive.

The men held tightly the cattle and horses,

That were the hope for the Hanis to cultivate new land.

The moving Hanis went through all kinds of hardships,

Shaking like the dragonflies' wings quivering in the rain.

The suffering Hanis didn't complain about the steep mountains and rapid rivers,

But the simple-minded and strubborn ancestor wumu.

199

扎纳阿波是聪明的乌木，
话语焐热了哈尼的胸膛：
"雨脚不停不能怪天，
只怪大雾罩在天上；
地下不平不能怪地，
只怪处处站着山冈；
世上不平不能怪乌木，
只怪腊伯黑心黑肠。

记着吧，我的后辈儿孙，
家里的事只能在家里说，
哈尼打失权帽绶带的话，
不能去对外人讲。
快走吧，亲亲的兄弟姐妹，
只要手不折，
就不会饿肚肠，
只要脚不断，
就不愁走不到好在的地方！"
走了，
哈尼又抬起粗壮的脚杆，
走了，
哈尼又挺起厚实的胸膛。

宽脯的骏马，
一脚不能跑过一座大山，
十步百步，
也能跑过十座山梁；

Apo Zhana is a smart wumu,

His words warming up the Hanis' heart:

"You cannot blame the sky when it keeps raining.

It's all because of the heavy fog above.

You cannot blame the earth when it is uneven.

It's all because of the mountains everywhere.

You cannot blame the wumu when there is the injustice in the world.

It's all because of the black-hearted Labos.

Keep it in mind, my children and grandchildren:

"Don't wash the dirty linen in public.

How the Hanis lost their chief hat and sash

Should not be talked about with others.

Let's go! My dearest brothers and sisters.

As long as our hands are not broken,

We will not go hungry;

As long as our feet are not broken,

We should not worry about not finding a good place."

Moving forward again,

The Hanis had their strong legs lifted.

Moving forward again,

The Hanis had their thick chests up.

Even the best steed with wide chest

Can't cross a mountain with one big step.

But with hundreds of thousands of steps,

It can run across ten mountains.

硬脚的哈尼，
一脚不能涉过一道大水，
十步百步，
也能涉过十条大江；
走过数不清的高山大河，
哈尼找着生息的地方。

派去的人回来报信，
在远处就已笑响：
"哈尼啊，
喜欢起来吧，
再走七十七日路，
就到色厄作娘。"

"色厄有个海子，
海里翻着波浪，
海水又清又甜，
大鱼肥猪样胖。
大水名叫得威①。

木船漂在水上，
说来你们不信，
船也穿着大襟衣裳②！"

---

① 得威：又宽又大的水。得威在哈尼族民间文学中常被提到，如儿歌《阿密抽》中咒骂有钱有势的女人"吃水要吃得威的水"。
② 大襟衣裳：此处指帆。

Even the Hanis with strong feet

Can not wade through water with one big step.

But with hundreds of thousands of steps,

They can wade through ten big rivers.

After having gone through countless high mountains and big
rivers,

The Hanis found a place to settle down.

The scouts came back with good news.

Their laughters were heard from far away:

"The Hanis!

Cheer up!

With another seventy-seven-day journey,

We will arrive at Se'ezuoniang.

"There is a big lake in Se'e,

With rolling waves.

The lake water is clear and sweet.

The fish in it are as fat as pigs.

The big lake is called Dewei①.

Many wood boats are floating on it.

You may not believe this,

But the boats there wear clothes② too!"

---

① Dewei: Wide and big water. It is often mentioned in the Hani folk-
lore, e. g. in the children's song *Amichou*, the rich and powerful woman is
described as "only drinking the water of Dewei".

② It refers to the sails of the boat.

听说的人个个惊奇，

"哦嗬哦嗬"一片赞扬。

说话的人比手画脚，

像窝小雀吵吵嚷嚷：

"得威海边有九个大坝，

像九颗珍珠放出金光，

个个坝子又宽又平，

都像朝前伸平的手掌。

最大的坝子住着哈厄①，

脸皮好像白鸡的翅膀，

见着我们就嘻嘻地笑，

又是拉手又牵衣裳。"

哈尼的笑声像大河淌水，

乌木又有新的担心：

"一道山箐只养一对箐鸡，

一对老虎守着一座山冈。

哈尼从远处搬来，

哈厄给不给歇气的地方？"

"哈厄有笑眯眯的乌木，

喜欢哈尼同住一方，

答应把最高的佐甸②，

----

① 哈厄："哈"（读上声，hǎ），此处意为鸡；"厄"，水。"哈厄"意为住在水边像白鸡样白的人。

② 佐甸：山名。

People who heard this were all surprised,

Their praise sounded "Oho Oho".

The scouts gesticulated with hands and feet,

Like a flock of twittering sparrows.

"By the Dewei Lake there are nine big bazies,

Like nine pearls glowing with golden lights.

Each bazi wide and flat,

Like open and flat palms.

By the biggest bazi live the Ha'es①,

Whose complexions are like the wings of the white chickens.

They giggled on seeing us,

Holding our hands and pulling on our clothes. "

The Hanis' laughters were like a river with running water,

And the wumu had new worries.

"One valley can only live one pair of pheasants.

One mountain is guarded by only one pair of tigers.

The Hanis came from afar.

Will the Ha'es let us have a rest here?"

"The Ha'e wumu always has a smile on his face

And has said that they like to live with the Hanis.

He has promised to let the highest Zuodian②

---

① Ha'e: "Ha" in the third tone means chicken; "e" means water.
"Ha'e" means people who lived by the water were as white as chicken.

② Zuodian: The name of a mountain.

给哈尼来做神山。"

扎纳召集头人，
把大事细细商量：
哈厄会不会像腊伯，
对哈尼撒下拿鱼的大网？

头人们想过七遍，
七个人一个主张：
"走路人说不得坐下的话，
打猎人顾不得坡陡路长，
逃难的哈尼走脱了七层厚皮，
驮子也磨通了马的脊梁，
事事小心不会出大错，
找个地方歇歇又讲。"

扎纳点点白头，
把哈尼分做三帮，
约好在佐甸山脚会齐，
三队人朝着三个方向。①

众人：
萨——依——萨！

---

① 歌手解释，这样可以避免腊伯追赶。

Be sacred mountain for the Hanis."

Zhana gathered all the headmen
To discuss about this in detail.
Will the Ha'e be another Labo,
Casting the net to catch the Hani?

The headmen thought it over seven times,
All seven of them having one idea:
"Those walking cannot talk like they were sitting down.
And hunters cannot worry about the steep slopes and the long
distance.
The fleeing Hanis have peeled off seven layers of skins,
And the loads have rubbed the horses' back raw.
Caution won't lead to big mistakes,
So let's have a rest and talk it over."

Zhana nodded his head of white hair
And divided the Hanis into three groups.
They agreed to meet at the foot of the Mount Zuodian
And the three groups took three different routes.①

Audience:
Sa—ee—sa!

---

① The singer's explanation: This way the Hanis could avoid being
chased by the Labos.

（二）

歌手：

萨——依——

走走停停，停停走走，

哈尼走过七十七天马路；

停停走走，走走停停，

哈尼来到佐甸山冈。

到了说定的日子，

有一队人却不知去向。

等过一日又等两日，

等伴的母鸡已经抱蛋；

等过两日又等三日，

等伴的母牛已经下儿——

可惜没有等来失散的兄弟，

只等来流不尽的泪水和悲伤。

哈尼是一树的枝丫，

一根也不能折断；

哈尼是一窝的嫩雀，

一只也不能飞散。

乌木派人四处去找，

焦心的喊声四处回荡。

七天七夜过去，

哈尼回到佐甸，

5.2

Singer:

Sa—ee—!

Walking and stopping, stopping and walking,

The Hanis had gone through seventy-seven days;

Stopping and walking, walking and stopping,

The Hanis had arrived at the Mount Zuodian.

But on the appointed day,

One group of people were missing.

One day passed, and then another,

And now it had been as long as the hen had already laid

eggs.

Two days passed, and then another,

And now the cow had already given birth to a calf—

Unfortunately, the Hani lost brothers never came,

Only the endless tears and sadness.

The Hanis were like the branches on the same tree,

So none should be broken.

The Hanis were the fledglings of the same nest,

So none should get strayed.

The wumu sent search teams to go in all directions.

The anxious calling echoing everywhere.

Seven days and seven nights had passed.

The search teams returned to the Zuodian.

四方找过三面，
只找着雀飞水淌；
九天九夜过去，
朝前找的人回到营寨，
个个像雨中竹子，
低着头弯着脊梁。

领头人说出了痛心的话，
句句话哈尼永世难忘：
"我们找到远远的前方，
望见哈尼留下的脚印，
那脚迹里清水已经灌满；
又望见哈尼留下的灰堆，
那灰堆已是灰饼一摊。
我们爬上最高的山顶，
把亲亲的弟兄呼唤，
只听见自己的声音，
听不到他们的回答；
我们又下到最宽的河边，
把亲亲的姊妹呼唤，
只听见一阵阵浪声，
听不见她们的回响。"

佐甸山脚的哈尼，
一齐放声痛哭，
泪水像大雨落地，
浸湿了佐甸的土壤。

Three of the four directions had been searched,

But they found only the flying birds and the running water.

Nine days and nine nights had passed,

The team searching the forward direction came back.

Everyone was like the bamboos in the rain,

With their heads hanging and backs bending.

The lead person said the heart-breaking words,

Each being unforgettable by the Hanis:

"When we got far ahead,

We saw the footprints our brothers left,

But the footprints had been filled with clear water.

We also saw the ash heaps our brothers left,

But the ash heaps had become a pile of ash cakes.

We went to the highest mountain top,

And called our dearest brothers.

But we only heard our own voice,

Not their answers.

We then went by the widest river

And called our dearest sisters.

But we only heard the laps of waves,

Not their responses."

The Hanis at the foot of the Mount Zuodian

All bursted into tears,

Which, like the heavy rain,

Soaked the earth of the Zuodian.

啊哟，亲亲的兄弟姊妹，
一娘生的哈尼子孙，
先祖传下了弟兄失散的古今，
叫后人不要把他们遗忘，
有钱有米就背着去找，
不要怕磨通我们的脚掌！

众人：
萨——依——萨！

歌手：
在哈尼心疼的日子，
贤惠的祖母扎纳玛唱起了哈八：
"萨——依——萨——
哈尼的后人哟，
我的儿子姑娘，
快止住眼中的泪水，
快忍住心头的悲伤，
快拿起尖角的锄头①，
重建新的家乡。

"打失的孤雁会调头，
打失的哈尼会找着佐甸山冈。

———————

① 尖角的锄头：哈尼族因居处山区，为开坡地方便，好用短柄、两尖角的锄头。

Alas, my dearest brothers and sisters,

The Hani descendants born from one mother!

The ancestors passed down this story of our lost brothers,

So that the descendants would never forget them.

Go to search whenever money and rice are ready.

Don't be afraid of rubbing our feet raw.

Audience:

Sa—ee—sa!

Singer:

During those heart-breaking days,

The virtuous grandma Zhana Ma started to sing the Haba,

the drinking song:

"Sa—ee—sa—

The Hani descendants!

My sons and daughters!

Hold back your tears

And your sadness.

Pick up your hoe with sharp blades①

To rebuild our new homeland.

"The stray goose will turn around,

And the missing Hanis will find their way to the Mount Zuo-

dian.

---

① The hoe with sharp blades: The hoe the Hanis use has a short handle and two sharp blades, which make it easier for the Hanis to work in the
fields in the mountainous area.

快喂肥黄牛大猪，
等亲亲的兄弟来吃；
快栽出红米玉麦，
等亲亲的姊妹来尝！"
听见扎纳玛的歌声，
女人揩干眼泪，
男人挺起胸膛，
大人小娃齐声响应：
"萨——依——萨！"

（三）

歌手：

萨——依——
为了在色厄住下，
扎纳和哈尼商量，
他头戴高高的帽子，
穿着新染的衣裳，
脱下棕片编成的鞋，
换上新鞋一双。

七个头人跟着乌木，
好像小鱼尾着大鱼，
身上银饰驮子样重，
走起路来叮叮当当。
哈厄寨子又宽又大，
整整齐齐像座蜂房，

Fatten up the cattle and pigs,

To wait for our dearest brothers to enjoy when they are back.

Plant the red rice and wheat,

To wait for our dearest sisters to taste when they are back."

On hearing the song by Zhana Ma,

Women wiped away their tears,

And men squared their shoulders.

All people, adults and children, responded together:

"Sa—ee—sa!"

5.3

Singer:

Sa—ee—!

To settle down in Se'e,

Zhana discussed with his people.

He put on the tall hat,

And the newly-dyed clothes.

He took off the palm leave shoes,

And replaced them with a new pair.

Seven headmen followed the wumu,

Like the small fish following the big fish.

The silver ornaments weighed on them like the loads of car-

gos,

Tinkling and jingling when he walked.

The village of the Ha'e was wide and big,

Tidy and neat like a hive.

不住哈尼的三层房子，
用木头搭起两层楼房。

头人的在处最高最大，
远远就望见它的模样，
白白的墙脚高又齐，
木楼的尖角像斑鸠张开翅膀。
哈厄头人站在门口，
见着哈尼又说又讲，
喜喜欢欢像喝醉米酒，
眼睛鼻子放出红光。

哈厄头人说：
"哈尼人呀，
你们从远方走来，
就请坐到哈厄的桌旁，
哈厄的美酒哈尼一同来喝，
哈厄吃肉哈尼一同来尝，
两家人在一处也不怕，
阿哥阿弟可以同坐一条凳上。"

扎纳唱起好听的哈八，
把哈尼的情意说出，
又牵过膀宽腰壮的牯牛，
把诚心的礼品送上。

They did not have the Hani three-story houses
But built two-story log cabins instead.

The house of the chief was the highest and the biggest,
Which could be seen from far away.
The white walls were tall and orderly.
The overhanging eaves were like turtle doves with outsprea-
ding wings.
The Ha'e chief stood at the door,
Friendly and welcoming to the Hani when he saw them,
Rejoicing as if intoxicated with the rice wine,
Eyes and nose turning red.

The Ha'e chief said:
"The Hanis,
You came from afar,
So please sit at our table.
The Ha'es' wine is to share with you, the Hanis,
And the Ha'es' meat is also to share with you.
Don't worry, as we two families can get together,
Just like brothers can sit on one bench."

Zhana sang the melodious Haba the drinking song,
Telling the appreciation of the Hanis.
He then called a strong wide-waist bull over
And gave it as the gift to show the Hanis' sincerity.

哈尼像蚂蚁找食，
找着色厄作娘，
佐甸山脚是宽宽的坝子，
正合哈尼种地开荒。
哈尼把大寨立在这里，
照着规矩立下秋房，
赶紧砍树烧出火地，
抢着节令种下玉麦高粱。

奔走的哈尼没有人心疼，
心疼哈尼的是满田庄稼；
吃苦的哈尼没有人喜欢，
喜欢哈尼的是遍山牛羊。
哈尼的庄稼老实好，
像罗比草盖满凹塘；
哈尼的牛羊老实壮，
像乌山草撒满山冈。

哈尼哈厄情投意合，
就像两窝雀共一树，
两寨的女人爱在一处说话，
两寨的男人爱在一起商量。

一年的三月，
是哈厄赶街的月，
街子摆在得威海边，
人来人往像鱼群钻浪。

The Hanis were like the ants looking for food

And finally finding Se'e Zuoliang.

At the foot of the Mount Zuodian was a wide bazi,

Suitable for the Hanis to plough and to plant.

The Hanis set their village here

And set up the sacrifice house qiufang according to their customs.

They hastened to cut trees and burn out the fields,

Working against time to plant the wheat and sorghum.

No one cared about the busy Hanis,

Except the crops all over the the field.

No one liked the suffering Hanis,

Except the flocks and herds all over the mount.

The Hanis' crops grew really well,

Like the Luobi grass covering the aotang.

The Hanis' flocks and herds were really strong,

Like the Wushan grass blanketing the hills and slopes.

The Hanis and the Ha'es hit it off,

Like two families of birds living on one tree.

The women of the two villages loved to chat with each other,

And the men loved to discuss matters together.

Every third month of the year

Was the time for the Ha'es' fair.

The fair was set by the Dewei Lake,

Crowded people coming and going like schools of fish cha-

sing the waves.

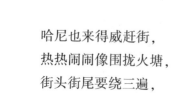

哈尼也来得威赶街，
热热闹闹像围拢火塘，
街头街尾要绕三遍，
大背小背满满当当。

哦哦，亲亲的哈尼儿孙，
记住这快活的时光，
赶街的日子是喜欢的日子，
一年到头只有这一趟，
赶街的日子是玩耍的日子，
一年到头只有这一场。

哦哦，一寨的兄弟姊妹，
你们问得威街的样子，
再会说我也难说像，
听听赫则大词①怎样唱吧，
那里说得仔细周详：

"最好听的是三月的弦子，
最好玩的是三月的街子，
女人喜欢的五彩丝线，

———————————

① 赫则大词：哈尼族古代宗教、文学、艺术、经济、生产的综合概括，亦可称哈尼族古典百科全书，共一万余句，又称"赫则一万句"。

The Hanis came to the Dewei fair too,

Bustling with the same excitement as if being around the fireplace.

They walked around the whole street for three times,

Filling up their big back baskets as well as the small ones.

Oh oh, the dearest Hani offsprings,

Remember these happy times.

The days of the fair were the joyful days,

Only once in the whole year.

The days of fair were the days to play,

Only once in the whole year.

Oh oh, the brothers and sisters in a village,

You ask what the Dewei street was like.

But no matter how good I am at telling stories, I could hardly
describe it.

Let's listen to the Heze Encyclopaedia①

Where it is explained in detail:

"The best melody comes from the strings in the third month,

And the most fun comes from the fair in the third month.

The colors of the silk threads that women are fond of,

---

① Heze Encyclopaedia: A classical encyclopedia of the Hanis including the ancient religion, literature, art, economy and production. With a total of more than 10,000 sentences, it's also known as "Heze Ten Thousand
Sentences".

在那里像彩虹一样齐，
男人瞧着的锄头，
在那里像太阳一样亮，
阿波阿匹喜欢的吃食，
那里一样也不缺，
扎谷扎密喜欢的穿戴，
那里一样也不少，
好东西街头摆通街尾，
要什么只消指指不消讲。"

扎实好啰，哈尼人！
难怪今日哈尼的在处，
三月的街子都有一个，
先祖赶过的色厄街子，
是哈尼三月街子的亲娘。

高能的扎纳阿波，
在三月里最苦最忙，
他叫拢姑娘伙子，
甜甜的话细细讲：

"离圈的牛马找不着歇处，
离家的哈尼漂流四方，
无儿的老虎守不住山岭，
无后的哈尼不会兴旺。

Are as many as the colors of the rainbow.

The shine of the hoes that men look at,

Are as bright as the sun.

The food that apo and api like

Is all there without one missing.

The clothes that zagu and zami like

Can all be found there.

The fabulous goods are displayed from the head of the street to the end,

And, to buy anything, one only has to point with no word."

That was really good, the Hanis!

No wonder wherever the Hanis live today,

There is a street for the fair in the third month.

The Se'e fair our ancestors went

Was the mother of Hanis' Third-month Fair.

The capable Apo Zhana

Was the busiest and the most hard-working person in the third month.

He gathered all the boys and girls,

Slowly giving his speech with sweet themes:

"Without the pens, the cattle and horses could not find a place to rest;

Without a home, the Hanis could but wander about.

Without cubs, the tigers can't keep their territory on the hill;

Without offsprings, the Hanis won't prosper.

哈尼的姑娘伙子哟，
听阿波把害羞的事情讲讲。

"看那得威的海水，
绿得像块玉石，
看那佐甸的山坡，
桃花像彩霞飘满，
爱唱的花雀成对，
爱跑的花鹿成双。
三月是哈尼找伴的月，
快快去到心爱的人身旁。
我权威的乌木说下话来，
许你们不去种地放羊，
快去结成甜甜的夫妻，
阿爸阿妈不准阻挡。
不单伙子可以来娶，
姑娘也可以挑新郎——
姑娘们，
瞧着哪个伙子赶紧来认，
扎纳阿波帮你们结对成双！

得了乌木的话，
姑娘走出大田，
伙子走下山冈，
尖声的树叶①吹透老林，

---

①　树叶：哈尼族乐器。

Hani boys and girls,

Don't be shy about what apo is about to tell you.

"Look at the Dewei water,

As green as jade.

Look at the Zuodian slope,

With the peach blossom like the flowing rosy clouds,

The canaries who love to sing are in pairs,

And the sika deer who love run as couples.

The third month is the mating season for the Hanis.

Go and be with your loved one.

I, the authoritative wumu, give you the permission

Not to farm the filed or herd the sheep

But to get married to your sweet heart.

Dad and Mum are not allowed to stop you.

Not only can young men pick the bride,

But young women can also pick the bridegroom—

Young women,

Hurry and find your favorite young man,

And Apo Zhana will help you pair up."

On hearing the wumu's words

The young women walked out of the fields.

And the young men walked down from the mountains.

Those who played the leaves① made a shrill sound through-

out the forest,

_____

①　Leaf: A Hani musical instrument.

粗声的巴乌①顺风飘荡，

口弦②说着悄悄话，

三弦细细来商量，

得威的波浪和海风，

把巴布、巴查③的歌声送到远方。

众人：

萨——哝——萨！

歌手：

佐甸的嫩竹一天天冒尖，

哈尼的小娃一天天增多；

竹笋转眼发成大竹，

小娃也一天天长大。

哈尼的小娃不会得闲，

放牛放马常到山上，

两山的箐鸡不会不斗，

一坡的小娃不会不嚷。

哈厄小娃也放羊放马，

---

① 巴乌：哈尼族乐器。

② 口弦：哈尼族乐器。

③ 巴布、巴查：情歌。哈尼族情歌分巴布、巴查两种，巴布为谈情时双方有了误会所唱的怨情歌，巴查为双方情投意合时所唱的恋歌。

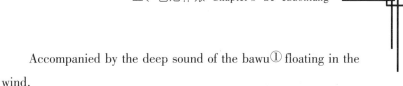

Accompanied by the deep sound of the bawu① floating in the
wind.

Those who played the kouxian② sounded like someone whis-
pering

To those who played smooth music of three-string lute.

The waves and winds of the Dewei Lake

Spread the love songs Babu and Bacha③ far and wide.

Audience:

Sa—nong—sa!

Singer:

The bamboo shoots in Zuodian had been growing day by day,

So had the number of the Hani children.

The bamboo shoots grew up quickly,

So did the children.

The Hani children were not idle,

Often in the hills herding horses and cattle.

Bamboo pheasants from two mountains had to fight,

And the children were the same.

The Ha'e children also herded their cattle and horses,

---

① Bawu: A Hani musical instrument.

② Kouxian: A Hani musical instrument.

③ Babu and Bacha: Love songs. The Hani love songs are of two
types: Babu and Bacha. Babu is resentful because lovers have misunder-
standings, while Bacha is happy because they get along with each other.

嫩嫩的草坡被它们把光，
哈尼要去吆牛吃草，
日日挨着他们的棍棒。
打嘛重重的不打，
骂嘛重重的不骂，
拿着细细的树枝，
好像追赶坡头的小羊。

望见小娃挨打受气，
哈尼老实心疼，
想起诺马阿美，
心中又苦又凉。

先祖在满三年，
哈厄也有提防，
头人走进哈尼大寨，
说出的话叫人心伤：

"哈尼啊，
走过你们的大田，
望见谷穗像马尾下奔；
走过你们的园子，
望见姜叶像乌鸦翅膀黑亮。
和你们一桌吃饭，
挟着的肉有一拃厚；
和你们一桌喝酒，
倒出的酒像大水淌。"

Which ate up the grass on the hills.

When the Hani children herded their cattle to the pasture,

They were beaten with sticks everyday by the Ha'e children.

They didn't beat too hard,

Nor did they berate the Hani children too badly.

Using the thin sprigs,

They chased the Hani children like chasing the sheep on the

slope.

Seeing the little children being abused,

The Hanis were in distress.

Recalling Nuoma Amei

They felt the bitter chill in their heart.

The ancestors had lived in Zuodian for three years,

And the Ha'es also became wary.

The Ha'e chief went to the Hani village one day

And said the disheartening words:

"Dear Hanis,

When we walk by your fields,

We see ears of millet hanging like the horses' tails.

When we walk by your gardens,

We see your ginger-leaves as shiny-black as crows' wings.

When we eat with you,

We pick up thick pieces of meats.

When we drink with you,

We pour the wine like spring water.

"不是哈厄变心变肝，
做客也有散席的时候，
哈尼歇饱了力气，
应当去找自己的家乡；
得威水里再没有你们的鱼虾，
佐甸山脚你们再不得栽秧！"

哈尼个个伤心，
扎纳来把话讲：
"牛多了要分圈，
蜂多了要分房，
我们喜喜欢欢遇在一处，
也要欢欢喜喜走开两旁。"

扎纳召拢哈尼，
高声说出主张：
"色厄坝子再宽再平，
也不是哈尼的家乡，
得威海水再凉再甜，
哈尼也要把它遗忘。
哈尼人啊，
不是自己的房子不能久住，
不是自己的红米不能久尝，
拉上你们的牛马，
背上你们的背箩，
让我们走吧，
走到远远的地方。"

"It is not that the Ha'e people changed their minds,
But even a feast must end.
Once the Hanis are rested,
Go and find your own homeland.
The Dewei Lake is no longer where you should fish,
And the foot of the Mount Zuodian is no longer where you
can farm!"

Everyone of the Hanis was saddened,
So Zhana said:
"When there are too many cattle, there must be more pens;
And when there are too many bees, there must be more
chambers.
We met them happily
And let's part our ways happily as well."

Zhana gathered the Hanis
And announced his plan loudly:
"As wide and flat as the Se'e bazi is,
It is not the Hanis' homeland;
As cool and sweet as the water of the Dewei Lake is,
It has to be forgotten by the Hanis.
Ah, my Hanis,
The house that's not ours we cannot stay for too long,
And the red rice that is not ours we cannot taste for too long.
Lead your cattle and horses
And carry your panniers.
Let us go,
Go to a distant place."

231

哈厄的头人也舍不得，
话像糯米又软又香：
"鸭子白鹅各游各的，
它们也共过一个水塘；
麂子黄牛各走各的，
它们也共过一座山冈。
哈尼哈厄都是兄弟，
不管你们去到哪方，
年年三月色厄街子，
哈尼可以来赶来玩，
年年得威水涨鱼肥，
哈尼可以来拉大网!"

听说又要搬迁上路，
哈尼女人哭倒路旁：
"七月的河水又浑又急，
哈尼像河水四处流淌；
我们的儿子是不争气的儿子，
把诺马家园打失在远方!
我们的男人是不能干的男人，
带来的苦难像大山一样!"

乌木扎纳走上寨堡，
他的声音苍老又雄壮：
"哈尼家家有人死去，
他们是战死在战场，
哈尼男人图的是名气，
子子孙孙也不会忘!"

The Ha'e chief also felt hard to let the Hanis go,

Saying words soft and sweet like the glutenous rice:

"Ducks and geese go their own ways,

Even though they used to share the same pool.

Muntjacs and cattle part their own ways,

Even though they used to share the same mountain.

The Hanis and the Ha'es are brothers,

So no matter where you go,

The third month of every year,

Se'e's fair is open to the Hanis.

When the water is high and the fish are fat in the Dewei every year,

Hanis are welcome to come net-fishing."

On hearing that they had to migrate again,

The Hani women cried so hard that they fell by the roadsides:

"The river water in the seventh month is murky and swift,

And the Hanis are like the river running in all directions;

Our sons are not able,

And lost our homeland Nuoma to the distant past!

Our men are not capable,

And brought us hardships like big mountains!"

Wumu Zhana went up to the village castle,

His voice deep and majestic:

"Every Hani family has had people who passed away,

And they died in the battle fields;

The Hani men aim at glory

That could not be forgotten by the Hani descendants."

233

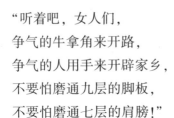

"听着吧，女人们，
争气的牛拿角来开路，
争气的人用手来开辟家乡，
不要怕磨通九层的脚板，
不要怕磨通七层的肩膀！"

"听着啊，
见多识广的阿波阿匹，
快快扶起不愿上路的姑娘媳妇；
听着啊，
一样也不怕的兄弟姊妹，
快快牵起不愿出圈的骡马牛羊。
走啊，跟着我年老的扎纳，
去寻找爱在的地方！"

走了，亲亲的兄弟，
先祖又走在搬迁的路上；
走了，哈尼的儿孙，
先祖离开了色厄作娘。

哈尼的先祖是硬气的先祖，
再深的大水也难把他们隔断；
哈尼的先祖是自豪的先祖，
再高的大山也难把他们阻挡！

众人：
萨——哝——萨！

"Listen! Women,

The best among the cattle use their horn to find a way,

And the best among us use their hands to build their homeland.

Do not be afraid of taking great pains in your feet,

Do not be afraid of taking great pains on your shoulders. "

"Listen!

Wise apos and apis,

Hurry and help the reluctant young women and wives to get on their feet.

Listen!

Brave brothers and sisters,

Get the unwilling mules, horses, cattle, and sheep.

Come and follow me, the old Zhana,

To look for a place filled with love!"

Leaving, dear brothers,

Our ancestors were on their migrating journey once again.

Leaving, the Hani descendants,

Our ancestors left Se'ezuoniang.

The Hani ancestors had strong backbones:

No matter how deep the river is, they were not afraid of crossing it.

The Hani ancestors had pride:

No matter how high the mountain is, they were not afraid of climbing it.

Audience:

Sa—nong—sa!

六、谷哈密查

歌手：

萨——依——！

唱了，

一娘生的兄弟姊妹！

讲了，

一寨的哈尼子孙！

先祖走过的路，

像哀牢山的青藤又苦又弯，

先祖传下的歌，

像艾乐坡的泉水源源不断。

围拢来啊，

今晚要唱那有名的谷哈密查，

这好听的名字啊，

像白鹇洁白的羽毛一片。

（一）

歌手：

萨——依——萨！

离开得威海水，

Chapter 6　Guha Micha

Singer：

Sa—ee—!

Let us sing songs,

Brothers and sisters who came from the same mother!

Let us tell stories,

The Hani descendants who came from the same village!

The roads trod by the ancestors

Were bent and bitter like the vines in the Ailao Mountains.

The songs passed down from the ancestors

Are endless like the spring water from the Mount Ailepo.

Come,

And I am going to sing about the famous Guha Micha to-night.

This sweet name

Is like a plume of the silver pheasant, clean and white.

6. 1

Singer：

Sa—ee—sa!

Leaving the waters in Dewei,

离开佐甸田园，
先祖纷纷起程，
处处马嘶人喊。

大群的先祖走在路上，
好似象群走上平原；
大群的哈尼搬迁，
又像牛群走出大圈。

在那哈尼搬迁的日子，
色厄响起惊炸的大雷；
在那先祖离去的日子，
色厄的大雨遮地盖天。

停停走走，走走停停，
先祖像一窝白鹇觅食，
走走停停，停停走走，
先祖像一群大鱼游转。
顺着山尾朝下走，
走过七十七日牛路，
随着水尾朝下搬，
走过七十七日马站。

大山千座万座，
哈尼吃的山有一座，
大水千条万条，
哈尼吃的水有一条，

Leaving the fields in Zuodian,

The ancestors started on the journey,

With horses neighing and people calling.

Big groups of the ancestors were on the road

Like herds of elephants starting to migrate towards the plain.

Big groups of Hanis were moving,

Also like herds of cattle walking out of their pens.

On the day the Hanis set out,

Thunders clapped in Se'e;

On the day the ancestors left,

Torrential downpour hit Se'e.

Stopping and going, going and stopping,

The ancestors were like groups of silver pheasants seeking

food;

Going and stopping, stopping and going,

The ancestors were like schools of fish swimming around.

Walking down along the back of the mountains,

The ancestors passed seventy-seven cattle roads.

Walking down along the end of the river,

The ancestors passed seventy-seven stagecoach stations.

Though there were tens and thousands of mountains,

One would provide for the Hanis;

Though there were tens and thousands of rivers,

One would provide for the Hanis.

察访的兄弟把消息传来，
新的好地已经不远。

先祖走下一道山梁，
睁大酸涩的双眼，
哈哈的笑声像山洪暴发，
喊喊的赞叹像鸟雀啼啭：
脚下是一片宽平的大坝，
三个缅花戚哩①也望不到边，
满坝土地腊肉样肥，
抓把尝尝蜂蜜样甜，
野桃野梨挤满平地，
树下生着野姜野蒜；
花尾的箐鸡见人不躲，
林边草地挤满白鹇，
青青草地深齐腰杆，
马鹿野羊到处望见。

六条大河哈哈笑着，
走在这片坝子中间，
大河纵横交错流淌，
好像巴掌上的纹线。

---

① 缅花戚哩：一目所及的范围。

The scouts had sent the news

That the new land was not far away.

The ancestors walked down from a mountain ridge

And opened their tired eyes:

Their loud laugh sounded like the explosion of the mountain

flood,

And their admiring whistling sounded like the twitter of the

birds.

Under their feet was a piece of bazi big and wide,

Wider than what three Mianhuaqilies① could see.

The soil in this field was as rich as bacon

As if it were sweet as honey.

The land was filled with wild peach- and pear-trees,

With wild ginger and garlic growing under their feet.

Birds with colorful tails were not afraid of people,

Countless silver pheasants crowding the grassfield by the

woods.

The grass grew waist high,

Horses, deer, and wild sheep everywhere.

Six rivers were laughing

As they run through the bazi.

The big rivers were crossing each other,

Like the lines on the palm.

----

① Mianhuaqili: As far as one's eyes can see.

在那坝子的尽头，
碧绿的大水有一片，
白日望去太阳样亮，
黑夜望去天空样蓝，
三个得威不比它大，
七个得威不比它宽；
七十七斤的青鱼像沙子样多，
八十八斤的黄鱼像芭蕉成串，
长条的公鱼跳水喘气，
好像利箭划破水面，
滚圆的母鱼钻草摆子，
好像月亮浇水洗脸，
数不清的大鱼大虾，
像百花盛开在宽阔的水面。

这块地方扎实好啰，
先祖叫它谷哈密查，
扎实出名的好地谷哈，
永远牢记哈尼心间。

众人：
萨——侬——萨！

At the end of the bazi

Was a patch of wide and jade-like waters.

During the day it looked as bright as the sun,

And at night it was blue like the sky.

Three Deweis would not be as big as it was,

And seven Deweis would not be as wide as it was.

Black carps of seventy-seven jin① were as many as sands,

And yellow fish of eighty-eight jin came in bunches like bananas.

The long male fish jumped breathlessly,

Like arrows piercing the surface of the water.

The fat female fish swam through the lake weeds

Like the moon slashing the water to wash their faces.

Countless fish and shrimp

Were like hundreds of flowers blossoming on the surface of the water.

This land was really good,

And the ancestors named it Guha Micha,

A truly famous place

That will be remembered by the Hanis forever.

Audience:

Sa—ee—sa!

---

① Jin: (Notes from translater) A unit of weight, the equal of 0. 5 kilograms.

歌手：

谷哈坝子住着蒲尼①，

他们是手脚黄黄的人，

不爱撵山打猎，

只爱开荒种田。

蒲尼的阿篇②叫罗扎，

头上的帽子鸡冠样鲜艳，

衣裳裤子宽又长，

脚上鞋子厚又软，

出门上路坐着高轮马车，

一把遮阳像鸡顶在上边。

千万蒲尼见他要磕头，

阿波阿匹也要弯腰，

七层楼房是他的在处，

高房盖在大海旁边。

哈尼来到谷哈密查，

罗扎心里老实盘算，

差人来到哈尼住地，

硬话说过七遍八遍：

---

① 蒲尼：异族，一说是汉族。据考，可能指包括汉、彝等民族
在内的民族先民。

② 阿篇：大头人。

Singer:

In the Guha bazi lived the Puni① people,

With rather tanned feet and hands.

They didn't hunt

But loved cultivating the land and growing the crops.

The Punis' Apian② was called Luoza,

Whose hat was as bright in color as a cockscomb.

His shirts and pants were oversized,

And his shoes were thick and soft.

He went out by a carriage with high wheels

And a sunshade like a cock head on the top.

Tens and thousands of Punis kowtowed to him on seeing him,

And apos and apis bowed as well.

His home had seven stories,

A tall building by the sea.

When the Hanis arrived at Guha Micha,

Luoza thought carefully

And sent someone to where the Hanis stayed

Who said tough words repeatedly:

---

① Puni: An ethnic group. One possibility is they were the Hans. According to research, it may refer to the ancestors of many ethnic groups including the Han and Yi nationalities.

② Apian: The title of the Puni chieftain.

245

"谷哈土地比天还大，
蒲尼人只有鸡窝星一点，
在不完的地方由你们在，
盘不完的田地尽你们盘；
只是手粗脚粗的哈尼，
要当我罗扎的帮手，
谷哈密查的事情，
样样由我阿篇掌管。"

大头人①的妻子扎纳阿玛，
对丈夫说出心里的挂牵：
"亲亲的男人啊，
老人的话留给了后代，
老人的事记在我心间，
哈尼不能当外人的帮工，
自己的羊群要自己来管！"

扎纳阿波摸着白头，
对女人说出自己的意愿：
"女人啊，
老人死去十七日，
事情出了十七样，

---

① 不知出于什么原因，此后诗中再没出现"乌木"的称呼，这
里的大头人扎纳与诺马划界的乌木扎纳是否为一人亦不详。

"Guha's land is bigger than the sky,

And the Puni population is so small that it could fit in a

chicken coop.

You may live where we live not

And cultivate where we have not.

But the clumsy Hanis must assist me, Louza.

Everything in Guha Micha

Must be managed by me, the Apian."

The wife of the chieftain①, Zhana'a Ma

Told her husband her concerns:

"Dear husband,

The words of the elderlies have passed on to the descend-

ants,

And they are in my mind.

The Hanis cannot be the helpers of others:

They must tend their own sheep!"

Stroking his white hair

Apo Zhana told his wife his thoughts:

"Woman,

After an old man has died for 17 days,

Things have changed in 17 ways;

---

① For some reason, the title of "Wumu" disappears in the epic from
this part on. It is also unclear whether the Chieftain Zhana here is the Wumu
Zhana who marked the Nuoma.

247

老人变出十七色，①
规矩天天都改变。

"哈尼是匹骏马，
也跑得汗淌气喘，
哈尼是只老象，
也走得脚疼腰酸，
你瞧最壮的汉子，
蹲下去膝盖抵住双肩；②
再走不得了，
再累不得了，
哈尼要和蒲尼同在，
哈尼要给罗扎来管，
不是我不想守住自己的羊群，
是羊群放进别家的田园。"

听说哈尼愿在，
罗扎有七层喜欢，
坐着高轮的马车跑来，
对哈尼说话又甜又软：

---

①　指老人死后皮肤改变颜色。
②　形容过度劳累已无法支持，只好采用这种姿势以免睡倒。

The old man has changed in 17 shades of color,①

And rules have changed ever since.

"The Hanis are a fine steed,

But still they are sweating and breathless from running.

The Hanis are an old elephant,

But still they are sore from walking.

Look at even the strongest men

Who are squatting now with their knees supporting their

shoulders.②

We cannot walk any more,

Cannot be more tired.

The Hanis will coexist with the Punis

And let their affairs be run by Luoza.

It is not that I am unwilling to tend my sheep

But that my sheep are in others' field."

On hearing that the Hanis were willing,

Luoza was very happy.

Riding his carriage with high wheels,

He came to speak to the Hani sweetly and softly:

---

①　It refers to the change in the color of an old person's skin after death.

②　This describes being overtired and having to take this position to avoid falling asleep.

来吧来吧,

哈尼人!

大大的水塘在得下多多的鱼,

宽宽的坝子歇得下多多的哈尼,

爱攀山就把大山分给你们,

爱种田就把坝子划出半边;

你们快快丢下大刀,

快把长矛卸下双肩,

亲亲热热地在不用大刀帮忙,

喜喜欢欢地在长矛只会戳眼。"

扎纳阿波挥挥手,

哈尼把大刀长矛丢在脚前,

但是先辈的往事怎能忘记,

哈尼连夜把武器掩埋。

从此世代哈尼,

都把这里叫谷哈密查①,

不管走到多远,

都把这名字带到多远。

---

① 谷哈密查:埋藏武器的地方。"谷",三尖叉,泛指武器;
"哈",此处意为埋藏;"密查",地方。谷哈密查指今昆明,今天哈尼
族仍称昆明为谷哈。具体解释有二,一为哈尼族一到昆明就埋下兵器,
以示友好;一为哈尼族战败后埋下兵器,认为兵器会带来灾难。(来
自原诗)

"Come,

The Hanis!

The large pools can hold many fish,

And the wide bazi can hold many Hanis.

You like to hunt, so the mountains can be yours;

You like to cultivate the land, and the half of the bazi will

be yours;

Quickly put down your broadswords

And the spears on your shoulders.

Friendliness needs no broadsword,

And in happiness spears may only poke the eyes."

Apo Zhana waved his hand,

The Hanis put down their broadswords and spears in front of

their feet.

But they could never forget the ancestors' past,

So they buried the weapons that night.

From then on, all Hanis

Called it Guha Micha.①

However faraway they have moved,

They have brought that name with them!

---

① Guha Micha: The place where the weapons were buried. "Gu", trident, refers to weapons in general; "Ha" refers to bury; "Micha", place. Guha Micha refers to Kunming. The Hanis today still call Kunming "Guha". There are two explanations: one is that the Hanis buried their weapons as soon as they arrived in Kunming to show their friendship; the other is that the Hanis buried the weapon after their defeat, as they thought the weapon would bring disaster. (Here we choose the version in the original epic.)

按照惹罗的古规，
哈尼举行安寨大典，
先祖把走来的大山，
选作万能的神山，
从驮子里拿出基石，
稳稳地放在神山上面，
这吉祥幸福的基石，
陪伴了哈尼千年。

哈尼的寨址也选好，
紧靠在大山旁边，
那鸟窝样的凹塘，
永远给哈尼温暖。

寨头也安下了神台，
先祖来这里祭神，
寨脚安下了高秋，
远处就能望见。

安寨的贝壳立过了，
划界的狗也拖过了，
豹子不会来拖猪抬羊，
魔鬼也不敢进寨游转。

大寨立起了三天，
寨头有雀鸟来唱，
大寨立起了三夜，
寨脚有马鹿来唤。

According to the ancient rules of Reluo,

The Hanis held the ceremony for the settlement.

The ancestors treated the mountains they arrived at

As almighty sacred mountain.

They unloaded the foundation rock that they carried all the way

And put it firmly on top of the sacred mountain.

This auspicious stone

Had accompanied the Hani people for thousands of years.

The site of the Hani village had been chosen:

By a big mountain,

The aotang, like a roost,

Would always bring warmth to the Hanis.

An altar was installed at the head of the village,

Where the ancestors went and worshiped.

A high sacrifice house was installed at the foot of the village,

Which can be seen from afar.

The divination shell was set up,

And the dog was dragged along to mark the borders.

Leopards would not come to steal the pigs and sheep,

And the ghost would not dare to haunt the village.

On the third day after the village was built,

Birds came to sing at the head of the village;

On the third day the village was built,

Red deer came to bleat at the foot of the village.

去世的先祖留下古规，
新地要找新的水源，
找水要最好看的扎密，
她才能跨进水娘的门槛。

扎密打出第一眼水井，
这就是谷哈出名的窝尼井①，
井水像扎密的眼睛黑亮，
井水像扎密的心意甘甜；
女人吃着这口井水，
笑声像水花串串，
男人吃着这口井水，
哈哈的笑声像水源不断，
阿波吃着这口井水，
脸上放出异样光彩，
扎谷吃着这口井水，
身子比牦牛还要健壮。

这些事情虽然古老，
弯腰的阿波还能记全，
哈尼扎密的水井，
如今还是谷哈最甜的清泉。

众人：
萨——依——萨！

---

① 窝尼井：据说昆明有著名的"窝尼井"，今已难寻。

The ancestors had left ancient rules：

In a new land, new source of water should be sought.

Looking for it required the prettiest zami,

The only one who could enter the gate of the Ms. Water.

The zami dug the first well,

Which is the Woni Well① that Guha is famous for.

The well water was shiny and black like the eyes of the zami,

Sweet like the heart of the zami;

Women who drank from the well

Laughed with sound like the spray of water,

And men who drank from the well

Laughed like the water running endlessly.

When the apos drank from the well,

Their faces glowed.

When the zagus drank from the well,

They were stronger than the bull.

Even though these happened in ancient times,

The humpbacked apos could still remember them all.

The well dug by the Hani zami

Is still the sweetest spring water in Guha.

Audience：

Sa—ee—sa！

---

①　The Woni Well：It is said that there was a famous "Woni Well" in Kunming, but it cannot be found today.

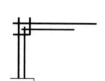

歌手：

神山淌下一股大水，
像围腰把寨子围在中间，
清清的大水喂饮着牛马，
亮亮的大水鹅鸭成片。

大水给先祖带来欢喜，
大水给先祖带来吃穿；
寨脚开出块块大田，
一年的红米够吃三年，
山边栽起大片棉地，
一年的白棉够穿三年。

谷哈成了哈尼的家乡，
哈尼在这里增到七万，①
先辈的规矩一样不少，
哈尼又把新事增添：
谷哈有大大的红石，
蒲尼背来炼铁，
哈尼学会烧石化水，
也学会造犁铸剑。②

哈尼寨子天天长大，

---

① 说当时昆明总人口为四万，哈尼占其小半。（来自原诗）
② 据哈尼创世史诗载，炼铁打制铁器是哈尼族先民自己的发明。

Singer:

The sacred mountain let out a big stream of water

That was circled around the village like an apron.

Plenty of clear water fed the cattle and horses,

And on the shiny water were gaggles of geese and ducks.

Ths water brought the ancestors happiness

And brought them food and clothing.

At the foot of the village were pieces of cultivated land

That produced the red rice in one year enough for three.

Along the mountains were planted large cotton fileds

That produced the white cotton in one year enough for three.

Guha became the homeland of the Hanis,

And the population increased to seventy thousand.①

None of the ancestors' ways was forgotten,

But the Hanis also added some new ones:

Guha had big red rocks,

And the Punis used them to smelt iron.

The Hanis learned to melt the stones

And also to make ploughs and swords.②

The Hani village expanded day by day,

---

① It is said that the total population of Kunming at that time was 40,000, with the Hani accounting for almost half of it. (Here we choose the version in the original epic.)

② According to the Hani genesis epics, smelting or forging iron was the invention of the Hani ancestors.

谷哈坝子占去一半，
大寨生出窝窝小寨，
好像小鸡围着阿妈游玩，
哈尼后代天天变多，
好像细沙难得数完，
不管走到哪山田坝，
"伙哑麻哑"① 处处听见。

（二）

萨——依——萨！
哈尼手杆再粗，
也是罗扎的帮手，
哈尼脚杆再硬，
也是罗扎的跑腿；
罗扎有碗大的贪心，
把哈尼的红米撮完，
罗扎有盆大的狠心，
把哈尼牵空了畜圈。

老实不佩服啊，
哈尼睁大眼睛，
几百人一队，
几十人一群，
天天找着头人阿波，
人人诉说新的屈冤。

---

① 伙哑麻哑：哈尼族的习惯性问候，意为"吃饭没有"。

Taking up half of the Guha bazi.

The big village gave rise to smaller ones,

Which were like chicks playing around the hen.

The Hani descendants became more and more day by day,

Like the countless sands.

No mater where in the field and bazi,

The sound of "Huoza maza"① could be heard.

6. 2

Sa—ee—sa!

No matter how strong the Hani arms were,

They were to help Luoza;

No matter how strong the Hani legs were,

They were to run for Luoza.

Luoza was so greedy

That he took all the red rice from the Hanis,

And Luoza was so cruel

That he emptied the livestock pens of the Hanis.

Unwilling,

The Hanis opened their eyes.

Lined up by the hundreds,

Bonded together by the tens,

They went to the Chieftain Apo every day

To complain about the new grievances.

---

① Huoza maza: A Hani greeting, meaning "Have you eaten yet?".

哈尼又换过三代头人，
这一代是有名的纳索，
他是扎纳阿波①的独儿，
是哈尼人里的好汉。

纳索落地就会说话，
七十个贝玛来教他贝②，
纳索生来力大无穷，
七十个工匠教他锻炼③；
他嚼过一箩的虎心，
他咽过一背的豹胆，
没有翅膀也会飞，
没有尖头也会钻。

纳索头人一天天长大，
身子像攀枝花树伸展，
宽宽的肩膀比岩石硬，
千斤力气藏在粗粗的腰杆，
圆圆的眼睛有数不完的主意，
直直的鼻子表示他的忠心赤胆。

纳索结了一门亲事，
讨回的姑娘不同一般，
她在哈尼人中排名第一，

---

① 此处所说扎纳是否是前面提到的大头人亦不甚明确。
② 贝：贝玛念咒称"贝"（或"背"）。
③ 锻炼：指打铁炼铁。

After the Hani chieftain had changed three times,

It came the famous Nasuo and his generation.

He was the only son of Apo Zhana①

And a Hani hero.

Nasuo was able to talk as soon as he was born,

And seventy beimas taught him to "bei"②;

He was born with superb strength,

And seventy blacksmithes trained him.③

He chewed a basket of tiger hearts

And swallowed another basket of leopard gallbladders.

He could fly without wings,

And dig without drills.

The chieftain Nasuo grew up day by day,

His body growing like the kapok stretching.

His wide shoulders were tougher than the rock,

And most of his strength lay in his thick waist.

His round eyes had countless ideas

And his straight nose showed his loyalty and courage.

When Nasuo got married,

His bride was unique.

Number one among the Hanis,

---

① It is unclear whether Zhana here is the chieftain mentioned above.

② Bei: The beima's incantation was called "bei".

③ It refers to training him to smelt and forge iron.

戚妮的名声永世流传。

戚妮阿爸是厄戚①头人，
他的大寨安在水边，
厄戚是哈尼第二大寨，
排在纳索的大寨后面。

戚妮扎密生在十五，
那晚月亮又白又圆，
戚妮的白脸就像满月，
她是月神来到人间。

戚妮长大越发好瞧，
一棵金竹栽在门前，
细长的脖颈像嫩白的竹节，
灵巧的双手像蝴蝶翩翩，
滑滑的辫子像黑蛇盘绕，
颤颤的腰肢像棉花样软。

戚妮在阿爸身边长大，
学会的本事老实不凡，
一把嘎得②神出鬼没，
撵山的阿波也不抵她一半。

---

① 厄戚：意为戚支系的、在水边的。
② 嘎得：弩箭。

She was Qisi, a name to be passed on from generation to generation.

Qisi's father was the headman of Eqi①,
A village by the water.
Eqi was the second largest Hani village,
Right after the village where Nasuo lived.

Qisi was born on the 15th of a month,
When the moon was white and round.
Qisi's white face was like the full moon,
A goddess of the moon descending onto the earth.

Qisi grew to be even more beautiful looking,
Like a golden bamboo planted in front of the house.
Her elegant neck was like a part of the fresh bamboo,
And her adroit hands worked like flying butterflies.
Her black braids were wound up like black snakes,
And her swaying waist was soft like cotton.

Qisi grew up by her father's side,
So she learned extraordinary skills.
She was so good at using the "gade"②
That even an hunting apo was not half as good as she was.

---

① Eqi: It means the Hani branch Qi, who lived by the water.
② Gade: Crossbow.

六月里的黑夜，
天像煮布的蓝靛，
晒台上有说有笑，
戚奴和阿爸谈地讲天。

阿爸说她年纪还小，
刚刚学会开弓搭箭；
戚奴抿嘴笑笑，
像朵才开的白莲，
"嘘"地吹响鸟哨，
一只血娜飞来，
等到血娜飞远，
戚奴射出竹箭，
只听一声尖叫，
血娜被射穿嗓管；
从此在她面前，
人人难夸弓箭。

戚奴的聪明蜜蜂难比，
她的善良马鹿一般，
都匹玛雅①没有她鲜艳，
她是百鸟里的白鹇。
戚奴嫁给纳索，
像月亮和太阳一般，
帮助丈夫管理大事，
纳索对她佩服又喜欢。

---

① 都匹玛雅：山茶，详见后诗。

One night in the sixth month,

The sky was as dark-blue as the dye.

On the balcony were laughters

As Qisi and her father were chatting happily.

Papa said she was still young,

A beginner at using the crossbow.

Qisi smiled,

Her face like a newly bloomed white lotus.

She whistled a bird wistle,

And a xuena-finch flew towards them.

She waited till it flew away

And then shot an arrow at it.

A squeal was heard,

And the bird had the arrow through its neck.

From then on and in front of her,

Hardly anyone could brag about their skill at bow and arrow.

Qisi was smarter than the bee

And kinder than the red deer.

Dupimaya① was not as beautiful as she was.

She was like the silver pheasant among hundreds of birds.

When Qisi was married to Nasuo,

They were like the moon and the sun.

She helped her husband with important affairs,

And Nasuo admired as well as loved her.

---

① Dupimaya: Camellia. For details, see below.

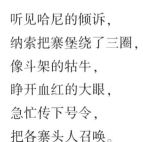

听见哈尼的倾诉，
纳索把寨堡绕了三圈，
像斗架的牯牛，
睁开血红的大眼，
急忙传下号令，
把各寨头人召唤。

打着灯笼火把，
头人个个来齐，
寨堡再宽再大，
人也坐到门槛；
点亮粗壮的松明，
吃起辣辣的黄烟，
天黑说到鸡叫，
话还没有说完。

话有几样说法，
像牛角有平有弯，
有人要和罗扎打架，
有人说还不到时间。

戚姒说出主张，
排解男人的疑难：
"水大才能养出大鱼，
坝宽才能开出大田，
会打的只打一架，
不会的天天纠缠；

On learning about the Hani people's hardship,
Nasuo walked around the village three times.
Like an angry bull,
He saw red.
Quickly, he sent an order
To gather all the village headmen.

With lanterns and torches,
All headmen came one by one.
The village castle was big,
But still some were sitting on the sills of the doorways.
Lighting up the pine-oil lamp
And the spicy pipes,
They talked from the evening to the dawn
But still did not finish about what they had to say.

There were different views,
Like some cows horns were straightforward and others were
not.
Some wanted to confront Luoza,
While others wanted to wait for a better time.

Qisi offered an idea
To resolve the dilemma facing the headmen:
"Only enough water can raise the big fish,
And only wide bazi allows large paddy fileds.
Those skilled at fighting battle only once,
While the unskilled get entangled in a never-ending problem.

老辈说做罗扎的帮手，
是为哈尼的子孙后代，
不要看小娃换上新衣①，
他是嫩竹身子还软，
谷哈人像树叶样多，
蒲尼人占了大半，
耐耐性子忍忍气，
哈尼才会得平安。"
戚姒说话扎实合理，
纳索把事情做了决断。

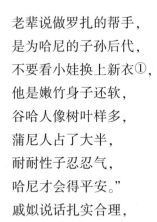

（三）

萨——依——萨！
罗扎生着七双耳朵，
天天打听哈尼的事情，
听说头人商量，
忙把主意想全。

平背的大猪杀倒，
圆腿的大羊绑翻，
最花的大鱼煎好，
最甜的米酒倒满，
请纳索头人来做客，
说话老实叫人喜欢：

---

① 为小孩换上新衣是他长大成人的标志。

The older generation agreed to be Luoza's helpers

Because they wanted to protect the descendants.

Don't only look at the children wearing new clothes①,

But they are still tender like the bamboo shoots.

People in Guha are as many as the leaves,

And more than half are the Punis.

Patience and endurance

Will bring peace to the Hanis."

Qisi's words were strong and reasonable,

And Nasuo made a decision.

6.3

Sa—ee—sa!

Luoza had many ears

Listening for the Hani affairs everyday.

On learning about the meeting of the headmen

He immediately started working on a plan.

He killed the fat pigs,

Bounded up fat sheep,

Fried the best big fish,

Poured out the sweetest rice wine.

He invited the chief Nasuo to have dinner

And spoke most pleasantly:

---

① Putting new clothes on a child symoblized that the child had grown up.

"哈尼的大头人啊，
高能的纳索好汉，
自从你来领头，
哈尼事事兴盛。

"瞧那伶俐的小娃，
成双成对地出来，
瞧那欢跳的牛马，
成伙成群在山间；
大田里的谷子，
鸡蛋一样肥大，
园子里的蒜头，
像添饭的小碗；
吃不尽的牛干巴，
把蘑菇房梁压断，
喝不完的糯米酒，
像打不干的清泉。
纳索啊，
我是一匹老马，
白头垂在胸前，
想和英雄攀亲戚，
把独囡嫁到你身边。"

纳索赶紧推脱，
说出心里的不愿：
"不真的话不是哈尼话，
哈尼说话句句实在，
你的好意我不敢领，

"The chieftain of the Hani people,

The able Nasuo,

Since you became the leader,

The life of the Hanis has prospered.

"Look at the lovely children

Who came out in pairs.

Look at the lively cattles and horses

That are in the mountains by herds.

The crops in the field

Have ears as thick as the eggs.

The garlic heads in the garden

Are as big as the small rice bowls.

The beef jerky more than you can eat

Could break the beams of the mushroom houses.

And the rice wine more than you can drink

Is like the spring water that never stops coming.

Nasuo,

I'm an old horse

With its head hanging in front its chest.

I would like to make friend with a hero

By letting my only daughter marry you and live by your side."

Nasuo refused right away,

Explaining his unwillingness:

"The untrue words are never uttered by the Hanis,

Whose every word is honest.

I could not possibly accept your kindness,

271

纳索的蘑菇房早有聪葵扎密①掌管！"
话还没有说完，
有人拉开门帘，
罗扎的姑娘走进来，
一朵白茶花开放在眼前。

罗扎的姑娘马妠，
美名到处流传。
一双手像嫩嫩的藕节，
圆圆的脸像绽开的红莲，
薄薄的嘴唇能说会唱，
斜斜的眼睛会悲会欢，
头上金钗太阳般亮，
两边耳环月亮般弯，
两只小小的绣花鞋上，
百花开出一片春天。

马妠扎密张开小嘴，
说话就像画眉婉转：
"宽眉大眼的纳索啊，
不要背对人家的笑脸；
瞧你宽厚的肩膀，
好像坚强的石岩，
瞧你明亮的眼睛，
发出神光一片；

---

① 聪葵扎密：贤惠的姑娘。

For the Nasuo's household has long been run by the congkui zami①!"

Before he finished,

Someone opened the door curtain.

Luoza's daughter came in,

Like a white camellia blossomed in front of his eyes.

Luoza's daughter Masi

Was famous for her beauty.

Her hands were as tender as the lotus,

And her face was like a red lotus flower.

The thin lips were good at speaking and singing,

And her willow-leaf eyes could be sad or happy.

The gold hairpin in her hair was sparking like the sun,

And the earrings on each side were like the crescent moon.

On the pair of her colorful embroidered shoes

Were hundreds of spring flowers.

Masi opend her small mouth,

Her voice as beautiful as the sound of a thrush.

"Handsome Nasuo,

Don't turn your back on my smiles;

Look at your broad shoulders

As hard as the rock.

Look at your bright eyes,

Shiny with sacred light.

---

① Congkui zami: Virtuous woman.

和你一处吃饭，
干饭也比肉香，
和你一处喝水，
清水也比蜜甜；
听你说话暖人心房，
同你共处我老实心宽，
家中有女人也不要怕，
叫她阿姐我也心甘！"

好听的话像好喝的酒，
纳索被说得心软；
罗扎又说另一番心意，
纳索就把头来点。
"纳索啊，
不是亲戚不在一处，
豹子黄牛难共一圈，
不做姑爷就做仇敌，
快领着哈尼朝别处搬迁！"

纳索回到寨堡，
把话说给戚姒，
戚姒仔细思量，
细细把丈夫来劝：

"头人商量的夜晚，
寨里的狗咬不断，
守寨的兄弟来讲，

Dining in the same house with you,

I will feel the dry rice taste more delicious than the meat.

Drinking in the same house with you,

I will feel the water taste sweeter than the honey.

Listening to you I feel warm at heart;

Living with you I will feel very safe.

I don't mind you already have a wife

And I am willing to call her my elder sister!"

The sweet words were like the tasty wine,

And Nasuo changed his mind.

After Luoza said more,

Nasuo agreed.

"Nasuo,

If we are not relatives, we don't live together,

Just as cattle and leopards don't live in the same den.

Unless you are my son-in-law, we are enemies.

If so, quickly lead your Hani people and move to another

place!"

Nasuo returned to the village castle

And told everything to Qisi.

Qisi thought carefully

And said to her husband patiently:

"The night the headmen met,

The dogs in the village kept barking.

According to the village guards,

罗扎来过三转，
哈尼说话被人偷听，
旧事未了新事又添。

"罗扎请客不是结交朋友，
硬嫁姑娘也另有打算；
纳索啊，
他的肠子像弯弯的老藤，
望得见一截看不见一半，
他的心眼像密密的蜂窝，
数得清一边数不清一边。

"纳索啊，亲亲的男人，
哈尼和外人打交道，
吃亏的是哈尼人，
记得诺马的老事，
哈尼把乌木恨了百年；
那时腊伯讨走哈尼的扎密，
也把哈尼的诺马讨进家门，
今天蒲尼嫁出姑娘，
也怕生着一样的心眼。

"听你的女人说句话吧，
不要再做憨憨的人，
竹筒不能当枕头，
蒲尼不能交朋友；
你要一日欢乐，
早上不能喝酒，

Luoza came three times.

He eavesdropped on the meeting,

So new trouble has arrived before the old was resolved.

"The purpose of Luoza's invitation was not to befriend you,

And forcing you to marry his daughter was a ploy.

Nasuo,

Luoza is tricky like an old vine,

Half of which can be seen but not the other half;

He is like a beehive,

Half of which could be counted clearly but not the other half.

"Nasuo, my dearest husband,

When the Hanis dealt with others,

The Hanis have lost.

Remember the story of Nuoma,

For which the Hanis resented the wumu for a hundred years.

Back then the Labo man married the Hani zami

Together with the Hanis' Nuoma.

Today when the Puni tries to marry off the daughter,

I'm afraid it is the same ploy.

"Do listen to your woman

And not to be foolish again.

Bamboo tubes cannot be pillows,

And the Punis cannot be our friends.

If you want a happy day,

Do not drink in the morning.

你想一家欢乐，
不能讨两个老婆，
你想一辈子欢乐，
不能讨那扎密做女人。
纳索啊，
我的话句句实在，
愿你装进耳朵里面!"

——听啰，
亲亲的兄弟姐妹，
自从先祖戚姒说出了话，
它就牢牢记在哈尼心间，
哈尼走遍天涯海角，
都会说出这句格言!①

众人:
萨——哝——萨!

歌手:
好话金子般宝贵，
纳索却没有听见，
哈哈的欢笑飞出寨堡，
惊起了树头的鹊燕:

---

① 由于哈尼族有过长期遭受外族欺凌的历史，所以形成了以上流传甚广的格言。当然，中华人民共和国成立后由于民族地位、关系的根本不同，这一情况已不复存在。

If you want a happy family,

Do not have two wives.

If you want a happy life,

Do not marry that zami as your wife.

Nasuo,

Every one of my words is honest,

And I hope you hear them!"

—Listen,

Dearest brothers and sisters.

Ever since the ancestor Qisi said these words,

They have been remembered by the Hanis.

The Hanis everywhere

Know this motto! ①

Audience:

Sa—nong—sa!

Singer:

Good words as precious as gold

Were not heard by Nasuo.

The village was filled with laughters,

Which startled the birds on the tree tips.

---

① Due to the fact that the Hani people have a long history of being bullied by other ethnic groups, there are popular sayings like this. Of course, after the founding of the People's Republic of China, the status of and relations among ethic groups have changed fundamentally, so this situation no longer exists.

"好看的扎密，
心爱的妻子，
你像河边的龙子雀，
听见水响也飞上天。
罗扎心黑对我设圈套，
怎肯把独囡嫁给我？
罗扎如把扣子下，
怎说要把谷哈给我掌管？"

"高能的纳索，
亲亲的阿哥，
一棵粗粗的树，
不能一夜长成，
一天长成的大树，
会被大风吹断；
一个聪明的人，
不能爬得太高，
爬上高处的人，
会把腰杆跌断！

"哈尼在谷哈七代①，
人还没占一半，
谷哈坝子的四角，
哈尼只有两边，

---

① 一说三代，一说十多代。

"Beautiful zami,

My dear wife,

You are like the dragon-finch by the river,

Flying to the sky even on hearing the sound of the river.

If Luoza tries to trap me,

Why marry his only daughter to me?

If Luoza wants to trap me,

Why let me be in charge of Guha?"

"Able Nasuo,

My dear,

A big strong tree

Could not have grown up in one night.

If one could grow up in one day,

It would be broken by the wind.

A smart man

Would not climb too high.

The one who climbes too high

Could fall and break the back!

"The Hanis have lived in Guha for seven generations①

But are still less than half of its population.

Within the four corners of the Guha bazi,

Only two sides belong to the Hanis.

---

① There are other sayings about the generations the Hanis had lived in Guha for, one is three generations, and another, more than ten generations.

蒲尼怎肯让出好地，
听凭你去主管！
纳索啊，
没有老象的身子，
就不要去占老象的地盘，
领着哈尼好好地过吧，
不要听罗扎的花言巧语！”

痴心的纳索听不进劝说，
美丽的马姒迷住他的心眼；
穿起新染的衣裳，
把马姒迎进家门。

祝贺的哈尼来了，
只是人来心不来，
望见纳索红红的脸，
阿波说：“瞧瞧，
圆圆的太阳花，
开遍他的脸！”
望见纳索滑亮的衣裳，
阿匹说：“看看，
亮亮的水明星，
哪有他鲜艳！”

从此哈尼人，
不对纳索把腰弯，
从此哈尼人，
只对戚姒把头点。

The Puni won't let their good land
Be managed by you!
Nasuo,
Without the body of an old elephant,
One should not claim the territory of an old elephant.
Lead the Hanis to live a quite and good life
And do not fall for Luoza's clever words!"

The infatuated Nasuo could not take in her advice.
Blinded by the beautiful Masi,
He put on the newly dyed clothes
And married Masi into his household.

The Hanis came to send congratulations,
But not sincerely.
Seeing Nasuo's red face,
An apo said: "Look,
A round sunflower
Is all over his face!"
Seeing Nasuo's beautiful new clothes,
An api said: "Look,
A mercury star
Would not be as bright!"

Ever since then, the Hanis
Would not bow to Nasuo;
Ever since then, the Hanis
Only nodded at Qisi.

（四）

萨——依——萨！
日子像谷哈的大水，
转眼淌到二月间，
九山九寨的哈尼，
染新衣用去成背的蓝靛；
扎密穿戴得像漫坡的鲜花，
伙子打扮得攀枝花树样矫健，
那最怕羞的女人，
也妆扮得比彩霞鲜艳；
各家各户来啰，
人人都来祭树，
在这热闹的日子，
哈尼祭祀祖先。①

最热最闹的地方，
要数纳索的大寨，
香香的菜大碗抬来，
甜甜的酒大壶提来，
竹兜里装满金黄的糯米饭②，
老老小小坐在神树旁。

---

① 每年二月属龙日，是哈尼族最盛大的祭祀日，又叫"艾玛突的日子"。
② 哈尼族用一种乔木泡出黄汁浸染糯米，再蒸成黄饭，以示吉利。

6. 4

Sa—ee—sa!

The time passed like the water in Guha,

And it was already the second month.

The Hanis of the nine villages and hills

Used much indigo to dye clothes.

The zamis looked like the colorful flowers all over the hills,

And the young men looked as active as the kapok trees.

The most shy women

Also dressed up, more colorful than the pink clouds.

Every family came

And everyone offered sacrifice to the tree.

On this festive day,

The Hanis worshipped their ancestors.①

The most festival place

Was the head village where Nasuo lived.

The Hanis used large bowls to hold delicious dishes,

And large pots to hold the sweet wine.

In the bamboo containers were the golden glutinous rice②,

And people old and young sat around the sacred tree.

---

①　The Dragon Day in the second month every year is the biggest sacrificial day for the Hanis, also known as "Aimatu Day".

②　The Hani people soak the arbor and use its juice to dye the glutinous rice yellow. They then steam the yellow rice, which is considered auspicious.

肥肥的胖猪献上，
三筒的清水打来，
全寨男人庄严地站好，
听那高能的咪谷诵念：

"万能的寨神啊，
哈尼站在你的面前，
高大的神树啊，
哈尼来把你祭献。
虔诚的寨人献上一片诚意，
请你赐给哈尼一片喜欢，
猪鸡牛羊满圈满岭，
金谷玉麦站满大田，
哈尼儿孙像树叶一样稠密，
哈尼人人像大树一样雄健！"

祭祀已经结束，
哈尼摆开酒饭，
精致的篾桌排好，
像一群高飞的大雁。

咪谷阿波又唱起哈八，
哈尼端起亮亮的酒碗：
"萨——依——萨——
好喝的酒有了，
好听的歌有了，
神佑的哈尼寨人，
像喜鹊一样喜欢。

The fat pigs were offered as sacrifices,
And three tubes of water were fetched.
All the males stood solemnly,
Listening to the respected Migu's recitation:

"The almighty god of the village,
The Hanis are standing in front of you.
The tall sacred tree,
The Hani people are offering sacrifices to you.
The pious villagers offer you their sincerity,
Pleading to you to bless the Hanis with happiness,
With pens full of pigs, chickens, cattle, and sheep,
With fields filled with corns and wheat standing tall,
With the Hani descendants as many as leaves,
And with the Hanis as healthy as the big trees."

When the ceremony was concluded,
The Hanis had a feast.
The exquisite bamboo-strip tables were lined up
Like the flying wild geese.

The apo Migu sang Haba the drinking song,
And the Hanis raised their shiny wine bowls:
"Sa—ee—sa—
With the good wine
And the beautiful songs,
The Hani villagers, blessed by the gods,
Are as happy as the magpies.

"快拿尖嘴的花雀,
来做喝酒的天神,
雀嘴插上黄饭,
雀脚伸进竹筒,
献过的雀头放进碗,
它把喝酒的令来传,
雀嘴对着哪一个,
哪个就把碗喝干!"

好听的哈八不歇口,
唱过天地又唱祖先,
咪谷的喉咙干了又润,
祝福的话把寨人耳朵装满,
欢乐的哈尼放声唱:
"萨——依——萨——"
歌声飞上白云间。

山下突然传来马嘶人喊,
一阵马蹄响到面前,
是谁不守哈尼的规矩,
竟把寨神的威严冒犯?

大马上跳下一个人,
他就是蒲尼罗扎阿篇,
手里的大刀才磨快,
雪白的锋口亮得戳眼。

"Take the colorful bird with the sharp beak

As the drinking god of heaven,

With its beak in the rice,

And its claws in the bamboo tube.

Put its head in a bowl,

And then it can give orders.

Whoever the bird's peak is facing

Must empty his bowl of wine!"

Nice Haba the drinking song went on,

Toasting to the heaven and then to the ancestors.

Migu's throat was dried and then moistened.

The blessings were filling the Hanis' ears,

And the happy Hanis were singing to their hearts' content:

"Sa—ee—sa—"

The songs flew up into the clouds.

All of a sudden neighing and shouting came up to the moun-

tain,

And the sound of horses' hoofs came right in front of them.

Who dared to violate the Hani rules

And defy the majesty of the sacred village god?

A man jumped off the horseback,

The Puni Luoza Apian.

The sword in his hand was just sharpened,

Its snow-white blade dazzling the eyes.

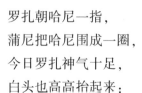
罗扎朝哈尼一指，
蒲尼把哈尼围成一圈，
今日罗扎神气十足，
白头也高高抬起来：

"听着，有名的纳索！
听着，我的姑爷！
你们从远处搬来谷哈，
是一窝麂子被狗追撵，
好心的蒲尼把你们收留，
分给你们好地好田，
是我威严的谷哈阿篇，
使得你们好吃好在
是我高能的罗扎阿波，
保护你们子孙增添，
我还把天神一样的姑娘，
嫁给你哈尼大头人！

"哈尼啊，你们听好，
好心要有好报，
不能忘记蒲尼的恩典，
牛羊想啃青草，
就要顺着大山，
哈尼想在谷哈，
就要顺着阿篇！

Waving his hand at the Hanis,

The Punis surrounded the Hani villagers.

Today Luoza was full of pride

And held high his head of white hair:

"Listen, famous Nasuo.

Listen, my son-in-law!

You moved to Guha from afar,

Like a litter of muntjacs chased by dogs.

The kind Punis took you in

And gave you good land.

It is I the dignified apian of Guha

Who made it possible for you to eat and live well.

It was I the capable apo Luoza

Whose protection made it possible for you to have more chil-

dren.

I also marry my goddess-like daughter

To you the Hani chieftain!

"The Hanis, listen carefully.

I expect good return for my kindness,

So don't you forget our Punis' kindness.

The cattle and sheep that want to graze the grass

Must follow the mountain.

The Hani people who want to live in Guha

Must obey the apian!

"你们要当我的帮手，
要把猪鸡牛羊进献，
要拿来软和的厚布，
要拿出白细的吃盐，
撵山要献头和腿，
拿鱼要交最肥的一串；
不准再来这山上祭祀，
钻云的神树要砍翻，
谷哈密查样样属我，
我要来把大庙兴建!"

千百个哈尼不出气，
就像石头一样沉默，
千百个哈尼火了，
都望着自己的头人。

"尊敬的阿篇罗扎，
纳索亲亲的丈人，
蒲尼的好心哈尼不忘，
我们才当了帮手百年。

"帮你砍出大块火地，
帮你开出大片良田，
帮你插秧种谷，
帮你栽树植棉，
帮你盖出厚砖大瓦的楼房，
帮你打出金丝亮晃的首饰，

"You have to be my assistants,

Bringing me pigs, chickens, cattle and sheep.

You must bring me rich and soft cloth,

And white fine salt.

From what you hunt, you must bring me the heads and legs;

And from what you fish, you must bring me the biggest.

You are not allowed to make sacrifices in this mountain any-more,

And your skyscraping sacred trees must be chopped down.

Everything in Guha Micha belongs to me,

And I will build a big temple!"

Thousands of the Hanis kept silent,

As quiet as the stones;

Thousands of the Hanis were mad,

Staring at their chieftain.

"Respected Apian Luoza,

Dearest father-in-law of Nasuo,

The Hanis didn't forget the kindness of the Punis,

Which allowed us to assist you for a hundred years.

"We helped you burn and level large pieces of land

And cultivate large crop fields.

We helped you transplant rice seedlings

And plant cotton.

We helped you build brick houses

And make shiny jewels.

你吃得甜甜油油地吃，
穿得厚厚暖暖地穿，
在得安安逸逸地在，
玩得喜喜欢欢地玩！
——这些都不说了，
还来要我们的神山！
哈尼是棵大树，
神山是它的根；
你要厚布哈尼给你织布，
你要吃盐哈尼给你熬盐，
你要神山哈尼绝不给，
任你把七层嘴皮说穿！"

听见纳索说话，
罗扎老牛一样气喘，
白亮的大刀举起，
要把纳索砍翻。

山脚响起吼声，
"哝嗬！哝嗬！"像撵山，
吼声震撼老林，
罗扎吓出冷汗。
三千个哈尼上来，
把罗扎围在中央，
领头的人是戚姒扎密，
锋利的弩箭对准罗扎的心肝。

You eat tasty food,

Wear warm clothes,

Enjoy life leisurely,

And play happily.

—We never complained about any of this,

But now you want to take away our sacred mountain!

The Hanis are like big trees,

With the sacred mountain as their root;

You can take the thick cloth weaved by the Hanis,

The fine salt made by the Hanis,

But you cannot take the sacred mountain,

Not matter how long you will talk about it!"

Hearing the words of Nasuo,

Luoza became out of breath like an old bull.

Raising the white and shiny sword,

He tried to kill Nasuo.

A roar sounded from the foot of the mountain,

"Nonghe! Nonghe!" like the sound of hunting in the mountains,

Shaking the ancient forests,

Scaring Luoza to sweat the cold sweat.

Three thousand Hanis came up

And stood around Luoza.

Led by the zami Qisi,

They had their sharp arrows aimed at Luoza's heart.

罗扎赶紧上马，
领着蒲尼下山，
来时比老虎还凶，
走时像小羊一般。

原来戚姒早有提防，
过年过节也不松闲，
望见罗扎领人出门，
她就跑进厄戚蒲玛①，
领来多多的兄弟，
把罗扎撵下神山。

哈尼回到寨里，
把罗扎咒过千遍，
弟兄们围住纳索，
久久不肯走散。

纳索转来转去，
心像牛滚塘样乱，
痛恨罗扎变心变肠，
给哈尼带来苦难。

罗扎的姑娘马姒，
嫁来已经半年，
已怀三月身孕，
走起路来也很艰难。

① 蒲玛：大寨。

296

Luoza got back onto his horse in a hurry
And led the Punis running down the mountain.
Coming, he was more ferocious than a tiger,
But leaving, he was like a sheep.

Turned out that Qisi was long prepared,
Never letting down her guard even during the holidays.
As soon as she saw Luoza leaving with his people,
Qisi went to Eqi Puma①.
Bringing with many of her brothers
To drive Luoza off the sacred mountain.

When the Hanis returned to the village,
They cursed Luoza thousands of times.
Surrounding Nasuo,
They would not leave for a long time.

Nasuo walked back and forth,
His heart agitated like a pond with a buffalo rolling in it.
He ditested Luoza for changing his heart
And bringing misery to the Hanis.

Masi, the daughter of Luoza,
Had been married for half a year.
She was three months pregnant,
And now walked with some difficulty.

---

① Puma: Big villages.

住进哈尼寨子，
马奴喜喜欢欢，
拉着戚奴叫阿贝①，
亲热得像块红炭；
见着老人"阿波""阿匹"地叫，
见着小娃"扎谷""阿妮"地喊，
遇着扎密长长地说话，
遇着伙子笑得很甜；
她和纳索相亲相爱，
笑脸像开不败的鲜花，
说话像画眉婉转啼鸣，
日日抬酒又递烟。

听见纳索咒骂，
马奴哧哧笑出声音：
"阿爸是棵老树，
外头粗壮里头枯，
老人做事样样糊涂，
他也无心把你冒犯。

"老羊想啃嫩草，
老人想吃好菜，
他想要的东西，
你就给他献上，
就算尽点孝心，

---

① 阿贝：小妹妹、小姑娘。

298

Since moving into the Hanis' village,

Masi was delighted.

Holding Qisi by hand, she called her abei ①,

As warmly as a piece of glowing charcoal.

Seeing the elderly, she called them "apo" and "api".

Seeing the kids, she called them "zagu" and "ani".

Meeting the zamis, she chatted with them for a long time.

Meeting the young men, she smiled sweetly.

She and Nasuo loved each other,

Her smile like flowers that never fade,

Her voice like a thrush singing cheerfully,

And she served him drinks and tobacco day after day.

Hearing Nasuo's curse,

Masi chuckled:

"Daddy is an old tree,

Looking strong but being dried-up inside.

The old man was a fool in every way.

He didn't mean to offend you.

"Old sheep want to chew the tender grass,

Like old men want to taste good food.

What he wants,

You offer it to him.

Think of it as being filial,

---

① Abei: Little sister, little girl.

礼节也要周全，
说到神山他怎么会要，
城里大庙还多得用不完！

"蒲尼对哈尼有说不尽的好处，
难道你就忘记干净？
你要细细心心地想，
不要急急忙忙地干，
逗火了阿篇阿爸，
他会把哈尼来撵！"

戚姒回到寨堡，
心里的话说出嘴边：
"今天出的事情，
我已说在前面，
你的树长得太快，
风一吹就倒在路边；
你的地位坐得太高，
掉下来就把脚杆跌断。
我早早劝过你，
不要把罗扎当兄弟；
我早就说给你，
不要讨他家人的女人。
瞧啊，
他要把姑爷砍倒在神树前！
瞧啊，
他要把哈尼撵出谷哈平原！"

Observing ritual propriety.

How could he want the sacred mountain?

The many temples in the city are more than enough!

"The Puni has done the Hani a world of good.

Have you forgotten them all?

You have to think very carefully,

Instead of acting recklessly.

If you push my apian daddy too hard,

He could chase Hani away!"

Qisi returned to the village castle,

Words moving from her heart to her lips:

"What happened today

Was what I said before.

Your tree is growing so fast,

When the wind blows, it falls by the wayside.

You sit so high,

When you fall, you break the leg.

I told you before,

Not to treat Luoza like a brother.

I told you before,

Not to marry the woman of his family.

See,

He is going to cut down my man in front of the sacred tree!

See,

He will chase the Hani away from the Guha plain!"

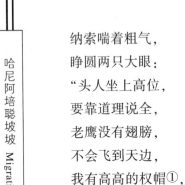

纳索喘着粗气，
睁圆两只大眼：
"头人坐上高位，
要靠道理说全，
老鹰没有翅膀，
不会飞到天边，
我有高高的权帽①，
不服罗扎掌管，
我去和他说理，
天神会做判断！"

"说起讲理的话，
哈尼伤心不完，
憨憨的纳索啊，
讲理你讲不赢罗扎，
他会说谷哈是蒲尼的家乡，
不是哈尼先祖的田园；
他会说抢去神山合理，
山上他埋过蒲尼老人。
再说也是枉然，
他随时想把哈尼来赶；
再讲也是白讲，
今日的事你也亲眼望见！"

---

① 权帽：此处指哈尼和蒲尼在谷哈以大河划界，两方各制一顶
高帽，表示对所辖领地的占有权。

Nasuo gasped,

And opened two eyes wide:

"The headman can sit on the high position,

Only because he's in the right.

Eagles without wings,

Cannot fly to the end of the sky.

I have the tall power hat①,

And I don't think Luoza is in the right.

I will go to argue with him,

As the gods will be the judge!"

"Speaking of being in the right,

The Hanis' hearts were broken.

Artless Nasuo,

You won't win the argument with Luoza.

He would say that Guha was the home of the Punis,

Not the fields of the Hanis' ancestors;

He would say it makes sense to take away the sacred mountain,

Since he buried the old Punis there.

It is useless to argue more,

As he was ready to chase the Hanis away any time;

It is in vain to speak more,

As you have seen with your own eyes what happened today!"

---

① The power hat: When the Hani and the Puni used the big river in Guha as their border, they made two top hats to indicate their possession of the territory.

"纳索啊，
听我一句良言，
小鸡和老鹰不能共一林，
黄牛和豹子不能共一圈，
快快带领哈尼走吧，
趁着罗扎没有动手；
快快带领哈尼搬吧，
趁着哈尼没有死人；
不要贪图好在的谷哈，
到别处兴建哈尼的家园！"

"你是聪明的扎密，
一向生着多多的心眼，
你是聪慧的女人，
怎会说要搬迁？
先祖来到谷哈密查，
经过去百年，
淌下的汗能使大河涨水，
出过的力能操倒大山，
你不说保住先祖的土地，
倒说要退出谷哈平原！

"纳索的女人啊，
亲亲的戚姒扎密，
我已打定主意，
决不离开谷哈。
哈尼要挖出埋下的武器，
把先祖的威风流传，

"Nasuo,

Take a word of advice from me.

Chickens and eagles cannot share one patch of woods;

Cattle and leopards cannot be kept in the same barn.

Quickly lead the Hanis away,

Before Luoza starts any scheme;

Quickly lead the Hanis to move away,

Before any Hani dies;

Let go what is good in Guha,

And build the Hani's home somewhere else!"

"You're a smart zami,

Always with a lot of wisdom.

How can a wise woman like you

Propose to move away?

Our ancestors came to Guha Micha

A hundred years ago.

Their sweat could make the river swell,

And the work could push down a mountain.

Now you don't talk about protecting our ancestors' lands,

But propose to withdraw from the Guha plain!"

"The woman of Nasuo,

My dear Qisi zami,

I've made up my mind

Never to leave Guha.

The Hani will dig up the buried weapon,

To show our forefathers' pride.

不打不走的才算哈尼，
要给罗扎尝尝哈尼的刀剑！"

"听见你威严的声音，
我的耳朵炸雷样响；
瞧见你发怒的神情，
我心头簌簌发颤。

"男人做事只图痛快，
女人才会知道艰难。
豹子和老虎咬架，
豹子要血流遍地；
哈尼和蒲尼打架，
哈尼要头落满山。

"啊哟，亲亲的纳索，
难道诺马的事情又要重现，
哈尼又要出大批寡妇？
难道喊杀的声音又要响起，
吃奶的小娃又要见不着阿爸的脸？"

"哎，女人！
水牛和老虎咬架，
老虎肚子也会被抵穿；
公鸡和老鹰搏斗，
老鹰也会被啄瞎双眼；
哈尼和仇人较量，

The real Hanis will not retreat without a fight,
But will render Luoza a taste of the Hani sword!"

"Your majestic voice
Is thundering in my ears;
Your angry face
Is shaking my heart.

"Men tend to act on impulses,
While women know what's tough.
When a leopard and a tiger fight,
The leopard's blood will cover the ground.
When the Hanis and the Punis fight,
The Hanis' heads will cover the mountain.

"Alas, dear Nasuo,
Is what happened in Nuoma going to happen again?
Will there be many Hani widows again?
Is the battle cry going to be heard again?
Will there be many nursing babies who won't see their dad's
face again?"

"Ah, woman!
When a buffalo and a tiger fight,
The tiger's belly could be pierced;
When a cock and an eagle fight,
The eagle could be pecked blind;
When Hanis and their enemies battle,

手脚从来不软。
多话不要再说，
快为男人祝愿!"

（五）

萨——依——萨!
哈尼吹响了牛角，
号声震动了山川，
牛角是大头人的嘴，
把紧急的命令来传:
"嗒嗒呜——嗒嗒呜——
静下来! 静下来!
树也静下来，
水也静下来，
话的大门打开了，
哈尼的好汉聚寨前!

"嗒嗒呜——嗒呜——
快点! 快点!
住在东边的哈尼，
歇在西边的哈尼，
快快挖出先祖的大刀，
快把先祖的志气来显!"

七沟七箐的哈尼来了，
九山九岭的哈尼来了，

The Hanis are never soft-hearted.

Say no more,

But wish your man luck!"

6.5

Sa—ee—sa!

The Hanis blew the buffalo horn,

Its sound shaking the mountains.

The horn was the mouth of the chieftain,

Passing on the urgent orders:

"DADAWU—DADAWU—

Keep quite! Keep quiet!

Trees, keep quiet.

Water, keep quiet.

The gate of words is open,

And the Hani heroes gathered in front of the village!

"DADAWU—DAWU—

Hurry up! Hurry up!

The Hanis who lived in the east,

And those who rested in the west,

Quickly dig up the broadswords of the ancestors,

And show the spirit of the ancestors!"

Presently came the Hanis from the seven gullies and seven

valleys,

And came the Hanis from the nine mountains and nine hills,

像淌山的十股大水，
汇合到谷哈平原。

打了，一娘生的兄弟姐妹！
打了，亲亲的哈尼后人！
树多多的山上也打了，
树少少的山下也打了；
草旺旺的坝头也打了，
草稀稀的坝脚也打了；
清清的河头也打了，
浑浊的河尾也打了；
不打的一处也没有了！
不打的一日也没有了！

瞧啊，亲亲的兄弟，
瞧啊，亲亲的姐妹，
大刀长矛像蚂蚱乱跳，
快箭飞标像蜂子遮天！

人叫出了老虎的声音，
马吐出了老象的气喘。
谷哈密查抖起来了，
好像一个打摆子的人！

Like ten streams running down from a mountain,
Converging in the Guha plain.

Fight, brothers and sisters from one mother!
Battle, my dear Hani descendants!
They fought up the hills where the trees were many,
And down the hills where the trees were few;
They fought at the head of the bazi where the grass was
thick,
And at the foot of it where the grass was thin;
They fought in the upper reaches of the river where the water
was clear,
And in the lower reaches of it where the water was turbid;
There was no place where there was no fighting,
And no day when there was no battle.

Look, my dear brothers,
Look, my dear sisters,
The broadswords and the spears were bouncing like frantic
grasshoppers,
And the arrows and darts covered the sky like a swarm of
bees!

The men called out with their tigers' voice,
While the horses breathed out the old elephants' breath.
Guha Micha shivered violently,
Like a person with serious illnesses.

311

起头开战是清水河边，
那里就是划定的地界，
深深的界草已被点着，
长长的河岸像火龙升天，
青青的界石也被烧炸，
轰隆的声音传出很远。

接着开仗的是叙纳罗坝子①，
这块地方最平最宽，
打架为了把这里争夺，
这里的土地最肥最软。

两边派出最恶的人，
仗也打得最凶最狠。
纳索亲自去吹号督战，
号声像大雨铺地盖天：
"嗒嗒呜——嗒嗒呜——
冲上前！冲上前！
哈尼的好汉冲上前！
不要让麂子老熊跑掉，
要把老虎骨头敲断！
我哈尼的大头人领着你们，
万能的天神在我们中间！"

---

① 叙纳罗坝子：地名，所指不详，可能是谷哈坝子中的一块地方。

The battle began by the Clear Water River,

Where the demarcation line was marked.

The deep boundary grass had been set alight,

The long banks of the river becoming a fire dragon flying to heaven,

And the green boundary stones were exploding,

The cracking sounds of explosion spreading far away.

The next battle happened in Xunaluo Bazi①,

Which is the flattest and widest.

They fought over this place,

Because the land here was the most fertile and softest.

Both sides sent the most ferocious men,

Who fought most fiercely.

Nasuo himself went to blow the horn and oversee the battle,

The sound of horn covering the sky like the heavy rain:

"DADA—WU—DADA—WU—

Rush forward! Rush forward!

Hani heroes, rush forward!

Don't let the muntjac and the old bear run away,

Do break the tiger's bone!

The Hani chieftain is leading you,

And the almighty god of heaven is among us!"

---

① Xunaluo Bazi: The name of a place unknown today. It may be a piece of flat land in Guha Bazi.

冲啦！冲啦！
杀啦！杀啦！
哈尼的大刀砍朝前！
哈尼的长矛戳朝前！
哈尼的棍子打朝前！
哈尼的三尖叉剁朝前！
还有那哈尼的流星，
在敌人头上飞转！

亲亲的弟兄们，
先祖在叙纳罗打得老实硬气，
杀翻的敌人一片连着一片。
哈尼宽片的大刀，
砍断了敌人的手杆；
哈尼齐眉的棍子，
打断了敌人的脚杆；
哈尼的流星套住敌人的脖子，
拉到面前又拔刀砍翻；
哈尼三五拃的长矛，
挑得敌人的肠子花蛇一样乱钻！

罗扎打不赢哈尼，
又派出新的兵马，
个个穿上厚厚的皮甲，
哈尼的竹刀竹矛戳不穿；
先祖吃亏啰，
几十个弟兄被绑，

Charge! Charge!

Fight! Fight!

The Hanis' broadswords wielded forward,

And their spears stabbed forward!

They hit forward with sticks

And cut forward with tridents!

The Hanis' lassos as well

Circled over the enemies' heads like meteors!

Dear brothers,

The ancestors fought hard at Xunaluo.

Numerous enemies were cut down in big waves.

The Hanis' wide-blade broadswords

Cut off the enemies' arms;

Their sticks as tall as the eyebrow

Broke the enemies' legs;

Their lasso meteors caught the enemies around the neck,

And then they roped them over and cut them down;

Their long spears

Pocked the enemies' bellies inside out!

Luoza saw that he could not beat the Hanis

And sent out new troops,

Each of whom wore a thick coat of leather

That the Hanis' bamboo broadswords and spears could not

pierce through.

The ancestors were defeated,

And dozens of brothers were caught.

蒲尼结起他们的头发，
像柴捆拖在马尾后边！

哈尼最老的阿波，
生着七十七层皱皮的老人，
望见情况紧急，
把哈八唱出嘴边：
"哈尼的英雄好汉，
豹子样勇敢的男人！
虽说我牙齿不剩一颗，
背脊也弯朝前面，
还听着你们呼喊，
还望着你们朝前！
记着哦，
老虎死了皮像鲜花，
白鹇死了毛像雪片，
先祖的志气不要打失，
死也要死在最前面！"

听见阿波的话，
哈尼的力气添，
早上捆去阿爸，
晚上儿子又上前！

打哟，
打了七个晚上！
打哟，
打了七个白天！

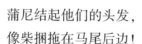

Their hair knotted together,

They were tied to the horses' tails like a bundle of firewood!

The oldest Hani apo,

An old man whose wrinkles had seventy-seven layers,

Saw the urgency of the situation

And started to sing Haba the drinking song:

"Hani heroes,

Brave men like leopards,

I have not a tooth left,

And my back bent forward,

But I'm still here listening to you roar,

And watching you rush forward!

Remember well,

The dead tiger's skin is like a flower,

And the dead silver pheasant's hair's like snowflakes.

Don't lose the spirit of your ancestors,

And die on the frontline if you have to die!"

Hearing the apo's words,

The Hanis felt stronger.

When in the morning the dad was caught,

In the evening his son came to the frontline again!

Fighting,

They had fought for seven nights!

Fighting,

They had fought for seven days!

哈尼难抵蒲尼，
退进大寨里面。

罗扎得意地笑了，
一句一回喜欢：
"咬人的老虎落进笼，
挑人的水牛关进圈，
会跑会跳的哈尼啊，
你还能朝哪里钻！"

（六）

萨——依——萨！
罗扎召集众多蒲尼，
把大寨围成一圈。
哈尼白天冲杀七回，
七回被打退；
哈尼晚上冲杀九回，
九回被打转。

七十七个弟兄被杀伤，
七十七个弟兄被砍翻，
七十七个弟兄被绑走，
纳索大头人愁眉不展。

头人们连夜商议，
寨堡里坐成一圈，

The Hanis could not beat the Punis
And had to retreat back to the village.

Luoza smirked,
And being very satisfied, he said :
"Like the tiger that attacks human has fallen into the cage,
The buffalo that gored people has been put in a pen,
The Hanis, who can run and jump,
Where can you escape now!"

6. 6

Sa—ee—sa!
Luoza gathered many Punis together
To besiege the village.
The Hanis tried to fight their way out seven times during the
day,
But seven times they failed;
They tried to fight their way out nine times during the night,
And nine times they failed.

Seventy-seven brothers were wounded;
Seventy-seven brothers were killed;
Seventy-seven brothers were captured;
The chieftain Nasuo was frowning with anxiety.

The headmen deliberated through the night,
Sitting in a circle in the village castle,

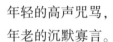
年轻的高声咒骂，
年老的沉默寡言。

戚姒扎密忙出忙进，
炒菜煮饭一点不闲，
等到头人吃饱喝足，
开口说出她的打算。

一句才说出半句，
听见有人气喘，
抬起亮亮的松明，
见马姒站在门边。
自从神山开战，
马姒忙得像飞燕，
头上插满金花银花，
耳朵戴上金环银环，
顿顿给男人切肉倒酒，
天天把纳索吃得头转。
戚姒叫纳索小心提防，
纳索说她不敢捣乱。

望见马姒悄悄偷听，
戚姒急忙转过话头：
"阿妹不要站在门口
天黑地黑风大天寒，
你有小娃不好走路，
还是进家歇歇腰杆。"

The young cursing loudly,
The old remaining silent.

Qisi bustled in and out,
Cooking meals non-stop.
She waited till the headmen had their fill
And then started to tell what she thought.

She had only said half of her first sentence
When she heard someone's shallow breathing.
Lifting the bright pine oil lamp,
She saw Masi standing by the door.
Ever since the war of the sacred mountain started,
Masi had been busy as a swift,
With gold and silver headdress flowers in her head,
And gold and silver earrings on her ears.
Masi served Nasuo meat and wine at each meal,
And kept Nasuo in a daze every day.
Qisi told Nasuo to be on his guard,
But Nasuo said Masi did not dare to play tricks.

Seeing Masi was eavesdropping,
Qisi quickly changed the subject and said:
"Don't stand in the doorway, sister.
It's dark and windy and cold there.
Being pregnant with your child,
You should go home and rest your aching back."

左说右说马奴才走，
脚虽走啦心里不愿。

戚奴关牢大门，
说出最好的主意，
头人们听得哈哈大笑，
一个个把膝盖拍酸。

扁脚掌的公鸭叫了三声，
旺脚毛的公鸡叫了三遍，
雾露浓浓的时候，
哈尼把寨门打开。

罗扎听说消息，
赶紧召拢人马，
几千个人一齐，
杀进大寨门槛。

突然听见一阵吼叫，
好像炸雷落在面前，
地皮变成一面大鼓，
震得人马难站上边。

浓雾里亮起千百双怪眼，
数不清的魔鬼冲到面前，
魔鬼生着一对尖角，
轻轻一挑人死马翻；
魔鬼还有阿爹阿妈，

After several rounds of persuasion, Masi left,
With her feet moving but her heart reluctant.

Qisi shut the door tight
And shared a wonderful idea.
In favor of it, the headmen laughed happily,
Slapping their knees sore.

When the drake with flat feet quacked three times,
The feather-footed cock crowed three times,
And the dew was thick,
The Hanis opened the gate of their village.

When Luoza heard about this,
He called up the troops.
Thousands of people together
Crossed the threshold of the village castle.

Suddenly they heard a roar,
Like thunder cracking in front of them.
The ground turned into a vibrating drum,
On which people and horses could hardly stand still.

In the heavy fog thousands of strange eyes lit up,
And countless demons rushed towards them.
With sharp horns,
The demons easily gored people and horses to death.
The demons also brought their father and mother,

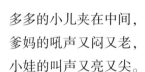

多多的小儿夹在中间，
爹妈的吼声又闷又老，
小娃的叫声又亮又尖。

哈尼不单放出魔鬼，
还在后头又杀又砍，
哦嗬哦嗬大声吼着，
把大群魔鬼吆到前边。

蒲尼的大队被魔鬼冲散，
像羊群被豹子遍山赶撵，
三个人里头，
一个被挑死踩死，
一个被烧伤踩烂，
还有一个——
被吓得脚瘫手软！

罗扎跳上快马，
一直跑到海边，
像被鹞鹰追赶的鱼雀，
朝着刺蓬乱飞乱钻。

太阳爬出大山，
照着谷哈平原，
哈尼把魔鬼叫回，
坝子里只剩一片白烟。

As well as many children in the middle,

The mothers' and fathers' roar sounding muffled and old,

While the baby's cry, sharp and shrill.

The Hanis did not only send out the demons,

But they also slashed their way through following behind the
demons.

Oho, oho, they shouted,

Driving the horde of demons over to the front.

The Puni troops were dispersed by the demons,

Like a flock of sheep, chased by a leopard, running all over
the mountain.

Of the three Punis,

One was gored and trampled to death;

One, burned and crushed;

And the last one—

His feet and hands, paralyzed by fear.

Luoza jumped onto the fast horse,

Running away to the lake,

Like a fishfinch chased by a hawk,

Flying and drilling towards the thorny woods.

When the sun climbed out from behind the mountain

And shone on the Guha plain,

The Hanis called the demons back,

Leaving only the white smoke in the bazi.

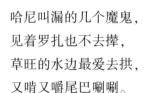

哈尼叫漏的几个魔鬼，
见着罗扎也不去撵，
草旺的水边最爱去拱，
又啃又嚼尾巴唰唰。

罗扎实在奇怪，
悄悄挨近旁边，
只见大鬼变成水牛，
背上披着蓑衣；
小鬼变成山羊，
身上蒙着披毡；
一只角绑尖刀，
一只角绑火把，
尖刀就是鬼角，
火把就是鬼眼！

众人：
萨——依——萨！

歌手：
讲了，亲亲的兄弟姊妹！
讲了，一寨的哈尼子孙！
在远古的谷哈密查，
戚姒布下了火牛火羊阵，
戚姒是高能的阿波，
她的美名世代流传！

Those demons that did not return

Did not chase Luoza when seeing him.

They would go to the grassy water's edge,

Grazing, chewing and swinging their tails.

Curious,

Luoza crept up towards them,

And found that the big demons had turned into buffalos,

With coir raincoat draping over their backs;

And the smaller demons had turned into goats,

With blankets covering on their bodies;

One horn was bound with a sharp knife,

And the other was tied with a torch.

The sharp knife was the demon's horn,

And the torch was the demon's eye.

Audience:

Sa—ee—sa!

Singer:

Let us tell the stories, dear brothers and siters!

Let us tell the stories, Hani descendants from the one village!

In the ancient Guha Micha,

Qisi employed the fire buffalo and goat tactic.

Her outstanding ability

Made her good name go through many generations.

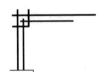

恨不得啰，
罗扎鼻子冒出火烟！
恨不得啰，
蒲尼又把大寨围团！

大头人纳索不紧不急，
叫哈尼牵出火牛火羊，
这回火把扎得更大，
刀也磨得更亮更尖。

样样整好打开寨门，
火牛火羊等在后边。
哦嗬——
这回出了怪事，
蒲尼不朝里钻！
寨门打开三回，
蒲尼一回也望不见。
他们是不打啦？
他们难道回家转？

哈尼放下大刀长矛，
火牛火羊也吆回圈。
茶水没喝一口，
烟筒刚刚冒烟，
蒲尼冲进来了，
大刀长矛飞转。

So angry,

Luoza had smoke coming out of his nose!

So furious,

The Punis laid siege to the main village again!

Chieftain Nasuo, quite relaxed,

Asked the Hanis to lead out the fire buffalos and goats.

This time the torches were bigger,

And the knives were brighter and sharper, too.

They got it all ready before opening the village gate,

With the fire buffalos and goats waiting behind.

Oho—

Something strange happened this time.

The Punis didn't rush in!

The gate of the village was opened three times,

But not once were the Punis seen.

Were they not going to fight?

Did they go home?

The Hanis laid down their broadswords and spears,

And drove the fire buffalos and goats back to the pens as

well.

Before they had a sip of tea

And took a draw on their pipes,

The Punis attacked again and rushed in,

With broadswords and spears flying and whirling in the air.

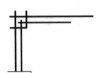
亏得纳索力气大，
流星舞得像刮风，
蒲尼退是退了，
哈尼的死人又添。

戚奴皱起眉头，
又叫纳索开战，
寨门打开像棕披，
火牛火羊拉出圈。

哈尼刚刚拔出刀，
她又把寨门关严，
忙出忙进三四回，
纳索也把她埋怨：
"哦嚓！①
哈尼的女人是酒醉的女人，
不会打仗只会闹着玩！"
他不知戚奴有聪明的主意，
嘴里调兵眼望四面。

她见哈尼牵出火牛火羊，
马奴就晒出大红被单，
哈尼歇下刀枪，

---

　　① 此处的"哦嚓"是讥讽嘲笑之意，而非感叹，"哦嚓"一词
在哈尼语中有多种意味。

Thanks to Nasuo's great strength,

His lasso meteor danced like the wind.

When the Punis retreated,

The Hanis found their casualty had increased.

Qisi frowned

And asked Nasuo to attack again.

The gate of the village opened like a brown cloak,

And the buffalos and goats were led out of the pens.

As the Hanis were just drawing their broadswords,

She closed the gate of village again.

In and out three or four times,

Even Nasuo began to blame her:

"Oho! ①

The Hani woman is a drunkard,

Not knowing how to fight and doing it for a lark!"

He did not know that Qisi had a clever idea.

When she gave orders to the troops she looked all round carefully.

She found that on seeing the Hanis let out the fire buffalo and goats,

Masi hung out a big crimson bedsheet.

On seeing the Hanis resting their swords and spears,

---

① Here "Oho" is used sarcastically, not an exclamation. The word "Oho" has many meanings in the Hani language.

马奴也把被单收卷；
被单是她的声音，
罗扎远处就听见。
收起是："来打得啦，
蒲尼定会打赢！"
晒出来是："来不得哟，
一来就打败战！"

纳索也看出奸细，
低头不语不言。
他扎实喜欢马奴，
不肯把她杀翻。

戚奴劝告丈夫：
"不怕狗会咬人，
只要主人会管。
她泄露得了一回泄露不了两回，
只消你把她提防在心间。"

纳索说给女人：
"箐里的花蛇好瞧，
心肠又毒又狠，
我只爱马奴的样子，
心肠我不喜欢。
戚奴扎密啊，
亲亲的妻子！
样子和心肠都美的，
只有你一个女人！

She rolled up the sheet.

The sheet was like her voice,

Which Luoza could hear from a distance.

When the sheet was rolled up, it said "Come and attack.

The Punis will win!"

When the sheet was hung out, it said "Don't come.

You will be defeated!"

Nasuo also spotted the spy,

But he bowed his head and said nothing.

He was quite fond of Masi

And couldn't kill her.

Qisi advised her husband:

"The dog that bites is nothing to be afraid of,

As long as its master can manage it.

She has let out the secret once but let there not be a second

time,

As long as you are wary of her."

Nasuo said to his woman:

"The colorful snake in the valley is beautiful

But poisonous and cruel-hearted.

I like Masi only for her good looks,

Not for her heart.

Oh Qisi zami,

My dear wife!

Beautiful both in appearance and in heart,

There is only one woman like you in the world!

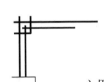
心里的话我只对你说，
不会漏给她一点半点！
妻子啊，
蒲尼又多又恶，
哈尼大难到来，
我要去木朵策果①，
把神奇的木人造出来，
哈尼是死是活，
就看这回能不能如愿！"

（七）

萨——依——萨！
遮天遮地的大树，
站满木朵策果高山，
大树笔直像筷子，
粗得像水牛腰杆。

造木人要找黄心树，
树头要有手样的枝，
树脚要有脚样的根，
还要生着敲得响的干。

找来七百棵合心的树，

---

① 木朵策果：山名，意为很高很高的大山，为谷哈最高山；又
可译为"像头上长着头发一样生满青草的高山"。

What's in my heart I only say to you,

Letting her know not a bit!

My wife,

The Punis were so many and so wicked,

And I'm afraid the great calamity of the Hanis is coming.

I will go to the Muduoceguo①

To make the magic woodmen.

Whether the Hanis will survive

Hinges on this one action! "

6. 7

Sa—ee—sa!

The big trees that shaded the sky and covered the earth

Stood all over the mountain of Muduoceguo,

Straight like the chopsticks,

Thick like the buffalo's waist.

To make wooden men, the trees must be yellow at the heart,

With the top branching out like the hands,

The root branching out like the feet,

And the hollow chunk that could make the tap-tap sound.

Seven hundred such trees were found

---

①　Muduoceguo: Name of a mountain, meaning a very high mountain. It's said to be the highest mountain in Guha, and it also means a mountain full of grass like hair.

造出七百个彪壮的大汉，
木人有手有脚，
鼻子嘴巴齐全，
手脚又粗又壮，
肩膀又厚又宽。

拿出祖传的本事，
纳索把工匠神祭献，
请高能的先祖工匠使力，
求万能的大神小神参战。
红冠的公鸡杀下一只，
血浸的红酒弹向四面，
咬开食指上的血肉，
在木人身上点了三点。

一滴点在眉心，
眼睛会望舌头会弹，
吼出"冲啰杀啰"的声音，
把山崖也震垮半边；
二滴点在手脚，
手也会抓脚也会踢，
舞动哈尼的长矛大刀，
上戳下砍快如闪电；
三滴点在心口，
会说会讲也会喜欢，
问出一句能答十句，
脑子会想心会打算。

And were made into seven hundred husky fellows.

These wooden men had hands and feet,

Nose and mouth,

With brawny and strong limbs

And thick and broad shoulder.

Using the skills he inherited from his ancestors,

Nasuo offered sacrifices to the god of the craftsman,

Asking the high-powered ancestral craftsmen for help,

And begging the almighty and the lesser gods for assistance.

A red-crowned cock was butchered,

And its blood in red wine was flicked in four directions,

Nasuo bit his forefinger

And dripped three drops of blood on each wooden man.

The first drop between the eyebrows

Brought the eyes and tongues to life, seeing and clicking

With the sound of "Charge! Fight!",

So loud the sound shook down half of the cliff;

The second drop on the hands and feet

Made them scratching and kicking,

Waving the Hani spears and broadswords,

Up and down, swift as lightning;

The third drop on the heart

Enabled them to talk and have likes and dislikes,

Ready to reply to one sentence with ten,

As they could think and plan.

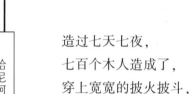

造过七天七夜，
七百个木人造成了，
穿上宽宽的披火披斗，
和真人难分难辨。

纳索领着木人回寨，
留下七十个弟兄把守高山，
再造七千个木人，
要把罗扎撵出谷哈平原。

——听啰，哈尼的子孙，
让我把好听的古今来传！
远古的先祖是高能的先祖，
做下的奇事一桩又一桩！

在谷哈宽平的大坝，
哈尼蒲尼站在两边，
蒲尼像水边的茅草，
排得又密又严，
哈尼像崖头的刺棵，
人马只有一点。

罗扎望见好笑，
骑马来到面前：
"纳索，我的姑爷！
找不着人来打架，
就答应我的条件，
哈尼只要像听话的牛马，

Seven days and seven nights had passed,
And seven hundred wooden men were made.
In the loose Pihuo Pidou garment,
They could hardly be distinguished from real persons.

Nasuo led the wooden men back to the village,
Leaving seventy brothers on the high mountain
To make another seven thousand wooden men,
So as to drive Luoza out of the Guha plain.

—Listen, Hani offsprings,
Let me pass on the stories of our ancestors!
Our ancestors were highly capable,
Creating one miracle after another!

On the wide and flat bazi at Guha,
The Hanis and the Punis stood on two sides:
The Punis were like the thatches at the water's edge,
In their tight rows,
While the Hanis were like a thorny tree on the cliff head,
With much fewer soldiers and horses.

Luoza was amused by what he saw
And rode his horse to the front:
"Nasuo, my son-in-law!
There's no need to fight,
If you agree to my terms.
As long as the Hanis work like the docile cattle and horse,

我就给你们山林大田!"

纳索拔出弯弯的牛角,
吹出"嘀嘀"的长声,
猛然间——
像天神来到谷哈,
七百个哈尼冲杀上前!

这些哈尼不比从前,
个个像豹子老熊力大无边,
罗扎还来不及细瞧,
蒲尼就被杀翻一片。

罗扎急忙下令,
蒲尼射出利箭,
支支长箭射中哈尼。

哈尼像刺猪大针插满,
可惜不见哈尼倒地,
鲜红的血也不见流淌,
你望我我望你嘻嘻地笑,
你帮我我帮你把箭拔完!

小狗遇着豹子,
罗扎吓破苦胆,
跑都跑不赢啰,
马脚也被跑断。

You will get the mountains and fields!"

Nasuo drew out his crescent-shaped horn,
Whistling a long "HOO—HOO",
Suddenly—
As if the god of heaven came to Guha,
Seven hundred Hanis charged forward!

These Hanis, unlike theselves before,
Were brawny and mighty like leopards and old bears.
Before Luoza could look at them carefully,
Many Punis had been killed.

Luoza hastened to give an order,
And the Punis released their arrows,
All of which shot at the Hanis.

The Hanis were like wild boars with big thorns,
But none of them fell down.
Nor were they bleeding.
Rather, they looked at each other and grinned,
Helping each other to pull out all the arrows!

Like a dog meeting a leopard,
Luoza freaked out
And ran away as fast as he could,
His horse's legs almost broken.

讲啰，亲亲的兄弟姊妹，
哈尼的木人一上阵，
就把蒲尼大队杀翻！
瞧啰，
在宽宽的大路上，
哈尼的木人把蒲尼堵截；
在窄窄的小路上，
哈尼的木人把蒲尼阻拦；
在滚滚的大河边，
哈尼的木人把蒲尼砍倒；
在平平的大田里，
哈尼的木人把蒲尼追赶！

众人：

萨——依——萨！

歌手：

嗬！嗬！
木人杀不赢的人一个也没有了！
木人攻不破的寨子一个也不见了！
谷哈阿篇啊，
被哈尼撵进他的大城；
谷哈罗扎啊，
望见哈尼就躲得老远！

听说阿爸打败，
又见哈尼喜欢，
马姒扎密的心哦，

Let me tell the story, dear brothers and sisters,

As soon as the Hani wooden men joined the battle,

The Punis' main troops were defeated!

Look!

On the broad roads,

The Hani wooden men cornered the Punis;

On the narrow paths,

The Hani wooden men blocked the Punis;

By the big rolling river,

The Hani wooden men executed the Punis;

In the flat fields,

The Hani wooden men chased the Punis!

The audience:

Sa—ee—sa!

Singer:

Wow! Wow!

The wooden men killed all their rivals!

They conquered all the villages!

Guha Apian

Was driven into his great city;

Guha Luoza

Avoided the Hanis on seeing them from afar!

Hearing her dad was defeated,

And then seeing the Hanis were excited,

Masi was grief-striken, her heart

像小鱼在铁锅里煎。

等到纳索回来,
马奴走拢男人,
像缠花绕树的蝴蝶,
左右前后打转。
抬来最甜的米酒,
点着最呛的辣烟,
巴掌肉喂进七块,
紫米饭喂进七碗。

马奴甜甜地问:
"亲亲的阿哥哦,
亲亲的男人!
哈尼打了胜仗,
我笑得手软脚软,
不知有兄弟受伤,
不知有人死在外边?"

纳索吃得打嗝,
饭饱酒足耳鸣眼花,
哈哈放声大笑,
戚奴的话忘记后面:
"扎密哟,憨人!

Like a small fish being fried in an iron pan of oil.

When Nasuo came back,

Masi approached him

Like a butterfly circling around a flower or fluttering around

a tree,

Following him, left and right, back and forth.

She carried in the sweetest rice wine,

Lit the most spicy tabacco,

Served him seven pieces of palm-sized meat

And seven bowls of the purple rice.

Masi asked sweetly:

"My dear brother,

My dear man!

Knowing the Hanis won the battle,

I laughed till my limbs were limp.

Were any of our brothers wounded,

Or did any die out there?"

Nasuo burped.

Full of food and wine, with ringing in his ears and blurred

vision,

He laughed out loud,

Forgetting Qisi's words totally:

"Zami, my silly girl!

打仗的是木人，
刀砍砍不死，
箭射射不穿，
怎会死在外边?"

马奴吓得心跳，
急忙细细盘问：
"豺狗家狗做一窝，
麂子黄牛做一处，
木人怎样分，
真人怎样辨?"

"真人会淌汗，
木人不淌汗；
真人流鼻涕，
木人鼻子干!"

纳索张开嘴，
就像水难断，
心里说"莫讲"，
嘴里说不完；
样样事事都讲啰，
样样事事都说全，
木朵策果的事情，
马奴扎密也听见!

马奴急得汗淋淋，
大火烧在眼面前，

It was the wooden men who fought,

Who couldn't be killed with the broadswords,

Nor pierced through by the arrows.

How could they die out there?"

Masi was shocked, her heart beating fast.

She hurried to ask for more details:

"It's hard to tell the jackals from the dogs.

It's difficult to separate the muntjac from the cattle.

How do you distinguish the wooden men,

From the real men?"

"Real men sweat,

While wooden men don't;

Real men are snotty,

While wooden men have dry noses!"

Nasuo opened his mouth,

Talked like running water that could not stop.

Thinking "Don't tell" in his heart,

But his mouth was unable to stop.

He told her everything,

Every detail of the whole story.

Even what happened in the Muduoceguo

was told to Masi!

Masi was so anxious that she sweated hard,

Like in front of burning fire.

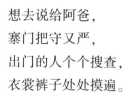

想去说给阿爸，
寨门把守又严，
出门的人个个搜查，
衣裳裤子处处摸遍。

马奻的心河沙样细，
马奻的心硬刺样尖，
脱下尖头的花鞋，
把机密写在里面，
又装作挑水洗菜，
把花鞋放在水边，
打听消息的蒲尼，
赶紧拿给阿篇。

罗扎打好主意，
领人又来开战，
甩出长长的套索，
把哈尼拖到马前。
打嘛也不打，
杀嘛也不杀，
先操去晒太阳，
瞧瞧会不会淌汗，
又拿鸡毛搔鼻孔，
瞧瞧淌不淌鼻涕，
会淌鼻涕会淌汗的，
马上拉去砍头，
不淌鼻涕不淌汗的，
赶紧推进大火里面。

She wanted to tell her dad,

But the gate was well guarded.

Every one going out would be searched

From head to toe.

Masi's heart was as detailed as the fine river sand,

And as hard and piercing as the thorn.

She took off her pointed embroidered shoes,

And wrote the secrets in the shoes.

Then she pretended to go carry water for washing vegetables,

And left her embroidered shoes by the water's edge,

Which was picked up by the Puni scout and

Hurriedly brought to the apian.

With countermeasures in mind,

Luoza led troops to resume the fight.

They threw out the long lassos

To rope in the Hanis before the horse.

They neither hit the captives,

Nor killed them.

Instead, they shoved the captives to under the sun

To see if they sweat,

And they scratched their noses with a feather

To see if their noses ran.

Those who had running nose and who sweated

Were beheaded at once;

Those who did not

Were pushed into the fire.

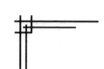

哈尼的七百木人啊，
眨眼就化成灰烟！

罗扎又派出人马，
围住木朵策果，
放起烧天的大火，
把一山木人烧尽！

苦啰，先祖的儿孙，
灾难来到哈尼面前！
惨啰，后世的哈尼，
伤心的事出在谷哈平原！

罗扎领着蒲尼来了，
一直打进厄戚蒲玛，
大人小娃被杀被砍，
牛马猪羊被拖被牵，
到处望见鸡飞狗跳，
平平的坝子堆满死人，
熊熊的大火烧红了天！

众人：
萨——依——萨！

歌手：
听啰，一寨的哈尼人！
在那木朵策果山上，
七十个哈尼为保护木人，

The Hanis' seven hundred wooden men

Turned into ashes in a wink!

Luoza again sent his troops out

To surround the Muduoceguo mountain.

They set fire that shot up to the sky and

Burned out a mountain of wooden men!

How painful it was, the offsprings of our ancestors,

That this disaster befell the Hanis!

How tragic it was, the Hani descendants,

That this sorrowful event happened in the Guha plain!

Luoza led the Punis

And advanced all the way to the village Eqi Puma,

Killing the adults and the kids,

Taking away the cattle, horses, pigs and sheep.

Everywhere cocks were seen flying and dog, jumping,

Corpses piling up on the flat bazi,

And the great fire burning the sky red!

Audience:

Sa—ee—sa!

Singer:

Listen to me! The Hanis from the one village!

In the Muduoceguo mountain,

Seventy Hanis, for protecting the wooden men,

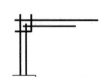

被砍死在高高的山巅，
七十个好汉流出七十股鲜血，
把木朵策果大山染遍。
一树树白花染红了，
像早上的彩霞耀眼，
哈尼把它叫做都匹玛雅，
谷哈的山茶花至今最红最艳！

众人：
萨——哝——萨！

歌手：
萨——依——萨！
讲了，一娘生的兄弟姊妹！
讲了，亲亲的哈尼寨人！
望见满山木人被烧倒，
瞧见满坝哈尼被砍翻，
纳索像中箭的老虎，
要带领兄弟们拼死在寨前！
聪明的戚姒劝说男人，
要他把哈尼带出谷哈平原：
"哈尼像被割断的草，
一排一排倒在田间，

Were killed on the top of the mountain.

Seventy heroes shed seventy streams of blood,

Which dyed the whole Muduoceguo mountain.

The trees with white flowers were dyed red,

Like the morning rosy clouds dazzling the eyes.

The Hanis named them Dupimaya,

And till this day the camellia in Guha is the reddest and the most brilliant!

Audience:

Sa—nong—sa!

Singer:

Sa—ee—sa!

Let's tell the story, brothers and sisters who came from the same mother!

Let's tell the story, dear Hani fellow villagers!

Seeing the wooden men all over the mountain burnt out,

Seeing the Hani fellows all over the bazi cut down,

Nasuo, like a tiger shot with an arrow,

Were determined to lead his brothers to fight to death in front of the village!

The wise Qisi began to persuad her man

To lead the Hanis out of the Guha plain:

"The Hanis are like the mowed grass,

Row upon row lying in the field.

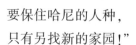
要保住哈尼的人种，
只有另找新的家园！"

听见戚姒的话，
哈尼都把头点：
"逃难吧，
谷哈没有哈尼的站脚处！
逃难吧，
能逃多远就逃多远！
这回啊，
哈尼不能成伙结队了，
为保住人种啊，
各人脸朝哪面就逃向哪面！"

七十个头人说话了，
七十个头人把头点：
"纳索啊，
你不是有福的头人，
我们不再听你指点！
你的心被鬼拿走了，
马姒的手蒙住你的两眼！

"那个女人啊，
心肠比毒蜂还毒，
快快把她杀掉，
她的鲜血才醒得了你的酒，
她的命才能抵哈尼的屈冤！"

To preserve the Hani race,

We have to find a new homeland!"

Hearing Qisi's words,

The Hani people nodded their heads:

"Let's flee,

As there is nowhere for the Hanis to stay in Guha!

Let's run away,

Run as far as we can!

This time,

The Hanis could not flee together.

To preserve the race,

Let us flee in whichever direction we happen to face!"

Seventy headmen had spoken,

And seventy heads nodded:

"Oh Nasuo,

You are not a blessed chief,

And we won't obey your order anymore!

Your heart has been taken by the ghost,

And your eyes have been covered by Masi!

"That woman,

Her heart is more poisonous than a poisonous wasp.

Kill her quickly.

Only her blood can sober you up,

And only her life can pay for the Hanis' grievances!"

头人纳索提起大刀，
头人纳索怒火烧天，
惹火的豹子龇起尖牙，
发怒的水牛角抵朝前，
三下两下扳倒马姒，
磨快的大刀抵在她胸前。

戚姒心肠最好，
她把大刀隔开，
说出大锤样重的话，
一句句打在纳索心坎：

"大头人哟，我的丈夫，
我一夜翻身五次，
十夜没有闭眼！
开头劝你不要讨马姒，
你偏偏把她领进家来，
后来劝你莫泄露机密，
你又把嘴凑到她耳边；
哈尼今天吃尽苦难，
只能怪你心短嘴快！

"纳索啊，
马姒肚里有哈尼的小娃，
你怎能把怀孕的妻子杀死？
难道丈夫杀死妻子的规矩，

Picking up his broadsword,

Chiefain Nasuo was boiling with rage,

Like an angry leopard baring its sharp teeth,

Like a ferocious buffalo thrusting its horns forward.

Pulling down Masi easily and quickly,

He laid the sharpened broadsword against her chest.

Qisi had the kindest heart.

She fended off the broadsword,

And uttered the words that were as heavy as a sledgeham-

mer,

Pounding on Nasuo's heart:

"Oh chief man, my husband,

I turned over five times in one night

And had not closed my eyes for ten nights!

In the beginning I entreated you not to marry Masi,

But you brought her home.

Later I told you not to divulge secrets,

But you put your mouth close to her ear;

The Hanis had to endure all these sufferings today,

And it is only because you are a near-sighted blabbermouth!

"But Nasuo,

Masi now is carrying a Hani baby,

And how can you kill your pregnant wife?

Will the practice of uxoricide

要从你高能的纳索开头？
难道阿爸杀死儿女的规矩，
要从你英雄的头人开端？
杀死马奴，
十条大江也洗不净你的臭名；
杀死马奴，
谷哈大海也洗不净你的黑脸！"

戚奴的话像熊熊的火塘，
烘红了头人纳索的脸，
纳索把大刀扔在地上，
头像老马垂到胸前。

戚奴对头人们行过大礼，
又把新的道理说了一遍：
"尊敬的头人阿波们，
哈尼的女人不会说话，
说不合心意不要当真。
马奴扎密犯下山样的大罪，
杀死恶人也合我的心愿。
可是阿波啊，
请你们留下马奴一条命，
请把她收进逃难的哈尼中间！
同耕一田的兄弟成冤家，
哈尼蒲尼成了仇人，

Start with you, able Nasuo?

Will the practice of filicide

Start with you, heroic chief man?

If you killed Masi,

Your infamy could not be washed clean by ten rivers;

If you killed Masi,

Your black face could not be washed clean by the Guha sea!"

Qisi's words were like a blazing fireplace,

Reddening the face of Chieftain Nasuo.

He dropped his broadsword on the ground,

And his head hung low to the chest like an old horse.

Qisi made a formal salute to the headmen,

And gave a new reason this time:

"The honourable headmen apos,

As a Hani woman, I am not good at talking like this.

If you do not like what I say, please forgive me.

Masi zami's crime is mountainous.

And killing the wicked is also what I want.

But apos,

I ask that you spare Masi's life,

And take her as one of the fleeing Hanis!

The Hanis and the Punis used to be brothers who plowed the same field,

But now they have turned against each other and become enemies.

杀死马奴扎密，
换不回哈尼的命，
杀死阿篇的独囡，
只会逗起两边的仇怨！"

戚奴的话扎实有理，
头人个个都已听见，
吸烟筒的搁在一边，
抬茶碗的放在脚前。

马奴扎密得了性命，
扎实感激戚奴的恩典，
说要做个低贱的人，
把洗脚水抬到戚奴面前。

戚奴和她说话，
样子还像从前：
"饭米糯米可以蒸一甑，
苦笋甜笋可以发一山，
不要做我的下人，
只要做我的姊妹，
不要帮着恶人，
只要帮哈尼一边！

"阿妹啊，
你我互相仇恨，
会带来儿孙的仇怨！

Killing Masi zami,

We still cannot bring the Hanis back from the dead;

Killing the only daughter of the Apian,

We will only stir up the hatred on both sides!"

Qisi's words sounded quite reasonable,

Which all headmen heard.

Those who were smoking set their smoking pipes aside,

And those who were drinking tea put down their tea bowls in front of feet.

The life of Masi zami was spared,

And Masi was deeply grateful to Qisi,

Saying that she would be a maid

To carry the water for Qisi to wash her feet.

Qisi spoke to her

The same way as before:

"Rice and glutinous rice can be steamed in one steamer,

And bitter and sweet bamboo shoots can grow in one mountain.

Do not be my maid,

But be my sister.

Do not help the wicked,

But help the Hanis!

"My sister,

If you and I hate each other,

We will bring hatred among our children!

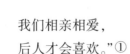
我们相亲相爱，
后人才会喜欢。"①

讲了，亲亲的兄弟们，
哈尼在谷哈把大事商谈，
烟筒的烟灰堆成三堆，
说出的话马驮不完，
七十七个头人一齐开口，
权威的话说在下边：

"谷哈密查是打失的好地，
哈尼要离开谷哈朝下搬迁。
纳索的妻子戚姒扎密，
是哈尼最英雄的女人，
全体哈尼要听从她的吩咐，
她叫走到哪边就走到哪边！"

头人的话刚刚出口，
"哦嗬！哦嗬！"欢声一片。
哈尼走到戚姒前面，
对她深深把腰弯。

望见哈尼的样子，
纳索怒气冲天：

———————————

① 戚姒生有一子，名叫卢威，马姒之子叫卢策，由于戚姒的宽
怀大度，卢威、卢策两个支系世世代代和睦相处，再无内部纷争。

If we love each other,

We will bring harmony to our descendants."①

Let us tell stories, dear brothers.

The headmen discussed the Hanis' affairs in Guha,

With the pipe ashes piling up in three heaps,

With words too many to be carried by horses.

Seventy-seven headmen spoke together,

But below are the words most authoritative:

"Guha Micha is a good place but we have lost it,

So now the Hanis are departing it and moving away.

Qisi zami, the wife of Nasuo,

Is most heroic among the Hani women.

All the Hanis must obey her,

And go wherever she asks us to go!"

The words of the headmen had just come out,

"Oho! Oho!" was the sound of great rejoicing.

The Hanis came in front of Qisi

And bowed deeply to her.

Seeing how the Hanis behaved,

Nasuo was furious:

---

① Qisi had a son named Luwei, and Masi had a son named Luce. Because of Qisi's generosity, Luwei and Luce, the two groups lived in harmony from generation to generation with no strife.

"哪个听见公鸡尾着母鸡叫？
哪个见过女人把男人鼻子牵？
戚姒本事再高再大，
也只是我纳索的女人！
不要听从搬家的话，
男人都跟我守住家园！"

戚姒抬起尊贵的手，
请全体哈尼安静下来，
金子样的好话说出口，
哈尼人人都听见：

"没有头人的哈尼，
像没有王的蜂群，
灾难来到的时候，
要围拢大头人身边！

"头人阿波们啊，
高能的扎纳去世了，
他的魂扛在纳索双肩，
我们要和纳索商商量量，
他还是哈尼的大头人！

"纳索啊，
头人不是没有教过的小牛，
爱跳就跳爱玩就玩，
你要听我戚姒的劝告，
快快领着哈尼搬迁！

"Who has ever heard cocks following a hen?
Who has ever seen a woman leading men by the nose?
No matter how capable Qisi is,
She is still my Nasuo's woman!
Don't listen to her talk about moving away;
All men guard the home with me!"

Qisi lifted up her noble hand,
Asking all the Hanis to be quiet.
Her words were as good as gold,
And every Hani was listening:

"The Hanis without the chieftain
Are like a swarm of bees without a king.
When disaster strikes,
We should stay closely around the chieftain!

"Headmen apos,
Since the capable Zhana passed away,
His soul is on Nasuo's shoulders.
We must discuss with Nasuo about our future,
As he is still the Hanis' chieftain!

"Oh Nasuo,
A chieftain is not an untaught calf,
Who jumps and plays as it wishes.
Take my advice
And lead the Hanis to move away quickly!

"雨有一天会停，
灾难有一天会解脱，
不能在坝子中心当一棵顶天的大树，
也可以到边远的大山上做一棵大树顶天。"

权威的戚岖把手一摆，
旁边走出八个哈尼，
八个人把纳索扛上肩头，
省得憨犟的头人又叫又哼。

趁着天黑雾大，
蒲尼望不见人，
哈尼马上起程前行，
悄悄离开谷哈平原。

众人：
萨——依——萨！

"The rain will stop one day,

As will the disaster end one day.

If we can't be a towering tree in the middle of the bazi,

We still can be a towering tree on the top of a mountain."

Then the authoritative Qisi waved her hand,

And eight Hanis walked out.

They lifted up Nasuo on their shoulders

So that this stubborn chieftain would not yell or whine.

While it was still dark, foggy,

And hard for the Punis to see anything,

They set out at once,

Quietly leaving the Guha plain.

Audience:

Sa—ee—sa!

七、森林密密的红河两岸

（一）

歌手：

萨——依——

谷哈不是哈尼的好地了，

哈尼又找着新的地方，

聪明的戚姒早已派人，

找到另一个山场。

好在的地方名叫那妥①，

天气没有谷哈凉爽，

三座大山围住平地，

竹篷密密站满山冈。

山下睡着宽宽的坝子，

就像朝前伸开的脚掌，

下方有潭碧绿的大水，

山头就能望见波浪闪光。

---

① 那妥：今通海。

Chapter 7　Dense Forest along the Red River

7. 1

Singer：

Sa—ee—

Guha was no longer a good place for the Hanis,

Who had found another place.

Smart Qisi had already sent out people,

Who had found another mountain field.

This good place was named Natuo①,

And it was not as cool as Guha.

The field was surrounded by mountains on three sides,

With lush green bamboo groves covering the mountains;

At the foot was the wide flat bazi,

Like the sole of a foot spreading forward.

The lower part was a pool of limpid blue water,

With sparkling waves that could be seen from the mountain top.

---

① Natuo：Tonghai County today.

瞧地的弟兄来说，
安寨的凹塘已经找着，
神山的基石已经埋好，
定界的石标已经栽上，
还顺手栽下哈尼的烟种，
黄烟是男人难离的伙伴，
只等大队去到新地，
就能把新烤的黄烟品尝。

听我说啊，亲亲的兄弟！
听我讲啊，一娘生的姊妹！
那妥阿惠①最香最软，
那妥阿惠最细最长，
你今天走去那妥瞧瞧吧，
先祖撒下的烟花还开在那方！

讲了，亲亲的兄弟姊妹，
哈尼大队来到那妥，
男人脸上沾满黄灰，
女人头发又乱又脏，
年老的阿波扎实火起，
说那妥是个不祥的山场。

老人的话金银样贵重，

---

① 阿惠：烟丝。

The brothers who found the new settlement reported:

The aotang for the village settlement had been found,

And the foundation stone on the sacred mountains had been buried;

The border stone had been erected;

The Hani tobacco seeds had also been planted,

Which is the men's inseparable partner.

It was only waiting for the arrival of the Hanis

Who could taste the newly cured tobacco.

Listen to me, dearest brothers!

Listen to me, sisters born from the same mother!

The ahui① of Natuo is the most fragrant and the softest,

The ahui of Natuo is the thinnest and the longest.

Go to Natuo today and see for yourself.

The tobacco flowers planted by our ancestors are still there.

Let's follow the stories, dearest brothers and sisters.

When the Hanis got to Natuo,

Men's faces were covered with yellow ashes,

And women's hair was messy and dirty.

Seeing this, an older apo was upset,

Saying that Natuo was not a blessed field.

The words of the elderlies were as valuable as gold and silver,

---

① Ahui: Cut tobacco.

他们的话能做药煨汤。
哈尼才开出大田，
各处的蒲尼①也随着搬来，
他们在平坝盖起大庙，
长声的钟鼓整天敲响。
这是些能干的查尼阿②，
不像谷哈的罗扎凶狂。
人人老牛般苦干，
个个喜鹊般会讲，
生着好心好肝，
有事也肯帮忙。

哈尼不愿和好人打架，
决定让出那妥地方，
查尼阿拉住哈尼的衣襟，
请先祖和蒲尼同在一方。

哈尼说小林难歇大象，
告别了蒲尼走向下方，
临走把最饱的烟种，
播在查尼阿的地上。

众人：

萨——依——萨！

---

① 蒲尼：此处的"蒲尼"专指汉族。
② 查尼阿：手艺人。"尼阿"二字连读，下面的"尼阿多"等
均如此。

As they were like the healing medicine and soup.

As soon as the Hanis cultivated the field,

The Punis① moved in from everywhere.

They built great temples on the flat place,

The bells and drums ringing all day long.

They were capable craftsmen Zhani'a②,

Not as ruthless as Luoza in Guha.

They worked hard like old cattle,

And could talk like magpies.

These warm-hearted people

Were always willing to offer help.

The Hanis did not want to fight with good people,

So they decided to give up Natuo.

The craftsmen Zhani'as pulled the Hanis' clothes

And asked our ancestors to stay with them.

The Hanis explained that a small grove could not accomodate elephants,

And then bid farewell to the Punis and moved down the mountains.

Before they left, they sprinkled the best seeds of tobacco

On the ground of the craftsmen Zhani'as' field.

Audience:

Sa—ee—sa!

---

① The Puni: Here it refers to the Han people.

② Zhani'a: The handicraftsman.

（二）

歌手：

萨——依——

像老鹰找歇翅的大树，

像胖鱼找喘气的水塘，

先祖走过下方的九山九岭，

哈尼涉过下方的大河大江，

靠着锄头样的脚板，

靠着甘蔗样的膝弯，

先祖来到了石七①，

又找着新的家乡。

石七的坝子巴掌样平，

石七的名字从不听讲，

山脚住着几家蒲尼，

山雀野猫和他们来往。

石七头人见着纳索，

脸上做出瞧不起的模样，

说话口气比水牛粗，

样样事情不爱商量。

听说哈尼要来同在，

张口闭口就要牛羊，

① 石七：今石屏。

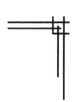

7.2

Singer：

Sa—ee—!

Like eagles looking for trees to rest,

Like big fish looking for pools to breathe,

Our ancestors crossed over nine mountains

And waded through the large rivers.

Relying on their feet that were like the hoes,

And knees that were like the sugarcanes,

Our ancestors came to Shiqi①,

Their new hometown.

The bazi in Shiqi was as flat as the palm of the hand,

And its name Shiqi was never talked about.

At the foot of mountains lived several Puni families,

Wild cats and titmice were their only neighbours.

When the chief of Shiqi met Nasuo

He had a look of contempt on his face.

He talked with a tone gruffer than a buffalo's moo

And refused to discuss anything with the Hanis.

As soon as he heard that the Hanis would like to settle here,

He started to ask for cattle and sheep.

---

① Shiqi：Shiping County today.

逗得纳索好气又好笑，
话像大刺一样硬邦：
"石七头人你竖起耳朵，
说话做事不要憨犟，
把你这小官放进眼睛，
还不如一颗细沙会梗会痒！"

石七头人害怕了，
赶紧强装笑样，
听说纳索汉姓姓李①，
也说："我和你姓一样。"
纳索问他李有十二李②，
十二李中姓哪样？
头人从来不听说，
张大嘴巴答不上。

哈尼在石七扎下，
大寨安在纳罗③山旁，
出名的大寨个个记得，
"纳罗普楚"④ 人人难忘。

---

① 中华人民共和国成立前许多哈尼人为躲避大汉族主义的压迫或钦慕汉文化而袭用汉姓，如本诗歌手和翻译者分别姓朱、卢而同时又有哈尼姓名。
② 十二李：哈尼按十二家支排列姓氏。
③ 纳罗：黑色的山，在今石屏县境内。
④ 纳罗普楚：黑山大寨，即今石屏哈尼大寨。

Nasuo felt mad but also amused.

So he sounded harsh like a thorn:

"Chief of Shiqi, prick up your ears,

Don't be stubborn when talking and acting.

Minor officers like you

Won't sting in the eye as much as a fine grain of sand does!"

The chief of Shiqi was afraid now

And hurriedly faked a smile.

He learned that Nasuo's Han surname was Li①,

So he said: "My surname is the same as yours."

Nasuo asked which Li was his

Among the twelve Li's②."

The chief had never heard of this

And so couldn't answer it.

The Hanis settled in Shiqi,

Setting up their village by the Naluo③ mountain.

The famous name of the village is known to all,

The unforgettable "Naluo Puchu."④

---

① Before the founding of the People's Republic of China, many Hani people used the Han surname to avoid the oppression of Han Chauvinism or to express their genuine admiration for the Han culture. For example, the singer and the translator of this epic had their own Hani names and also took the Han surname Zhu and Lu respectively.

② The twelve Li's: The Hani's family names are listed in twelve branches.

③ Naluo: The black Mountain, which is in Shiping County today.

④ Naluo Puchu: The big village in the Black Mountain; it is the Big Hani Village in Shiping today.

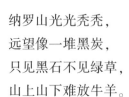
纳罗山光光秃秃，
远望像一堆黑炭，
只见黑石不见绿草，
山上山下难放牛羊。

哈尼不嫌石七穷苦，
先祖不怕纳罗荒凉，
寨头大山认作神山，
神明的基石好好安放，
山边寨脚开出平地，
盖起杀牛祭寨的秋房。

夜间坐拢一处，
男人女人商量，
穷处不是哈尼的在处，
要让石七好吃好住；
早上出去做活，
人人不怕出力，
荒凉贫瘠的石七，
一天变出七个样。

搬开黑亮的石头，
把大田开到山上，
引来清亮的泉水，
栽出绿绿的稻秧，
到秋风吹起的时候，
山上山下一片金黄。

The Naluo mountain was bare,

Like a pile of black charcoal seen from afar.

With black stones everywhere but no green grass,

The mountain was hardly a place for cattle and sheep could

graze.

The Hanis didn't mind the harsh environment of Shiqi,

Nor were they afraid of the desolation of the Naluo.

They deemed the mountain at the head of the village sacred

And placed the sacred foundation stone very well.

They cultivated and tilled some land by the mountain and the

village

And built up the village's sacrifice house qiufang.

At night, they sat together,

Men and women discussing.

A poor place was not for the Hanis,

So they must make Shiqi a good place to live in.

They left in the morning,

Not afraid of working hard.

The desolate and barren Shiqi

Changed seven times in one day.

The black shiny stones were removed,

And the terraces were built up on the mountain.

The sparkling spring was guided into the fields,

And the green rice seedlings were planted.

When the autumn breeze came,

The whole mountain was covered in golden.

有了好山好水，
盖起高高的蘑菇房，
有了好田好地，
阿妈把好儿生养，
看那高高的纳罗山上，
阿爸又把儿子的衣胞埋进土壤。

望见纳罗不穷，
望见石七变样，
望见哈尼吃着白亮的肉食，
望见哈尼喝着香甜的米酒，
石七头人心不来了，
要和先祖划开两旁。
七千哈尼只给一块地，
七百蒲尼拿去大地方，
还要哈尼给他做帮手，
还要拖走哈尼的牛和羊。
宽厚的先祖火冒三丈，
高能的纳索撸起臂膀；
两边又结成了冤家，
石七又变成了战场，
"嘀嘀"的牛角又吹起，
"上前"的吼声又叫响。

石七头人打不赢哈尼，
连夜从谷哈请人帮忙；
石七的蒲尼一下变多，
像纳罗的石头遍布山冈。

On the mountain and by the water,

The mushroom houses were built up high.

With the terraces and the fields,

Mothers gave birth and raised healthy children.

Look! On the high Naluo mountain,

Dads again buried their sons' afterbirth in the earth.

Seeing that the Nanuo was no longer poor,

Seeing that Shiqi had changed,

Seeing that the Hanis eat white and shiny meat,

Seeing that the Hanis drink the fragrant and sweet rice wine,

The chief of Shiqi was mad,

And demanded the land be divided between them and our ancestors.

The Hanis of seven thousand got the smaller half of land,

While the Punis of seven hundred got the larger half.

He also asked the Hanis to assist him,

Even required to take the Hanis' cattle and sheep.

The kind and generous ancestors were angry,

And the capable Nasuo rolled up his sleeves.

Once again the two sides became enemies,

Turning Shiqi into another battlefield.

"HOO—HOO—" the horns were blown again,

"Forward! Forward!" the roar rang out again.

The chief of Shiqi could not defeat the Hanis,

So overnight he asked for help from Guha.

The number of the Punis in Shiqi suddenly increased,

As many as the stones on the Naluo mountain.

哈尼阿培聪坡坡
Migrating Epic of the Hanis

打啰，杀啰！
哈尼又死去七十个兄弟！
杀啰，打啰！
哈尼又打失七十只牛羊！

新开的石七不能再往，
哈尼又要去到远方。
高能的戚姒召拢哈尼，
说出的话让人心伤：
"多灾多难的哈尼啊，
我们像细脚的麂子，
被人撵过数不清的山冈。
为了不给蒲尼杀完，
为了不让哈尼死光，
兄弟姊妹不能再欢聚一堂，
头人领着子孙各去一方！"

啊哟，心疼啰！
啊哟，扎实悲伤！
一处长大的兄弟要分开，
一处玩大的姐妹要离别；
阿波们不能再在一处咂烟闲谈，
扎密们不能再在一处把线纺！

分寨的日子哦，
像木刻刻在哈尼心上；

They fought, and they killed.

The Hanis lost another seventy brothers!

They killed, and they fought.

The Hanis lost another seventy cattle and sheep.

The newly-cultivated land in Shiqi could no longer be the place to live,

And the Hanis had to migrate to another far away land.

The capable Qisi had gathered the Hanis,

And what she said was heartbreaking:

"The Hanis who have suffered so much

Are like muntjacs with thin legs,

Being forced to cross countless hills.

To avoid all being killed by the Punis,

To prevent the Hanis from dying off,

Brothers and sisters could no longer happily stay together,

And the headmen must take their offsprings to different places!"

Alas! The hearts were broken!

Alas! It was really sad!

Brothers growing up together had to separate from each other.

Sisters growing up as playmates had to part from each other.

Apos could no longer smoke and chat together.

Zamis could no longer spin the threads together!

The date to divide the village

Was like the woodcut, engraved in the Hanis' heart;

分家的日子哦，
像烙铁烙在哈尼肝上。
石七的七千哈尼，
哭声震垮了纳罗山梁！

在高高的纳罗山头，
哈尼最后一次祭神；
在凹凹的纳罗山脚，
哈尼最后一次杀牛在秋房。
分寨的大典开始了，
七十个贝玛坐在高位上；
告别的时候来到了，
七十寨哈尼站在下方。
大大的水缸倒满清油，
碗粗的灯芯点得通亮，
神圣的灯光照着神山，
灯光映照在哈尼身上。

哈尼今后各走一方，
人人都把基石抚摸；
搬迁的哈尼背不走神山，
要把这神石放在心上。

瞧哦！
全体哈尼一齐跪下，

The date to break up the family,

Was seared, as if by a hot iron, into the Hanis' soul.

The seven thousand Hanis in Shiqi,

Cried so hard that the sound could break ridges of the Naluo mountain!

On the top of the Naluo mountain,

The Hanis made the sacrifice to the gods for the last time;

Down at the foot of the Naluo mountain,

The Hanis killed the oxen in the sacrifice house qiufang for the last time.

When the great ceremony of the village division began,

Seventy beimas were sitting in the high position.

When it was time to bid farewell,

Seventy villages of the Hanis were standing below.

A giant vat was filled with clear oil,

And bowl-thick wicks were lighted all bright.

Sacred light shone on the sacred mountain

And reflected on every Hani.

From then on, the Hanis went separate ways,

So everyone touched the foundation stone;

The migrating Hanis could not take the sacred mountain with them,

And they must put the foundation stone in their heart.

Look!

All the Hanis knelt

庄严的话对着神讲：
"不管我传到哪一代，
这神圣的基石不烂，
我不变哈尼的心肠！
不管我走到哪一方，
这高高的神山不死，
我永远认得哈尼的家乡！"

听哦！
七十个贝玛高声把话讲：
"分寨的哈尼人，
古规古矩最要紧，
后代的子孙来相认，
就看这古规忘不忘！

"不要忘啊，
一家最大的是供台，
一寨最大的是神山，
神山上块块石头都神圣，
神山上棵棵大树都吉祥，
砍着神树和神石，
抵得违犯了父母一样！

"不要忘啊，
建寨要照惹罗的规矩，
要竖那珍贵的贝壳①，

---

① 贝壳：哈尼的吉祥之物，详见第三章所述。哈尼族结婚一定要在箱底压上两个贝壳以示吉利。

386

Speaking solemnly to god:

"No matter how many generations I will carry on,

This sacred foundation stone will not crumble,

And my Hani heart and kindness will not change!

No matter where I go,

This sacred high mountain will live within me,

And I will always recognize the Hanis' homeland!"

Listen!

Seventy Beimas spoke loud and clear:

"The Hanis who are about to go in separate ways,

The ancient rites and rules are the most important.

Whether the future generations remain our descendants

Depend on whether they would forget all these ancient rites!

"Never forget—

The most important in a family is the altar,

And the most essential to a village is the sacred mountain.

Every stone in the sacred mountain is sacred,

And every tree in the sacred mountain is auspicious.

Damaging sacred trees and stones

Is the same as defying one's parents!

"Never forget!

When building a village, the rules in Reluo should be followed:

The precious shells① should be erected;

---

① Shell: An auspicious object for the Hanis. It is described in detail in Chapter Three. The Hani people must put two shells in the bottom of a trunk for good luck when getting married.

要拖那划界的肥狗，
要立那杀牛的秋房！

"哈尼人哦，
牢牢记住吧，
哈尼是老祖母塔婆的爱子，
大寨要安在那高高的凹塘；
寨头要栽三排棕树，
寨脚要栽三排金竹，
吃水要吃欢笑的泉水，
住房要住好瞧的蘑菇房！

"亲亲的哈尼人啊，
不能把哈尼的故乡遗忘：
不能忘记虎尼虎那的大水，
不能忘记惹罗普楚的山冈，
不能忘记诺马阿美的大田，
不能忘记谷哈密查的悲伤！

"哈尼人啊，
走到天边也要记住，
哈尼都是一个亲娘生养，
一个哈尼遭了灾难，
七个哈尼都要相帮！

The fat dog should be dragged along to mark the boundaries;

And the sacrifice house qiufang for killing the oxen should be built!

"The Hanis!

Keep in your mind,

The Hanis are Granny Tapo's favorite child.

The big village should be located highly in the aotang.

In front of the village three rows of palm trees should be planted,

And behind the village three rows of golden bamboo be planted.

Drink from the happy spring,

And live in the good looking mushroom houses!

"Dearest Hanis,

Do not forget our homeland;

Do not forget the waters of the Hunihuna mountain;

Do not forget the hills of the Reluo Puchu;

Do not forget the fields of the Nuoma Amei;

Do not forget the sorrows of Guha Micha!

"Ah, Hanis,

No matter how far you go, remember

That all Hanis were born from the same mother.

When one Hani is suffering,

Seven should help.

"啊啊！
叮嘱的话说完了，
我们的眼泪也流光！
快到四面八方去吧，
愿你们无论走到哪一处，
都像这遮天的竹篷一样茂盛；
愿你们无论去到哪一方，
都像这标直的棕树一样刚强！"

离了，离了，
亲亲的兄弟姊妹，
先祖离开了石七地方！

走了，走了，
亲亲的哈尼后代，
先祖像山水淌向四面八方！

众人：
萨——哝——萨！

<h2 style="text-align:center">（三）</h2>

歌手：
萨——依——
石七头人好似豺狗，
想把哈尼赶尽杀光，
领着蒲尼紧紧追来，
一日要打三次大仗。

"Ah!

All that should be said have been said,

And all the tears we have have been shed!

Set out in all directions.

Wherever you are,

May you prosper like this thick bamboo bush.

Wherever you go,

May you be strong like this straight palm tree!"

Leaving,

Dearest brothers and sisters,

Our ancestors left Shiqi.

Walking away,

Dearest Hani descendants,

Our ancestors were like the mountain spring flowing in all directions!

Audience:

Sa—nong—sa!

7.3

Singer:

Sa—ee—!

The chief of Shiqi was like a jackale,

Who wanted to kill all the Hanis.

He led the Punis to chase after the Hanis,

Who had to fight three battles every day.

戚妮率领哈尼大队，
去找新的地方；
纳索领着七百好汉，
把蒲尼追兵阻挡。

分手的时候到来了，
戚妮对丈夫把话讲：
"扎纳阿波已经死去，
高大的身子变冷变僵，
他把哈尼福气带去，
苦难像大山压在我们头上。

"纳索啊，亲人！
虽说你武艺高强力大如牛，
也千万不要贪打恋战。
我领着大队朝前去，
你打退蒲尼快赶上，
哈尼等你来做主，
羊群盼着领头羊。

"前头有条哈查①，
翻滚着红红的大浪，
在红水的两边，
是青青的大山。
那里有遮天的大树，

————————————

① 哈查：大江，指红河。

392

Qisi led the main team of the Hanis

To look for a new place;

Nasuo led seven hundred heroes,

To stop the Punis' pursuits.

When they parted their way,

Qisi said to her husband:

"Apo Zhana has died,

And his tall body is cold and stiff.

He took with him the Hanis' good luck,

Sufferings like a mountain weighing us down.

"Nasuo, my dear!

Even though you are skilled in fighting and as strong as a

bull,

Please don't enjoy doing it.

I will lead the team forward,

But you catch up with us as soon as you defeat the Punis.

The Hanis will be waiting for you to be their leader,

Just like the sheep long for theirs.

"There is a hacha① ahead,

Where huge red waves are rolling.

On both sides of the red water,

Are green mountains,

Where big trees shade the sky,

---

① Hacha: Big river. It refers to the Red River in Yunnan Province.

那里有暖和的凹塘，
恶鬼恶人难找到，
是哈尼中意的地方。
纳索啊，男人，
我丢掉百样珍宝，
只带上你的酒壶烟筒；
我打好软软的棕鞋，
等你穿鞋过江!"

细心的戚姒留下马姒，
叫她和头人纳索做伴，
她知道纳索脾气暴躁，
只有老婆能和他说话商量。

听说大队不在，
蒲尼追得更猛，
纳索边打边退，
去到建水山上。

几天几夜爬山，
脚杆又麻又酸，
几天几夜打架，
手杆又痛又胀。
哈尼又中毒气①，
个个睡倒山上，

---

① 毒气：指瘟疫。

And an autong provided warmth.

Evil spirits and wicked people could hardly find it,

And it is the kind of place the Hanis are looking for.

Nasuo, my man,

I left behind hundreds of treasures,

But brought with me only your wine pot and cigarette pipe;

I have made soft straw sandals

For you to wear when you cross the river!"

The very thoughtful Qisi made Masi to stay behind,

To accompany Chieftain Nasuo.

She knew that even though Nasuo had a quick temper,

His wife could still talk with him.

When the Punis learned the main team had left,

They intensified their chase.

Nasuo was fighting but also retreating

Back onto the Jianshui mountain.

Days and nights of climbing the mountains

Left them with numb and sore legs;

Days and nights of fighting

Left them with aching and swelling arms.

The Hanis were also decimated by poison gas[1],

Falling to the ground and falling asleep.

---

① Poison gas: It refers to plague.

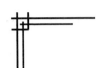

七百哈尼被捉，
手脚一齐被绑，
蒲尼不捉马妮，
她是阿篇的姑娘。

石七头人喜欢死啰，
提着大刀来找纳索，
找着纳索就找着金银，
好到谷哈密查领赏。
等到翻遍七百哈尼，
不知纳索去到哪方！

——听啰，一寨的兄弟，
纳索是天神的后人，
扎纳歇在他的肩上；
纳索是高能的哈尼，
会变千样万样。
他变成一棵大树，
阴凉铺满四方。

蒲尼热得冒烟，
坐到树下躲凉，
身子刚靠上树，
大刀架在脖子上，
转眼被砍死一片，
个个喊爹喊娘。

多多的蒲尼围拢，

Severn hundred Hanis were arrested,
Their hands and feet bound up.
The Punis did not arrest Masi,
For she was the Apian's daughter.

The chief of Shiqi was so happy
That he came with the broadsword to look for Nasuo.
If he found Nasuo,
He would be rewarded by Guha Micha.
He searched through the seven hundred Hanis
But could not find Nasuo!

—Listen! Brothers from one village,
Nasuo is the descendent of the god of the heaven,
With Zhana watching over him on his shoulders.
Nasuo was a super-Hani
Who could take on variable forms.
He became a big tree,
Shading everywhere around it.

The Punis were so hot
That they sat under a tree to cool off.
As soon as they leaned against the tree,
The broadswords were on the necks.
Many Punis were killed in a flash,
Every single one screaming and crying.

Many more Punis came up,

见着大树就砍光；
纳索又变成巨石，
平平地躺在路旁。

蒲尼砍得手软，
身子像朵棉花，
望见石头又平又滑，
争抢坐处又推又搡。
石头突然翻过身来，
把他们压死压伤。
石七头人发起狠心，
又把纳索围在中央，
见着石头就砍就剁，
不怕大刀砍缺砍断。

山腰走来马帮，
马铃叮咚作响，
驮子上驮着木头，
马锅头①单在马上，
纳索又变成木头，
在驮子上摇摇晃晃。

砍烂一山石头，

---

① 马锅头：红河流域对赶马人的习称，他们多爱骑单边马，即
双脚迈向一边，这是哀牢山区马帮的特点。

Cutting down all the trees they saw.

Nasuo turned into a boulder then,

Lying flat beside the road.

The Punis' hands were droopy,

Their bodies feeling cottony.

Seeing that the stone was flat and smooth,

They pushed and shoved their way just to sit on it.

The boulder suddenly flipped over

Injuring and crushing them all.

The chief of Shiqi turned cruel,

Giving the order to besiege Nasuo.

They also started to chop up all rocks they saw,

Their broadswords chipped, cracked, and broken.

Then a caravan of horses came from the hillside,

With the horse bells tinkling.

They were loaded with logs

And also those maguotous① riding with their legs on one

side.

Nasuo had changed to logs now,

Rocking and swaying on the back of the horse.

Having chopped up the rocks of the whole mountain,

---

① Maguotou: The nickname for the caravan in the Red River valley. These people like to ride the horses with both of their legs on one side, a practice that characterizes the horsemen in the Ailao Mountains.

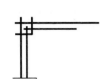

还是不见纳索，
石七头人又吼又叫，
好像饿虎纵下山冈：
"哈尼，
快快交出纳索！
不交，
就把你们杀光！"

纳索听见吼声，
把马奴悄悄叫到身旁：
"扎密啊，我的女人！
要救出七百哈尼，
只有我来偿命。
你叫蒲尼快快住手，
说我纳索就在身旁！"

自从跟随戚奴扎密，
马奴换了一副心肠，
已经不是蒲尼女人，
变成一个哈尼姑娘。

瞧见纳索变来变去，
马奴心里阵阵喜欢，
听说纳索要去抵命，
马奴一阵一阵悲伤：
"亲亲的男人哦，
高能的纳索！

The chief of Shiqi still found no Nasuo.

He roared

Like a hungry tiger running down the mountain:

"Hanis,

Turn in Nasuo!

Otherwise,

I will kill you all!"

Nasuo heard the roar

And quietly called Masi to his side:

"Zami, my woman!

My life is the only way

To trade for those of the seven hundred Hanis.

Ask the Punis to stop right away

Because I, Nasuo, am here."

Since she came under the influence of Qisi zami,

Masi had become kind.

She was no long a Puni woman,

But a Hani one.

Seeing Nasuo changed his forms,

Masi was very happy.

But on hearing Nasuo's decision to sacrifice his life,

Masi was very sad:

"My dearest husband,

My powerful Nasuo!

我怎能望着你去死，
我怎能去对蒲尼讲？
我没有这样的狠心，
我没有这样的狠肠！"

纳索的话像刀砍，
马奴没有了主张，
只好答应头人纳索，
去对蒲尼把话讲。①

蒲尼答应马奴，
松开哈尼的捆绑，
把纳索烧成灰堆，
又拿石槽②来装。

哈尼的大头人纳索，
死在建水山上，
后代子孙不忘祖先，
过山过水来到这地方。
山上盖起纳索大庙，
庙里供着纳索石像，
虔诚的大礼行过三遍，
黄黄的烟丝献上三撮，

---

　① 又一说马奴在迁徙途中仍出卖哈尼，纳索即被她出卖而死，
与原诗不符。
　② 石槽：石棺。

How can I watch you die?

How should I speak to the Punis?

I don't have such a cruel heart,

I don't have such savagery!"

But Nasuo's words were like the cutting of a sword,

And Masi wavered in her determination.

She ended up agreeing to follow his order

And to speak to the Punis.①

They did as Masi requested,

And untied the arrested Hanis,

Burned Nasuo into ashes,

And put them into a stone box②.

The Hani Chieftain Nasuo

Died on the Jianshui Mountain.

Later generations remembered their ancestor

And, crossing mountains and rivers, they visited this place.

A big Nasuo Temple was built in the mountain

And inside it was a stone statue of Nasuo.

Piously bowing three times,

They also offered three pinches of tobacco,

---

① Another version of the story is that Masi kept betraying the Hanis during the migration, and Nasuo died as a result of Masi's betrayal, which is inconsistent with the story in this epic.

② Stone box: Stone coffin.

过山过水的哈尼人啊，
会得纳索头人的保护，
爬山脚不酸，
下箐脚不软，
痨病能躲脱，
瘟病染不上！①

众人：
萨——依——萨！

（四）

歌手：
萨——依——
马奴领着七百哈尼，
翻过七座钻天大山，
在红水滚滚的江边，
把哈尼大队赶上。
听说纳索英勇战死，
七千哈尼痛哭悲伤，
红河两边深深的峡谷，
哈尼的呼喊久久回荡。

戚奴揩干眼泪，
下令马上出发，

---

① 据说中华人民共和国成立前建水山上的纳索庙还在。

The Hanis passing through those mountains and rivers

Would be protected by Nasuo.

They could go up the mountains with no sore feet

And come down the valleys without quivering legs.

They could be unaffected by consumption

Or escape from the plagues!①

Audience:

Sa—ee—sa!

7.4

Singer:

Sa—ee—

Masi led seven hundreed Hanis,

Crossed seven skyscraping mountains.

At the bank of the Red River of roaring red waves

They caught up with the Hanis' main team.

Hearing that Nasuo fought to his death,

The seven thousand Hanis burst into tears.

In the deep valleys along the Red River

Long echoed the shouts and cries.

Qisi wiped away her tears

And gave orders to move forward.

---

① It is said that before the founding of the People's Republic of China, the Nasuo Temple on the Jianshui Mountain was still there.

哈尼顺着红河，
走到江尾下方①。

下方天气扎实热，
好像背着大大的火塘，
牛马猪鸡张嘴喘气，
大人小娃身上发痒。

老林厚是厚了，
草也发得很旺，
只是到处爬大蛇，
沿途处处遇老象。

猪羊蹄子烂了，
骏马牙齿掉光，
公鸡不会啼鸣，
狗也不会汪汪，
母牛下儿难活，
母马养儿死光，
阿妈生下的小娃，
只能活过三早上！

下方在不得了，
哈尼又来上方，
趁着枯水的干季，
渡过红河大江。

_____

① 指红河下游地区，越南境内。

Following the Red River,
The Hanis came to the lower reaches①.

There it was such burning hot
As if a fireplace were on everyone's back.
Cattle, horses, pigs and chicken were all panting heavily,
And the Hanis, old and young, were itching all over.

The forests were indeed dense,
And the grass, vigorous,
But pythons appeared everywhere,
So did old elephants along the way.

The hoofs of pigs and sheep were worn out,
And the horses' teeth were gone.
The cock couldn't crow,
Nor could the dog bark.
The calves could hardly survive,
And all the foals died out.
The newborn babies
Could but see three mornings!

The lower land was no longer a place to stay in,
So the Hanis then moved to the upper land.
Taking advantage of the dry season,
They crossed the big Red River.

---

① It refers to the lower reaches of the Red River, within the borders
of Vietnam.

找着的第一块好地，
名字叫作"策打"①，
那是清水旺旺的山坡，
厚密的树林围着凹塘。

挖出大片坡地，
梯田开山上梁，
支起高高的荡秋，
盖起三层的寨房。

第一次丰收季节，
玉米堆得像山；
第二次收获的日子，
红米堆齐屋梁。
小狗也养成胖狗，
瘦羊也喂成肥羊，
小娃喜笑颜开，
老人脸上发光。

戚姒把策打让给马姒，
领着儿子找新的地方。
戚姒的恩情比哀牢山大，
马姒卢策永远不忘。

戚姒马姒比姊妹还亲，
卢威卢策像一娘生养，

——————————

① 策打：地名，不详。

The first good land they found
They named it "Ceda"①.
It was the hillside featuring clear water,
Thickets surrounding the aotang.

Cultivating a large piece of land on the hillside,
They built terraces up the mountain ridges.
Setting up high swing sets,
They also built the three-story houses.

The first harvest season
Had the corn piled up like a mountain;
The second one
Had the red rice piled up to the beam of the barn.
The puppies were fattened,
So were the sheep.
Little children smiled,
And the elderlies' faces were glowing.

Qisi let Masi stay in Ceda
And left with her son to find a new place.
Qisi had a heart bigger than the Ailao Mountains,
And Masi and Luce would never forget.

Qisi and Masi were closer than sisters,
And Luwei and Luce were like born from the same mother.

---

① Ceda: The name of a place. Its location today is unknown.

新寨老寨相帮相助，
代代子孙你来我往。

众人：
萨——依——萨！

<h1 style="text-align:center">（五）</h1>

歌手：
讲了，一寨的兄弟姐妹！
讲了，先祖的后代子孙！
好听的哈八唱过九天九夜，
唱歇了哀牢山上的大风，
唱平了红河里的大浪，
今晚单唱我们艾乐，
怎样找着尼阿多①家乡。

众人：
萨——依——萨！

歌手：
从前哈尼爱找平坝，

---

① 尼阿多：地名，今元阳县境内，是红河南岸最富饶、美丽的
地方，哈尼以其为骄傲；旧译"鸟多""丫多"，不准确。

The new and old villages helped each other,

Their descendants are close generation after generation.

Audience:

Sa—ee—sa!

7.5

Singer:

Let's tell stories, brothers and sisters of a same village!

Let's tell stories, descendants of the ancestors!

The pleasant Haba drinking song had been sung for nine

days and nights,

Which stopped the wind on the Ailao Mountains,

And calmed waves in the Red River.

Tonight I will only sing about our Aile,

About how the homeland Ni'aduo① was found.

Audience:

Sa—ee—sa!

Singer:

The Hanis used to be fond of flat bazi,

────────────

① Ni'aduo: The name of a place. It is in today's Yuanyang County. It is said to be the most fertile and beautiful place in the south bank of the Red River, which is Hanis' pride. The old translations "Niaoduo" or "Yaduo" are not accurate.

平坝给哈尼带来悲伤，
哈尼再不找坝子了，
要找厚厚的老林高高的山场。
山高林密的凹塘，
是哈尼亲亲的爹娘。

权威的戚姒领着哈尼，
走遍了江外所有大山，
处处都有好在的歇处，
戚姒要找最好的地方。

这天队伍停在山坡，
哈尼正在喝水歇凉，
树上飞来一只白鹇，
轻轻走过哈尼身旁。

白鹇走到戚姒面前，
摇摇身子抖动翅膀，
一片白云样的羽毛，
轻轻飘到戚姒手上。

白鹇抬起细细的红脚，
走一步拍一下翅膀，
白白亮亮的羽毛，
像银子闪闪发光，
银光闪闪的小路，
铺向树多的山冈。

Which brought them only saddness.

They now no longer looked for bazi,

But they looked rather for dense forests and high mountains.

The aotang surrounded by thick trees and in the high mountains

Became the dearest parents of the Hanis.

The authoritative Qisi led the Hanis

And went through all the mountains by the Red River.

There were places suited for settlement everywhere,

But Qisi wanted the best.

One day, the team stopped on a hillside,

And the Hanis were drinking and resting there.

A silver pheasant flew down from a tree,

Gently pacing along the Hanis' side.

It gently walked up to Qisi and standing in front of her,

It shook its body and flickered its wings.

A feather white like the cloud

Floated onto Qisi's hand.

The sivler pheasant started to move its slim and red feet,

Flapping its wings at every step.

The white and bright feathers

Shone like pieces of silver,

Paving the little path

That led to the hills covered with trees.

戚妣跟着白鹇，
走进旺旺的草丛，
绕过高高的老崖，
望见迷人的地方。

只见山坡又宽又平，
好地一台连着一台，
山梁又斜斜缓缓，
好像下插的手掌。
下头三个山包，
恰似歇脚的板凳，
中间空空的平地，
正是合心的凹塘。

再看高高的山腰，
站满根粗枝密的大树，
老藤像千万条大蛇，
缠在大树身上。

又看平缓的山坡，
淌过清亮的溪水，
舀起一捧喝喝，
甜得像蜜糖一样。

再看山头和山箐，
野物老实多啦：
细脚的马鹿啃吃嫩草，
大嘴的老虎追逐岩羊，

Qisi followed the silver pheasant
Into the lush grassy land,
Around the high cliffs,
And finally saw an amazing place.

The hillsides were broad and flat,
With fertile farm land terrace after terrace.
The ridges were stretched downward gradually,
Like the palm of a hand facing down.
The three hills towards the bottom
Looked exactly like a footrest.
In the middle was an open and flat land,
Precisely is the desirable aotang.

Behold, the high mountain sides
Were filled with ancient and dense trees.
Old rattans were like thousands and thousands of pythons
Winding themselves around big trees.

Behold, the gentle slopes of the mountains
Were marked by streams of clear and bright water,
Which could be scooped up
And tasted like honey candies.

Behold, the peaks and valleys of the mountains
Were the home of wild animals living harmoniously together:
Small-hoofed red deer grazing,
Big-mouthed tigers chasing the rock-climbing sheep,

狐狸在剑茅丛里出没，
老熊在大树干上擦痒；
岩脚深深的草棵里，
野猪呲着獠牙喘气，
坡头密密的竹林里，
竹鼠眯细眼睛把嫩笋尝；
大群鹦鹉在小树上嬉戏，
成对的鹧鸪在刺蓬里鸣唱；
披着黄衣的龙子雀，
在树枝上跳上跳下，
扇着黑翅的老鸹，
在树顶上哈哈笑响。
……

这边瞧过瞧那边，
上方听过听下方，
水淌雀唱的山窝，
戚姒把它爱上。

哦嗬的声音喊出欢喜，
嚓嚓的脚步走得匆忙，
劈开高高的刺蓬，
戚姒走进了凹塘。

凹塘里歇着大群白鹇，
好像白云飘落这方，
望见人来轻轻啼叫，
不飞不躲像把话讲。

Foxes hanging out here and there,

And old bears itching on the big trunk.

In the midst of the grass under the rocks,

Wild boars, fangs revealed, were breathing heavily.

In the dense bamboo forests,

Bamboo squirrels, eyes half closed, licked the tender bamboo shoots.

A large flock of parrots were playing on the small trees,

While pairs of partridge were singing in the thorns.

Dragon-finches, in yellow capes,

Skipping among the branches.

Crows, flapping their wings,

Laughing on the top of the trees.

...

Having checked out here and there,

Listened everywhere up and down,

This mountain with water running and birds singing

Qisi fell in love with.

Chuckling her joy happily,

Rustling her steps hurriedly,

Parting the high thorn bushes,

Qisi came to the aotang.

There were resting a large gaggle of silver pheasants,

Like the white clouds had befallen the place.

Seeing people approaching, the birds crowed gently,

Not fleeing but like speaking.

白鹇是吉祥的鸟，
白鹇是哈尼的伴，
白鹇喜欢的地方哈尼也喜欢，
白鹇的家乡也是哈尼的家乡。

顺着白鹇铺出的银路，
哈尼大队走进山场，
个个眼睛亮光闪闪，
把神灵的恩惠赞扬。

男人解开斜口的大襟，
脖子上揩了五把汗，
额头上揩了三把汗，
一边揩一边把嘴嗒响；
女人捧起清清的泉水，
脸上洗了三把凉，
头上洗了五把凉，
一面洗一面啧啧夸奖。

见着这块好地，
公鸡白日也叫了，
鸭子晚上也唱了，
大马也闻见青草香，
挣脱缰绳跑上山冈。

嗬嗬！
有十七层皱纹的阿波开口了，
认定这是哈尼合心的地方；

Silver pheasants are an auspicious bird,

Silver pheasants are companions of the Hanis.

The place they like is also liked by the Hanis,

Their homeland is also the Hanis'.

Following the silvery road paved by the silver pheasant,

The Hanis walked into the mountain.

Everyone's eyes were shining,

Praising the blessings of the gods.

Men untied their robes that tied on the side,

Wiped their sweaty necks five times,

And their sweaty foreheads three times,

While clicking their tongues.

Women scooped up the clear spring water,

Splashed it on their faces three times

And their heads five times,

While uttering praises.

Seeing this good land,

Roosters crowed at dawn

And ducks quacked at dusk.

Horses could smell the fragrance of the grass,

Freed themselves from the rein and made a dash to the hills.

Hah hah!

The apo with seventeen layers of wrinkles confirmed,

It was exactly the place for the Hanis.

缺掉十七颗牙的阿匹说话了，
认定这是哈尼合心的家乡；
共扶一架犁耙的十个男人开口了，
认定这是哈尼发家兴旺的宝地；
共操一架纺车的十个女人说话了，
认定这是哈尼子孙繁衍的地方！

嗬嗬！
哈尼把寨子立起来了，
寨基就安在窝窝的凹塘，
这是哈尼挂头名的好地，
江外再找不着更好的地方，
要说寨子的名字——
"尼阿多"比打雷响亮！

江外的哈尼聚集这里，
尼阿多是哈尼的靠望：
来啰！
脚跛的阿波，
气喘的阿匹，
腿软的扎谷，
生病的阿妮——
都来到这方！

来啰！
背着鸡鸭，

The api with seventeen missing teeth confirmed,

It was exactly the homeland for the Hanis.

Ten men who used the same ploughshare confirmed,

They were sure it was the treasure place where the Hanis would thrive.

Ten women who used the same spinning wheel confirmed,

They were sure it was where the Hanis would raise their children!

Hah hah!

The Hanis built the village,

With its center being set around the hollow aotang.

It was the number one place among the Hanis,

No better place than this could be found.

As for the name of the village——

"Ni'aduo" sounded louder than the thunder!

All the Hanis along the river gathered here,

And Ni'aduo was the hope of the Hanis.

Come!

The limpy apos,

Breathless apis,

Exhausted zagus

Unwell anis——

All come here!

Come!

Carry the chickens and geese;

吆着小猪，
牵着小牛，
拉着小羊——
都走拢这方！

来啰，来啰，
放下宽片的大刀，
拿起窄片的砍刀，
歇下三分的长矛，
扛起三尖的锄头，
先祖要丢掉逃难的日子，
哈尼要在新地栽种米粮！

瞧哦，
先祖又把古规在尼阿多传扬：
上头的山包做枕头，
下头的山包做歇脚，
两边的山包做护手，
寨子就睡在正中央；
神山神树样样不缺，
寨房秋房样样恰当。

先祖的古规十足十美，
尼阿多又添出新的一样：
从前庄严的阿玛突，
只把寨神供在上方，
今后哈尼的阿玛突，
要把尊贵的戚姒祭献颂扬！

Coax the piglets;

Lead the calves

And the lambs—

All come here together!

Come! Come!

Put down the broadswords,

And take up the narrow machetes.

Release the three-feet spears.

Pick up the three-point hoes.

Our ancestors wanted to stop running away

And the Hanis wanted to grow crops!

Look!

The ancestors proclaimed the ancient rules in Ni'aduo:

The top of the mountain as the pillow,

The bottom as the foot rest.

Hills on both sides as the hand guards,

The village slept in the middle.

Sacred mountains and sacred trees were all set,

The village houses and sacrifice houses were all built in order.

Although the ancestors' rules were perfect,

Ni'aduo added another:

The Amatus in the past

Only put on the altar the god of village,

The Amatus from now on

Would make sacrifices to praise the distinguished Qisi!

记住啊，亲亲的兄弟姊妹！
戚姒是哈尼最大的能人，
她的地位和寨神一样。
她是最直最高的大树，
威严地站在哈尼山上，
她有最大最多的神力，
保护着哈尼子孙牛羊。

众人：
萨——依——萨！

歌手：
瞧哦，亲亲的寨人！
尼阿多像山上的旺笋，
一天比一天长高长壮！
瞧那寨脚开出台台梯田，
层层稻秧比罗比草兴旺；
瞧那寨头开出片片坡地，
块块荞子比乌山草更旺；
猪鸡鸭鹅老实爱肥，
骡马牛羊老实爱壮；
小娃玩耍像猴子热闹，
老人吃烟像打雷样响。

哈尼在尼阿多不出三年，
名声随大风刮到四方。
鸡叫狗咬把生人引进寨子，

Remember, dearest brothers and sisters!

Qisi is the best among the Hanis,

Her status is the same as the village god.

She is like the most upright and tallest tree,

Standing with dignity at top of the Hani Mountain.

She gathered in her the most of the divine power

That protects the Hani descendants and their livstock.

Audience:

Sa—ee—sa!

Singer:

Look, dearest fellow villagers!

Ni'aduo was like the thriving bamboo shoots,

Growing taller and stronger day after day.

Look at the terraced fields at the foot of the village,

Layer upon layer of the rice seedlings more prosperous than
the weeds.

Look at the fields cultivated on the slops.

The buck wheat grew more vigorous than the wushan grass.

Pigs, chickens, ducks and geese were fat.

And mules, horses, cattle and goats were strong.

Children were playing as lively as the monkeys,

And elderlies were smoking as loudly as the thunders.

The Hanis had not been in Ni'aduo three years,

But their reputation was spread by the wind in all directions.

The sound of chicken and dogs led the strangers into the village,

做生意的蒲尼常来游逛。
他们挑来女人喜爱的丝线，
男人爱使的东西也各式各样。
哈尼换出的红米腊肉虎皮，
把蒲尼壮汉压得摇摇晃晃。

纳索玛①有七十个男人的智慧，
走遍了江外的大小山冈，
哀牢山上的块块石头，
她都熟得像手心的纹样。

纳索玛说给寨人：
"亲亲的子孙后代，
听我把要紧的话讲：
不要怕磨通脚上的九层老茧，
不要怕勒烂背箩筐的肩膀，
快去占下江外的地盘，
快去开发哈尼的家乡。
哈尼来到一处新地，
蒲尼也尾到这方，
不比马鹿快就撵不着马鹿，
哈尼要有快快的脚和硬硬的肩膀！"

---

① 纳索玛：纳索的妻子，即戚姒，这样称呼表示尊敬。

And the Puni merchants often went to visit.

They carried the silk threads that women loves

And things men liked were plenty, too.

The Hanis' red rice, preserved meat, and tiger leather

Weighed so much on the Punis that they were stambling a-round.

Nasuo Ma① had the smarts of seventy men,

Checking out all the mountains and hills by the river.

Every stone on the Ailao Mountains

She knew as well as her palm print.

She told her fellow villagers:

"Dearest descendants,

Listen to me on something very important:

Don't be afraid to grind through the nine-layered callus on your feet.

Don't be afraid to work your shoulders raw from carring the baskets.

Hurry and claim the territory down the river,

To develop the new homeland for the Hanis.

When the Hanis have come to a new place,

The Punis are to follow.

Unless you're faster than the red deer, you cannot catch up with them,

And the Hanis need faster feet and stronger shoulders!"

---

① Nasuo Ma: The wife of Nasuo. It refers to Qisi. Others address Qisi this way to show respect.

听见老祖母的吩咐，

哈尼像蜜蜂搬家分房，

分家的头人抱着白鹇，①

领着寨人去到新的山冈。

第一个能干的头人楚依，

领着哈尼去到瓦渣②，

由他传下的楚依这支，

至今还在瓦渣地方。

楚依头人多才多艺，

白鹇跳舞他也比样，

他是第一个编白鹇舞③的人，

"哈森阿波"④ 名扬四方。

楚依的儿子叫略博⑤，

把白鹇舞跳遍山乡，

---

① 因为白鹇为哈尼引了路，所以此后凡哈尼搬迁，都要抱着一
只小白鹇，认为白鹇是指引道路的神鸟。

② 瓦渣：红河县一地名。

③ 白鹇舞：哈尼族的代表性舞蹈，通过对白鹇各种动态的模仿，
借以表达哈尼对吉祥幸福的企望。

④ 哈森阿波：编舞的师傅。

⑤ 此处人物姓氏与哈尼族的父子连名制有出入，不详。

On hearing the words of the old grandmother,

The Hanis started moving and dividing their chambers like bees.

The headmen held silver pheasants①

And led the villagers to the new hills.

The first capable headman was Chuyi,

Who led some Hanis to Wazha②.

This Chuyi branch that followed him

Is still in Wazha today.

Headman Chuyi was a talented man,

Mimicking the silver pheasants when they danced.

He was the first one who choreographed the Silver Pheasant Dance③,

"Hasen Apo" ④ is the renowned name spread everywhere.

Chuyi's son was called Luebo⑤,

Who brought the dance to all mountain villages.

---

① The silver pheasant led the Hanis to find out their settlement. Since then, whenever the Hanis move, they carry a small silver pheasant, believing that the magic bird can guide their way.

② Wazha: The name of a place in Honghe (Red River) County.

③ The Silver Pheasant Dance: The Hani representative dance. By imitating the silver pheasant's dynamic moves, the Hanis express their aspiration for good fortune and happiness.

④ Hasen Apo: The master choreographer.

⑤ For some reason, there is a discrepancy between the names mentioned here and the customary Hani patronymic system.

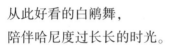
从此好看的白鹇舞，
陪伴哈尼度过长长的时光。

略博生下两个扎密，
好像天上一对月亮，
卢威瞧着最好的妹子，
把她讨进自己的蘑菇房。

讲了，先祖的后代儿孙！
自从楚依分了寨子，
尼阿多的哈尼各去一方，
江外最清最甜的水边，
哀牢最肥最软的土上，
到处有哈尼的子孙，
到处都有哈八在唱。

大寨生出小寨，
小寨生出新寨；
大寨是小寨的阿哥，
小寨是新寨的亲娘；
哈尼寨子布满哀牢山，
像数不清的星星缀在天上。

跟着分家的楚依头人，
罗纳头人也走出家乡，
领着术娃、罗纳两支，
扎在两个不远的山冈。

From then on, the beautiful Silver Pheasant Dance
Has accompanied the Hanis for a long time.

Luebo had two zamis,
Who were like a pair of moons in the sky.
Luwei fell in love with the most gorgeous girl
And married her to his mushroom house.

That's the story, ancestor's descendants!
Ever since Chuyi started the new village,
The Hanis in Ni'aduo went their separate ways.
By the clearest and tastiest water down the river,
And on the most fertile and softest soil in the Ailao
Mountains,
Hani's descendants were everywhere,
And Haba the drinking song was sung everywhere.

Big villages generated small ones,
Which generated new ones.
Big villages were the elder brother of the small ones,
Who were the mother of the new ones.
The Hani villages covered the Ailao Mountains,
Like the countless stars adorning in the sky.

Following the headman Chuyi,
Headman Luona also moved away from the homeland,
Leading two branches, Shuwa and Luona,
And settled in two hills not too far away.

罗纳是个宽厚的头人，
让彝族兄弟住在身旁，
从此罗纳的大寨，
成了两族的家乡，
"哈尼哈窝提玛札"①，
两族兄弟都爱讲。

第三个头人叫罗赫，
在竹鹿②安下了寨房；
策打的儿孙也搬来，
一处做活一起商量，
人多地少在不下，
兄弟又为分家忙：

早上分出去的是罗蒲寨，
下午分出去的是麻栗寨，
麻栗寨是世上最大的哈尼寨，
山腰上盖满七百个蘑菇房。

第二日早上又分出一支，
领寨的头人名叫必扎，

---

① 哈尼哈窝提玛札：这是流传在红河南岸哈尼族地区的名谚，
意为"哈尼族彝族是一娘生"或"老大老二一娘生"。
② 此处提及的竹鹿及下文提及的罗蒲、麻栗、必扎、洞铺等均
是元阳县境内地名，恕不详注。

Luona was a kind headman
And he allowed the Yi people to live nearby.
Ever since then, Luona's village
Became the homeland of the two ethnic groups.
"Hani Hawo timaza"①,
Both groups were fond of saying.

The third headman was called Luohe,
Whose village was settled in Zhulu②.
When the grandchildren of Ceda joined them,
They worked together but decided
That the space was not enough,
So they split again among themselves.

In the morning, the Luopu Village left,
And in the afternoon, the Mali Village did.
Mali became the largest Hani village in the world,
Seven hundred mushroom houses covering the mountainside.

The next morning another group moved away,
Its headman's name was Biza.

---

① Hani Hawo timaza: This is a well-known proverb used in the Hani region on the south bank of the Red River. It means "The Yi and the Hani were born from the same mother" or "the elder brother, the younger brother were born from the same mother".

② Zhulu mentioned here and Luopu, Mali, Biza and Dongpu mentioned below are all names of places in Yuanyang County.

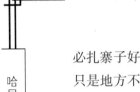

必扎寨子好是好了，
只是地方不够宽敞。
必扎、罗蒲和竹鹿，
三寨又走出哈尼三帮，
三股水合做一股，
在洞铺安下寨房。

围坐在火塘边上的哈尼，
亲亲的兄弟姊妹阿波阿匹，
这些人就是我们的直系先祖，
洞铺就是他们开辟的家乡，
要问哪家祖先是哪一个，
快把各人的家谱细背细讲！

众人：
萨——依——萨！

（六）

歌手：
萨——依——
讲了，一娘生的兄弟姊妹！
唱了，亲亲的哈尼后代儿孙！
好听的哈八唱到今晚，
该唱的已经唱过，
该讲的已经讲完，
长长的路已经走到了头，
会唱的喉咙也不能再唱。

The Biza Village found a good place,
But it was not spacious enough.
Biza, Luopu and Zhulu
Three villages split again,
Forming one group
And settling in Dongpu.

The Hanis sitting around the fireplace,
Dearest brothers and sisters, apos and apis,
They are our immediate ancestors,
Who built Dongpu.
If you want to know which ones were your ancestors,
You must know your own family tree!

Audience:
Sa—ee—sa!

7. 6

Singer:
Sa—ee—

Let us tell stories, brothers and sisters from one mother!
Let us sing songs, dearest Hani descendants!
Tonight, the nice Haba the drinking songs
Have sung what should be sung,
Have told what should be told.
So the long journey has come to the end,
And the skilled singer cannot sing any more.

一寨的亲人啊，

碗里的米酒已经喝干，

变暗的火塘不能再向，

明天还有要紧的活计要干，

各人应当回到自己的蘑菇房，

多余的话我还有一句，

只是不能用哈八来唱。①

---

① 搜集整理者按：接着歌手按规矩叙说了分寨的详情——纳索玛去世后，卢威、卢策派出两路人去占领各地，一路到了河口县的麻迷、玛拉、俄八、俄扎及越南境内的窝比和戚策蒲玛等地，一路到了绿春县的事尼阿、窝拖蒲玛及红河县的大黑弓、元阳的哈卡、皮甲等地。

Dearest fellow villagers,

The rice wine is finished,

And the fading flames in the fireplace should let be.

Tomorrow is another day of much work,

So let's each return to our own mushroom house.

There is one more thing I want to say,

But I can't tell in Haba the drinking song.①

---

① Notes from the compiler: Then the singer followed the rule and explained the details of the village division——After Nasuo Ma passed away, Luwei and Luce sent two teams to occupy the different regions, one team to Mami, Mala, Eba and Eza in Hekou County, and Wobi, Qice Puma, etc. in Vietnam, while the other to Shini'a, Wotuo Puma in Lvchun County, Daheigong in Honghe County, and Haka, Pijia, etc. in Yuanyang County.